Friends don't let friends
get eaten by vampires.

HUNTERS & PREY

Katie Salidas

IMMORTALIS SERIES: BOOK 2

Hunters & Prey
SECOND EDITION
Copyright © 2010 by Katie Salidas
Second Edition © 2015 Katie Salidas

Editing by Sharazade
Cover Art by Willsin Rowe
Interior Design by Katie Salidas

Published by Rising Sign Books, LLC.
http://www.RisingSignBooks.net
ISBN: 978-0-9851277-3-2

THE IMMORTALIS SERIES:
All 6 Books Are Available Now

Becoming a vampire is easy. Living with the condition... that's the hard part. Join Alyssa as she stumbles through the world of the "Unnatural."

BOOK 1: IMMORTALIS CARPE NOCTEM - Newbie vampire Alyssa never asked for this life, but now it's all she has. Rescued from death by Lysander, the aloof and sexy leader of the Peregrinus vampire clan, she's barely cut her teeth before she becomes a target. Kallisto, an ancient and vindictive vampire queen – and Lysander's old mate - wants nothing less than final death for her former lover and his new toy. She's not above letting the Acta Sanctorum, and its greatest vampire hunter, Santino, know exactly where the clan can be found. With no time to mourn her old life, Alyssa's survival depends on her new family. She will have to stand alongside Lysander and fight against two enemies who will stop at nothing to destroy them.

YOU ARE READING **BOOK 2: HUNTERS & PREY** - Rule number one: humans and vampires don't co-exist. One is the hunter and one is the prey. Simple, right? Not for newly-turned vampire Alyssa. A surprise confrontation with Santino Vitale, the Acta Sanctorum's most fearsome hunter, sends her fleeing back to the world she once knew, and Fallon, the human friend she's missed more than anything. Now she has some explaining to do. However, that will have to wait. With the Acta Sanctorum hot on their heels, staying alive is more important than educating a human on the finer points of bloodlust.

BOOK 3: PANDORA'S BOX - After a few months as a vampire, Alyssa thought she'd learned all she needed to know about the supernatural world. But her confidence is shattered by the delivery of a mysterious package - a Pandora's Box. Seemingly innocuous, the box is in reality an ancient prison, generated by a magic more powerful than anyone in her clan has ever known. But what manner of evil could need such force to contain it? When the box is opened, the sinister creature within is released, and only supernatural blood will satiate its thirst. The clan soon learns how it feels when the hunter becomes the hunted.

BOOK 4: SOULSTONE - It's a desperate time for rookie vampire Alyssa, and her sanity is hanging by a slender thread. Her clan is still reeling from the monumental battle with Aniketos; a battle that claimed the body of Lysander, her sire and lover, and trapped his spirit in a mysterious crystal. A Soulstone. Unfortunately, no amount of magic has been able to release Lysander's spirit, and the stone is starting to fade. Weeks of effort have proved futile. Her clan, the Peregrinus, have all but given up hope. Only Alyssa still believes her lover can be released. In despair, Alyssa begs the help of the local witch coven, and unwittingly exposes the supernaturals of Boston to unwanted attention from the Acta Sanctorum. The Saints converge on the city and begin their cleansing crusade to rid the world of all things "Unnatural." In the middle of an all-out war, but no closer to a solution to the dying stone, Alyssa is left with an unenviable choice: save her mate, or save her clan.

BOOK 5: MOONLIGHT - Good girls don't wear fur, or fight over men, and they certainly don't run around naked, howling at the moon. But then, no-one ever called Fallon a good girl. As a human unofficially mated to an Alpha werewolf, Fallon is being pressured to "become"...or be gone. Her mate Aiden, the interim leader of the Olde Town Pack, is in a position that demands he either choose a wolf mate...or leave the pack forever. No matter how hot the sex with Fallon is, he can't ignore centuries of tradition. Become a wolf or not. If only the choice were that simple. Fallon's options are further clouded by the overt presence of other females desperate to be the Alpha's mate. And when these bitches get serious, it's not just claws that come out. If Fallon wants to keep her man and take the title she'll have to exert a little dominance of her own.

BOOK 6: DARK SALVATION - A gathering storm of violence is on the horizon. Whispered threats of the Acta Sanctorum's return have the supernatural world abuzz. Only recently aware of the other world hidden behind our own, Kitara Vanders has barely scratched the surface of what being supernatural truly means. A special woman in her own right, she possesses unique telepathic abilities, gifts that have recently come under the scrutiny of the Acta Sanctorum, a fanatical organization whose mission is to cleanse the world of anything supernatural. Targeted, and marked for death, Kitara's only hope lies with the lethally seductive yet emotionally scarred warrior, Nicholas.

Knowing full well the atrocities the Acta Sanctorum is capable of, Nicholas is all too eager for the battle to begin. Fueled by pain and rage from the loss of his mate, he's itching for a fight, but one thing stands in his way, Kitara: a beautiful dark-haired woman with unique psychic abilities and an unusual link to the Saints. Despite his resolve to remain focused on his mission, a purely physical relationship binds them together in a way neither of them expected. And when her life hangs in the balance, Nicholas finds his own is teetering on the edge too.

To my husband, Nicholas.
You may hate your character, but I love both him and
the real man who inspired him. I couldn't ask for a
better or more supportive husband.

ACKNOWLEDGMENTS

To: Angela, Willsin, Brenda, Minnie, & Alice. This book would not exist without you. Thank you all for the help, hard critiques, and encouragement.

To my awesome editor, Shar. What can I say…you rock!! Thanks for putting up with me and all of my dumb questions.

1

Hot blood coursed through my veins as I gulped down the gushing fountain of my victim's neck.

He won't be hurting women anymore. I thought to myself as I swallowed each hot mouthful of blood. *How quickly the hunter becomes the prey.*

Using the power of my mind, I sent him feelings: waves of pain and grief for the murder he had committed. The human mind was easy to control, and I called upon all the skill I possessed to make him suffer.

Murderers and those who dealt in crime and abuse were my prey. It was because of them, those vile individuals, that I was a vampire. Memories of my own near-death experience and echoes of past wounds fueled me.

As a vampire, I had power, the power to stop bad people from doing awful, evil things. Fate has a way of working things out, and it gave my bloodlust a purpose. If I was to be this creature, I would ensure that my feeding stopped the unnecessary deaths of innocents.

I drained him slowly and painfully, savoring the honey-sweet elixir of his blood. Keeping him alert enough to feel every draw against his neck, I gnawed at the wound with my sharp teeth and dug my nails into his flesh. I wanted him to feel everything. I wouldn't let him go unconscious. He needed to know and understand the torment he had inflicted on others. I only wished I had found him, sooner before he ended the life of the poor woman lying at our feet. The fearful look in her dead eyes was a painful reminder of the men who had attacked me.

This man would pay with his dying breath.

My victim moaned pitifully. He beat against my back, struggling to free himself. I tightened my grip, locking his body in my deadly embrace.

He was going nowhere.

The heat from his blood coursed through my veins, strengthening me, warming me, giving me his life-energy. I savored this feeling: the tingling rush, the ecstasy, that filled my being.

Just as the wave of pleasure crested, his heart slowed to an erratic thump, and the gushing fountain became a trickle. I knew he wouldn't last much longer. His blood pressure was dropping.

I lifted my head and gazed into his fear-filled eyes. "It's no fun when you're on the receiving end, is it?" I smiled at him, licking the last few drops of his blood from my fangs.

My head swam with energy—his energy. I felt powerful, strong, and just.

The wretched man was like putty—just a lump of mush—in my hands. Weakly, he exhaled a final dying breath. The light of life in his eyes extinguished. His head lolled and then flopped backward.

I listened carefully. His heart thumped once, twice, and then … nothing.

I bit my tongue and swirled a mix of my saliva and blood across the wound on his neck, ensuring it would close. The evidence of my feeding would be gone by the time anyone found him.

A strange prickling sensation tickled the back of my neck. The hair on my arms stood straight on end. I had come to know this unmistakable feeling quite well since I'd been turned. Another vampire was close.

I dropped my victim unceremoniously on top of the woman he'd just killed and turned around to scan the area. Though the street was dark, my vampire eyes had no problem spotting another pair of pale eyes staring back at me from the shadows.

A footstep broke the silence. Still young, I'd had limited dealings with other vampires. Not all were friendly. I hoped the one watching me would be.

"I know you're out there," I called to the darkness. "Show yourself."

Raspy laughter crawled out of the shadow. "Are you sure you want me to do that, Alyssa?"

In the space of a second, realization hit me. My eyes went wide and my heart slammed into my chest.

Oh shit. Santino!

Another footstep echoed around me as he moved into the light.

A trademark of the vampire kind, his blue-gray eyes seemed to glow as he looked at me. A wild mane of salt-and-pepper hair jutted out in all directions on top of his head. Deep-creased wrinkles and scars covered an aged face that had seen many battles. His lips pulled back into a predatory smile, revealing a perfect set of sharp white fangs.

I was running before I could even comprehend the thought of it. I needed to get away. Fast.

***

As the sun began its ascent into the sky, I settled down, safely at home, preparing for sleep. But it wouldn't come peacefully. Somewhere, trapped between the dreaming and waking world, I felt his presence. The cold, prickling sensation. It crawled up my spine and raised the hairs on the back of my neck.

Not again. I tried desperately to rouse myself. I knew what would come next.

As if on cue, those cold, emotionless, blue-gray eyes appeared above me. They locked on me with contempt.

Santino.

I'd dreamt of him for weeks after our last battle. I thought I had finally escaped the daymares that had haunted me, but now they were back.

I knew every scar on that fearsome face, though I wished I didn't. I'd met him only once before, and against the odds, I'd lived to talk about it. That was something only a handful could claim. Santino was not one to leave anyone alive once he'd set his sights on them.

I willed myself to wake. But, just as before, the dream continued.

His piecing gaze bore into my skull. I was motionless; my body barely held the strength to gasp for air. Laid out like an offering, I was an easy target, ready to be slaughtered.

If I could have screamed I would have, but I was mute, destined to see the events unfold as they had when I had lived through them.

Santino's mouth formed a sinister smile. The tips of his fangs poked out from behind his lips, but I knew it was not his teeth I should fear.

Stuck again in this nightmare, I tried in vain to will myself awake. Paralysis had me frozen in place, helpless. Slowly, he reached out, grabbing my head, balling up a fistful of my hair. Strands snapped under his grip, pinching and pulling away from my scalp.

I needed to break free from his grasp. I needed to somehow get out of this dream.

Fear gripped me. He rocked my head from one side to the other, inspecting me. *Would this finally be the time? Would he finally kill me?* His eyes focused on my neck.

Wake up, damn it!

"Not going to be much of a fight, are you?" he said, pulling out his knife—a large thick blade with jagged edges. Blood from his last kill still coated it.

He made the sign of the cross and mumbled a prayer under his breath.

I willed my muscles to listen. *Move*, I yelled in my head. *Move, damn it. Wake up!*

My heart beat wildly, thundering in my ears as Santino's eyes opened and focused on me once more. Disgust flashed across his face, as if I were a mangy animal and it was beneath him to have to put me down. His lips again formed that sinister sneer. I shuddered. His gaze was like ice, sending a shiver slithering down my spine to the churning pit of my stomach.

He exhaled a growling breath that echoed in the room as he placed the cold, heavy blade to my neck.

***

No!

I awoke with a start, shooting upright in bed. My heart pounded, and my chest heaved with each sharp breath.

Disorientation fogged my vision. I struggled to compose myself and come back into reality.

It's over, he's gone.

If this had been merely a bad dream, the sight of my room and Lysander sleeping next to me would have been immediate comforts, but this wasn't just a dream. Those events were real. Re-living my first run in with Santino seemed to be my curse. The memories haunted me, playing out every detail of that bloody night, ending just before Santino attempted to finish me off.

He'd nearly destroyed my entire clan that night. I shuddered at the thought of him. Santino was well known as the Acta Sanctorum's best hunter—a vampire who made a career of killing his own kind. He and his team of hunters had tracked down and destroyed the largest coven of vampires known to exist.

He killed their leader, Kallisto, right before my eyes. I was supposed to have been next on his hit list. If it hadn't been for Lysander and the aid of our friends in the Peregrinus clan, I would have died.

I was lucky to have gotten away, and Lysander had almost paid for my escape with his life. Everyone assumed Santino either dead or too weak after that battle to continue his hunt.

Deep down, I felt differently.

I knew he had survived. He was the one I'd seen while hunting. I had run from him without a good look, but there was no doubt in my mind. It couldn't have been anyone else.

When are these dreams going to stop? I sighed, raking my hands through my hair, pulling away long red strands sticking to my clammy face.

Vampires aren't supposed to have daymares.

I ran the battle though in my memory. Even though months had passed since I had been pulled out of the burning building, it still felt like it had been only a day ago. I remembered Lysander's motionless body floating in the water. He had managed to escape the fire by diving out of a second-story window to the back yard pool below. It had taken us days to nurse him back to full health.

But Santino was never found.

Lysander believed Santino was gone, and that there was no reason to fear him anymore.

Faint rays of light seeped in through the sides of the curtains. Still daylight. The clock on Lysander's tall oak dresser flashed as the minutes changed, confirming the time.

Great, only noon. Sunset isn't for at least seven more hours. Damn these long summer days!

I rubbed my sleepy eyes and took a deep, cleansing breath. My heartbeat slowed, returning to a faint whispering thump.

No use trying to get back to sleep now.

A very groggy-looking Lysander rolled over to face me.

I looked into his sleepy eyes, allowing myself to feel the warmth—the connection between us. "Sorry, did I wake you?"

His face always looked so angelic among the sheets. I felt safe with Lysander. He was my guardian, my teacher, and my lover.

"Santino again? I thought you had finally escaped those dreams," he said, yawning as he stretched out his muscular arms. My midday waking had become routine for the last few months. I'd woken him up too many times with these daymares.

"Yeah. I still can't get the memory out of my head. What if he did survive? What if he is gaining strength?"

He sat up next to me. His dark chocolate-colored hair, messy from sleep, fell haphazardly around his pale face, highlighting his beautiful blue-gray eyes. The sheet fell to his waist, allowing for a full view of the defined ridges of his chest, corded arms, and broad shoulders. He reached up and gently stroked my face with a cool hand, tracing his thumb over my lips.

"Alyssa, please. We have had this conversation too many times." He gazed at me imploringly, begging me to go back to sleep. "Even if Santino is still out there, he is weak. The fire almost killed me. You and the Peregrinus brought me back with your blood. Santino wouldn't have that luxury. He will take months, if not years, feeding on the blood of animals to heal back to full strength again."

"Why do I keep dreaming about him? Why can't I get him out of my head?" I fisted my hands at my side, balling up bed sheets.

"You've had very traumatic experiences." His voice was soft and soothing. "It is normal for there to be some after-effects."

"It's not only that, I saw…"

He put an arm around me and pulled me close. I relaxed a little, enjoying the feel of his strong arms. Nuzzling into his chest, I listened to his heart. It beat in a slow, peaceful rhythm. I wanted to settle down, to lie there enjoying the comfort and pleasure of being close to Lysander. But the thought wouldn't leave my head.

The words spilled from my mouth before I could form cohesive thoughts. "I saw a man. Last night. He looked exactly like Santino. I was hunting."

"It's only natural that your mind is focusing on Santino." Lysander's voice remained soft, as smooth as velvet and as peaceful as a lullaby. He gently stroked my arm. "But you must trust me. If he is out there, he is too weak to hurt us."

What if he isn't? I shook my head.

Please relax, Alyssa. His voice was a whisper in my mind.

"Lysander, get out of my head," I warned.

I still hadn't mastered completely how to close off my mind. Any time I was emotional, about anything, I lost all control. Lysander knew this and usually pretended to avoid eavesdropping, but I knew he could listen in to my inner monologue at will. At well over two thousand years old, it was only natural for him to use his mental abilities. They were as common to him as a reflex.

"Alyssa, I do not need to listen to your thoughts to know you aren't letting this go. I can feel your tension. And I can see it in your frightened face."

I sighed. I needed him to take my concerns more seriously, but the fact that I was so young, so new to this life, worked against me. Lysander, as well as the others, though loving as family, tended to regard me as naive and inexperienced. They had centuries of life behind them, and at twenty-five, I was no more than a child in their eyes.

"Call it intuition or whatever. I just feel like these terrible dreams are a warning. I saw him. I know I did. Santino is still out there and stronger than we think."

Lysander let out small groan. "What would you have us do then? We cannot fight a ghost, a dream, or a figment of your imagination."

His patronizing tone aggravated me. "I don't know," I said through gritted teeth.

"Alyssa, my treasure." He softened his voice. "I did not mean to offend. I just do not think Santino is as much of a concern as you are making him."

I buried my head into his neck, absorbing the slow pulsing of his veins against my lips. For a brief moment, my thoughts turned to the feeling of ecstasy and need building inside me. I wanted a taste of Lysander's blood. I licked at my fangs, focusing on that want, but the thought of Santino would not escape my mind.

"I just can't shake this feeling. And you're not helping by making light of my concerns."

"You are my little trouble maker." He sighed. "You seem to draw in problematic situations and make things more than they are. I only think—"

"Is that how you think of me? As a magnet for trouble?" I tried to pull away from his body, but his arm held me tight.

He looked down, finding my sad eyes. "Would it make you feel better if I said that you have a penchant for making life more interesting?" He gave me a boyish grin. "Or, that your knack for finding danger has brought adventure back into my life?" His eyes narrowed slightly as if he was studying my face, no doubt hoping his back pedaling was working.

It wasn't.

I locked my eyes on his, trying to show him the worry I felt, willing my fear and the memory of my previous encounter to flow from me like a wave into his mind.

The corners of his lips dropped. His expression became serious. "Would it make you feel any better if we met with the Peregrinus about this? Maybe in counsel we can come up with an answer to your fears."

That might be a good idea.

I had avoided telling any of them of my dreams or my encounter with the man who looked like Santino for fear of inciting more worry, but the wisdom of the four remaining members of the clan might prove helpful.

"Yes." I smiled as I relaxed and leaned into Lysander's chest. "Maybe they'll know what to do."

"Then we will speak to them this evening." His hand glided up and down my arm. "Now, can we try to go back to sleep? Dusk is not for quite a while."

"You can." I shook my head. "I'm not sure I can get back to sleep. My mind is stuck on Santino. It's almost like he is the boogeyman come back to haunt me."

"Perhaps I can distract you from these fears." Lysander's voice carried an air of mischievousness. He tilted his head away, exposing his neck. The pulsing vein under his skin enticed me. He reached a hand up to the back of my neck and gently pulled me in closer—a silent invitation.

I opened my mouth against his skin and licked at his pulse. A low growl rumbled in his chest. I swirled my tongue on his neck, enjoying his salty taste before I sank my teeth in.

I loved the sensation that accompanied drinking Lysander's blood: the instantaneous head rush, the wild energy, and the cool tingling as it flowed down my throat. His blood was liquid euphoria, and since turning me, he shared it with me freely whenever I wished.

Ahh, yes, this is a pleasant distraction.

The thick sweet elixir washed down my throat. I let out a slight moan. My heart beat faster, pushing his powerful blood through my veins. It warmed me, filling my being with pleasure.

I pulled back gently from his neck and looked into his hypnotic eyes. The twilight blue-gray pools called out to me. Locking on to me with their pull, they compelled me and drew me to Lysander. A foggy sensation rolled into my head.

Ohh, You're not playing fair, Lysander.

His strength and practice in the mental arts showed as the blissful dizziness set in. I felt the lust he willed on me. Erotic images played in my head. Desire ignited inside me, heating my blood in anticipation of his kiss. He temporarily derailed the fearful thoughts that had gridlocked my mind with worry. All I could think of was Lysander. I needed him. I wanted him. All of him.

He laid me down gently on the pillows and towered over me before pressing his soft lips to mine. His tongue dipped into my mouth and playfully licked at my fangs.

The gentle pressure of his body against mine reminded me of pleasures of evenings past. I felt the stiff evidence of his desire pressed against my thigh. He nudged his hips forward, rubbing his thickness against me, hinting at his plans.

His hand trailed down my body. With feather-soft touches, he tickled and teased my bare skin. Each touch caused an eruption of gooseflesh, making me hot and ready for more.

"Forget Santino. Wouldn't you rather think of this?" His voice was magic, deep and husky with need.

I wanted to concentrate on Lysander. I loved his hands on my body, touching, exploring, teasing; but the mention of Santino's name broke his spell over me.

How quickly could he heal from animal blood?

Lysander nibbled at my ear and trailed slow kisses down my neck. My body reacted to his touch. Warmth spread between my thighs, my breast ached, and my nipples hardened to pebbles as he teased me. But my brain locked onto questions of Santino.

What if he found other vampires to feed on?

I felt the quick pinch of Lysander's teeth, sinking into my breast, followed by the warm caress of his velvety tongue, lapping at my blood.

What if there are more Saints out there than we expected?

Lysander groaned loudly, then suddenly stopped and sat up. Disappointment filled his eyes as he stared down on me. "You're not into this today, are you?"

"Huh? What?" His words brought me back into reality.

He let out a loud breath and licked a spot of blood from the corner of his mouth.

"Look into my eyes, Alyssa. Let me take you away from these thoughts."

"I can't. I can't let this go. I feel like this is a warning somehow. I can't ignore it."

Lysander sighed and collapsed next to me. He jerked the sheet over his body as he rolled over.

"I'm sorry." I rolled to face him.

"Well, I will say this. Your mind is getting stronger. You have never broken my control before." The magic had left his voice.

I never wanted to. "I wish I could say it was all my doing. I wasn't actively blocking you. It's just, you said his name and I snapped back into reality."

A puzzled look marked Lysander face. His eyes narrowed as he turned to me. "Really? You weren't trying to block me?"

Blood rush to my cheeks. "No, I was enjoying what you were doing."

Lysander's mental control had been unbreakable in the past. He had tried to show me how to block him, but

I had never been fully capable. I could block my thoughts well enough, but when it came to full control, I still had a lot to learn. He had told me it was because I was so young. As vampires age, our power increases. Someday I would be strong enough to fend off an attack from an ancient like him, but that could be centuries away.

He rolled toward me. "We will talk with the clan tonight. I can see that we will not get past this worry of Santino." I could hear the tension in his voice.

"Thank you," I said. I laid my head on his chest, listening for the gentle beating of his heart.

"Try to sleep then. There is not much to do till sundown."

Lysander wrapped his arms around me and gave a small squeeze.

Sleep was probably best, but I didn't know if it would come. I feared the memory; the daymare would return the moment I drifted back into unconsciousness.

Lysander's breathing became shallow. *I wish I could sleep like that again. Why is he not worried? How can he sleep so soundly?*

I rolled free of his grasp, easing myself out of bed. It would do no good to lie here awake, awaiting dusk. I knew sleep was not going to come. Throwing on some jeans, a bra, and a small red tank top, I left Lysander to sleep peacefully.

My life as a newborn vampire was probably not what most would consider standard. I doubted most newbies ever had to contend with the rage of a two-thousand year old jealous vampire like Kallisto or the hunters of Acta Sanctorum within a month of their turning. I'd done both and lived to talk about it. I should probably have counted my blessings and trusted that the older vampires knew what was best. Still, I couldn't help but listen to my intuition. Something was definitely wrong, and I had the sneaking suspicion it was about to come back to bite us all.

2

The day dragged on as I attempted, unsuccessfully, to keep myself occupied. Time moves slowly when you're trapped. Daylight is no friend to vampires, and the Las Vegas desert is not known for lending itself to many overcast days.

I knew very well the danger of leaving the house during the daytime hours. I had already experienced once, the blinding effects of direct light on my photosensitive eyes. The sun's rays were overpowering. Light stung me, like white hot pokers being shoved through my skull. Even when I could force my eyes open, through the pain, focusing was near impossible. Light bathed everything in white-wash creating an indistinguishable haze all around me.

Couple all of that with an almost immediate blistering sunburn, and there was plenty to make sure I would never want to venture outside again during the day. All I could do was sit and keep busy, waiting for dusk.

I paced the cavernous living room like a caged animal, wearing a track into the carpet with my boredom. The clock taunted, ticking at its slow pace. Each minute felt like an hour, and each hour was a small eternity to itself. Hoping for some relief to my boredom, I decided to do a little research.

My maker, Lysander, was also a historian who meticulously documented everything he experienced. He'd created quite an expansive library of vampire history—which I figured should give me plenty to look through.

Randomly, I took ancient tomes from the hand-carved oak bookshelf and brought them to the glass-top coffee table.

I collapsed on the large black leather sofa and began my research, hoping to find more information on Santino. Sadly, there was little more than the snippet of information I'd already learned. He'd been an Italian mercenary before he was turned, choosing immortality and servitude to the order of the Acta Sanctorum to overcome his age and eventual death. Unfortunately, as Lysander hadn't dealt much with him, there was little personal history to be chronicled.

What I knew of the Acta Sanctorum wouldn't be any more help to me. The Catholic Church may hold his leash, but they didn't control his everyday movements. It was the man—the hunter—that I needed to figure out.

Frustrated with the lack of help the books were providing, I settled down in front of the TV—another sad attempt to pass the time. Hours crawled as the clock continued mocking me. It felt like dusk would never come. I flipped through channels, searching through talk shows, soap operas, and day-time court TV, finally stopping on a news network.

Nicholas always watches the news. Perhaps I could get something out of it. If I could just remember that name. Who was it that he said works with Santino?

"Quentin." Nicholas's voice boomed from behind me. It startled me, shaking me from my thoughts. I hadn't expected any other clan members to be awake this early. I looked up to find him standing at the entrance to the hallway. He was a short man, but built like a soldier. His muscular frame filled the arched entrance to the hall. "His name is Quentin Kagan, and he doesn't work with Santino, he handles him, like a dog." Nicholas gave a snort of a laugh. "Santino reports to him."

"Thanks," I said feeling a little annoyed at the interruption. "Sorry, was I too loud out here? I didn't think anyone was up."

Nicholas quirked an eyebrow at me and walked over to the black, leather love seat next to me. "No, I was already awake. I heard the news and thought I should come out and see what's going on."

He sat and glanced at the TV, brushing away the dark, shaggy hair from his eyes. The glowing light from the TV cast odd shadows on his face emphasizing his permanent five o'clock shadow and cleft chin.

I drummed my finger on the plastic casing of the remote control. "I'm not really sure what I'm watching. I was just flipping through."

He shot me a sideways glance and crossed his arms in front of his chest. "Sounded to me like you were looking for clues."

"You know, it's not polite to go digging around in people's minds." I slumped back into the couch and let out a loud breath.

"I shouldn't have to." He cocked his head, and his eyes narrowed as he focused on me as if he were trying to stare right through me. "You shouldn't be hiding things from your family. I seem to remember another young fledgling who did the same thing. And can you tell me what happened to her? Remember Jessie?"

It was a low blow. I blinked a few times and turned away, pretending to look at the lamp on the side table. I remembered Jessie all right. She had tricked me into following her straight in to the hands of our enemy. Lysander wanted her ripped limb from limb for her treachery. She found death quickly once the clan had taken a vote.

"So, are you going to tell me what's got you looking for clues about Santino, or am I going to have to find out for myself?" His voice carried an air of menace.

Like all ancients, he had a wealth of power. I knew I was outmatched. It's hard to block them when they get you in their sights.

"Fine," I groaned. "Look, I uh, I've been having dreams… about Santino."

"Santino?" Nicholas turned to focus on the TV screen, but the corner of his mouth rose to a grin. "Does Lysander know you are dreaming of other men?"

"What? No! Not like that. Daymares."

"Poor little fledgling vampire, having daymares," he said with a laugh.

Does he always have to be such a jerk?

"Not really a day-nightmare, more like reliving the past."

"Post-traumatic stress," Nicholas said nonchalantly. He leaned back, crossed his legs and relaxed into the cushions of the loveseat.

"Yeah, Lysander thinks the same thing." I huffed. *Why am I bothering to talk to him? I can't expect him to listen to me. He only respects his fellow elders.*

"And you think there is more to these daymares, I assume?"

"Yeah!" *Whoops, said that a little too loud.* "I don't think Santino is gone. I think I saw him last night."

"He's not gone. For good that is." He waved his hand casually in the air as if to say this was common knowledge.

I was momentarily speechless. I hadn't expected Nicholas, of all vampires, to support my theory. "Wait, what? You're agreeing with me?"

"There was no body found at the fire. Am I correct? No body means no proof." He didn't bother looking at me as he spoke, but I had no doubt he saw me nodding in agreement. "You were there with me when we found Lysander."

"Yeah."

"Did you see Santino?"

I shook my head. "Well, no, I didn't."

"Did you sense his presence at all?"

I hesitated before answering. I hadn't even considered that fact. We can sense when others are around. I hadn't sensed him that night. "No."

"Then there was no proof of his death." He held up a finger, shaking it in the air, punctuating the words as he spoke. "If he isn't dead, he is still out there, somewhere."

"That's what I was saying, but Lysander says he's—"

"Too weak, right?"

"Yeah." I narrowed my eyes waiting for Nicholas to drop a bomb on me. *He's going along with this too easily.*

"Lysander's right about that…" He pointed a finger at me again.

Okay, here's where he tells me I'm stupid.

"Or." He brought his hand to his mouth. "At least he was right at some point. Santino would need to heal, just as Lysander and Rozaline did after the fire."

A pang of guilt struck me at the mention of Rozaline and the fire. She had forgiven me for accidentally burning her with a flame thrower during our previous battle with the Acta Sanctorum; but Nicholas, it seemed, still held a grudge. He'd been particularly mean to me ever since.

"Lysander says that could take a long time." I clenched my jaw, remembering how badly they had been burned.

Nicholas's eyebrow arched sharply. "And you don't believe him?"

"Well, umm…" I bit at my lower lip. I didn't want to speak against Lysander, but I felt deep down that he was wrong about Santino.

Nicholas's mouth twisted into a mocking smile. "Go ahead, say what you're thinking."

"No." I sighed, looking down to the carpet. "He's a vampire just like us. What if he, you know, drank from people, in a desperate attempt to heal?"

"I'm starting to like you, Alyssa. You're not as vacant as I originally thought."

"Vacant! Thanks for the vote of confidence, asshole! You know, for a second I almost forgot what a jerk you are."

"Flattery will get you nowhere. If you want my respect, you need to earn it. Now back on point. If Santino went rogue and started feeding from humans, he could easily have healed by now."

I nodded. "Okay, so he must have drank from mortals."

Nicholas gasped and put his hand to his cheek in an overly dramatic fashion. "But what of the Acta Sanctorum? What of the Church? They would not condone that. What would he tell them? Would he still be their crusader if they knew the bad things he had done?"

"Well, no. He wouldn't be able to work with them again if he fed from mortals." *Where is he going with this?*

"Right, then he could no longer be a— " Nicholas lifted his hands, making a quotation motion with two fingers."—Saint, and then he would be no threat to us."

I shook my head again. "You're talking in circles. Where is this going?"

"If you will shut up, I'll tell you."

I tapped my foot impatiently. "Fine. Go on, please," I said through gritted teeth.

"We can safely assume he did not break the law of the church or his order. And Santino is not like us, he won't kill humans even if they are criminals that deserve death. That would really put a cramp in his holier-than-thou attitude. All Santino has is the Saints and his mission."

"Okay then, how fast could he heal on animal blood?"

"You're interrupting again."

I clenched my hand tight around the TV remote, feeling the plastic casing crack under my grip.

"Forget animal blood, Alyssa. How did Lysander and Rozaline heal?"

"Oh, I'm allowed to talk now?"

"Only if you add something valuable to the conversation."

I groaned in frustration. "We fed them our blood."

"Bingo." He pointed a finger at me. "They healed because they drank vampire blood. And where could Santino get vampire blood?"

"I see where you're going with this. If we didn't kill all of the Saints, then they could have healed Santino."

He cocked his head to the side and gave me a mocking smile. "You do catch on quick, don't you? Keep this up and you just might get a gold star."

I bit back my annoyance.

"But didn't Rozaline say there were only a few immortal Saints? We had to have killed at least five of them, and that doesn't account for the ones that Kallisto's guard dealt with. There shouldn't be any more."

"What I believe Rozaline said was, the Acta Sanctorum wouldn't be so stupid as to have more than they can handle. That doesn't tell us how many they have. Five dead Saints is hardly enough to destroy the whole of the Acta Sanctorum."

That wasn't what I wanted to hear. Santino could be alive and well, and have another army of vampires and hunters to send after us.

"So if we assume he has healed, then he would be looking for us with his other minions?"

"We don't assume to know anything about his intentions."

I slumped back into the couch. "That's not an answer, Nicholas."

"I never said I had the answers, now, did I?"

"You certainly pretend to have them."

"I never pretend." The corner of his mouth rose in a smirk. "If I know something, I say it."

"So what do we do then?"

"Not sure at the moment." His eyes fixed back on the TV screen. "What time is it?"

I looked over to the clock on the bookshelf. "Just after five."

"Change it to local news."

"Yes, your highness." I snorted, pressing the buttons on the remote, careful not to crack the plastic casing further, and flipped back down the channel list to the local news report.

Maybe he will hear something important. I wish I knew what to look for.

"I doubt we will find any clues right now," Nicholas said with a sigh. "If he is out there, he's going to be working undercover. His last attacks drew too much media attention."

My memory flashed to the burning tower that had once housed Kallisto's coven. Vivid images of the charred, blackened top of the pristine white building and the huge plume of smoke that rose into the sky had been broadcast for days after the attack. The second fire, at Kallisto's safe house, was dwarfed in comparison, yet still drew the local media. Nicholas was right—Santino wouldn't want that kind of attention again. He would want to come after us in secret.

"What would we be looking for?" I wanted to do something. I couldn't just sit there twiddling my thumbs.

"It would be too complicated to explain to you. I'll know if I see something."

"Great, so I'll just sit here and do nothing." *That will make time move faster.*

"Shh, I'm trying to watch this."

Jerk!

The news was filled with the same everyday stories it always had. Reports of negligent mothers leaving their kids in hot cars while they ran into grocery stores, robberies, murders, the most recent million-dollar slot winner, and special deals being offered by the local casinos. There was nothing—not a single, noticeable clue to tell me if Santino was still out there looking for us.

Nicholas hardly took his gaze from the television. I couldn't tell if he was interested in the news or just trying to ignore my impatient sighs.

The annoyingly chipper female anchor was teasing the top story of the night, a dismembered body found near Industrial Road, when I heard a soft voice greeting me from the hallway.

"Good evening, Alyssa."

I looked over to see the smiling and sleepy face of Rozaline, Nicholas's mate. Her long brunette hair hung down, framing her milky white face. She wore a pair of pink flannel pajama pants that draped over her toes and a simple white camisole top. As usual, a variety of crystal point pendants hung from her neck on silver chains.

"I'm surprised to see you out here. Has Nicholas roped you into watching the local news now too?" she asked.

"No." I giggled. I wasn't the only one who picked on him for his obsession with the news. "I was already watching when he came out here."

"Alyssa has some suspicions about Santino," Nicholas added, his eyes still firmly locked on the television screen.

"Really? Santino?" Rozaline walked gracefully to the loveseat. Her necklaces clinked softly against one another as she moved. "What makes you worry about him, Alyssa?" She took a seat next to Nicholas and gave him a sweet peck on his cheek.

How does a nice woman like Rozaline fall in love with a rude and obnoxious man like Nicholas?

Nicholas shot me a mocking smile. No doubt he had heard that thought. He placed his hand on her knee, giving it a small squeeze.

I rolled my eyes and turned my attention to Rozaline.

"I've been having a recurring daymare, only it isn't just a bad dream. I think it's a warning. Nicholas and I were talking and we agree it's possible Santino's still out there, and there may be more Saints."

"Whoa, whoa, slow down," Rozaline said, holding up her hand. "If there is a chance that Santino is still out there, then there really is only one option."

"What?" I asked.

"We leave town for a while."

She's got a point there.

Rozaline continued, "You know we of the Peregrinus clan are travelers. We never planned to make Las Vegas a permanent home. Perhaps the timing is right to move on. Santino is too cunning a hunter, and I do not wish to fight him again. We will take you and Lysander with us."

"You'll have to get him to agree to that," I said with a small sigh. "He's not exactly of the same mentality. He thinks I'm worried for nothing."

"Lysander is not a stupid man," Rozaline said. "He will listen to reason. When the rest of the house is awake, we will discuss the options and come to an agreement on what to do. For now, just relax."

Rozaline leaned her head into Nicholas's chest, yawning. Her sharp fangs glinted in the lamplight as her mouth opened wide. At times it seemed odd to me that she was a vampire. She looked so young, no more than twenty; it was strange to think she was over seven hundred, and her mate, Nicholas, like Lysander, was well beyond two thousand.

"Nicholas dear," she cooed. "Can we please find something other than news to watch this evening?"

I stifled a snicker. Rozaline winked at me.

"Alyssa has the remote," he sighed.

"Here, watch whatever you want," I said, tossing the remote to her. I laid myself out across the couch while Rozaline flipped through the channels.

Will it be that easy to convince Lysander to leave? Will he willingly go? I hope this meeting goes well tonight.

Patience was never a virtue of mine, and waiting for the clan to come together for a meeting was unnerving.

I wanted Lysander to take my worry more seriously, and I needed the clan's support. I knew Lysander was not oblivious to the possible dangers out there, but he seemed to value the opinion of the other ancient vampires.

Nicholas and Rozaline lay cuddled together on the loveseat, watching TV sitcoms.

My eyes kept darting from the TV to the clock and back. It was past eight and Lysander had still not awoken for the evening.

I can't sit here cooped up all night.

"We should go eat soon," Rozaline said, looking back at me.

"Why go out, when you could just order in?" Nicholas taunted. "Pizza delivery boy sounds good."

"Nicholas!" Rozaline playfully slapped his arm.

"What? Too much fat? You watching that girlish figure?" he teased, tickling Rozaline's side.

She bucked and giggled as she slapped away his hands. "Nicholas, what has gotten into you?"

"Get a room you two," I laughed.

Even though I couldn't understand how anyone would be attracted to Nicholas, it comforted me to think that a couple could last so long and still seem so much in love.

Rozaline was right about one thing. It was time to feed. The small pangs of hunger reminded me that it had been more than a day since my last hunt.

I would need blood very soon. Unlike the elder vampires, my need for blood had to be sated frequently. I could manage a day or two without it, but not any longer. Animals could hold me over, but in a city, the only animals I would find would be stray dogs and cats, and I refused to harm an innocent little creature like that. I needed something much larger. Thankfully in the city of sin, criminals, my regular prey, were quite accessible.

"I'll leave you two to yourselves. Tell Lysander I'll return later for the meeting. I'm going to hunt. I'll stick close to home just to be safe tonight."

Rozaline and Nicholas barely noticed me getting up. They were too busy with each other on the couch.

3

I stepped out into the fresh night air and sucked in a deep breath. Dry asphalt, sweet lemon trees, and the heady perfume of roses enticed me. I loved the outdoors, especially after being trapped inside all day.

Small twinkling stars glittered in an endless navy blue sky. The moon glowed clear and bright, bathing the neighborhood in its soft silvery light. It was a perfect evening.

For safety's sake, I decided to stay closer to home and hunt on foot, rather than taking Lysander's Jeep all the way into the city. Anxiety over our upcoming meeting kept me on edge. I wondered if Lysander would submit to the idea of leaving town for a while. If Santino was truly back, that would certainly be a good reason to take off and allow Lysander to pick up his old memoirs. We'd known about them for months and still he had not planned our trip to Boston to retrieve them. It seemed the perfect solution and timing on all accounts. I knew the clan would have some influence on him, though the extent of that influence wasn't yet clear.

I wandered down the sidewalk, contemplating what traveling would be like with the Peregrinus, in their big

R.V. It would be a far cry from our current lifestyle, that was for sure. Our home was in a nice middle-class suburban neighborhood filled with one- and two-story homes.

Suburbs were quiet—not my first choice for a hunting ground—but there were still criminal elements to be found … if you knew where to look.

I glanced down, surveying my clothing: a pair of sandals, tight-fitting low-rise jeans, and a red spaghetti strap tank top. I adjusted my breasts under my shirt, wishing I had worn a better bra.

It's so much easier to attract the wrong type when your breasts look full and perky.

I giggled to myself and shook my hips, watching the turquoise jewel in my silver navel ring glint in the moonlight. My tank top ended just above the ring, allowing for a nice view of my lean midriff.

Rapists were easy targets. Flash a little skin, and they were all over you. They just loved innocent looking women walking alone at night. I should know. It was partially the reason I became a vampire.

Months had passed since that brutal attack, but the memory still caused a shiver to dance down my spine. I had been so weak, so helpless, and the two brutes that had attacked me enjoyed every minute of my suffering.

I wasn't weak anymore, thanks to Lysander's healing kiss. It was he who had taught me to hunt down criminals, partly as a vendetta and partly as a survival mechanism. After all, I had to drink blood; who better to take it from than those who had caused me to become a vampire in the first place?

Of course, I wouldn't dare hunt directly in the neighborhood of my home. Lysander forbade it because it might draw too much attention to myself and the rest of the clan. Our ability to blend in with normal people was the key to remaining a secret. It was the reason we lived right in the middle of a sprawling suburban neighborhood. We were well hidden in plain sight because we never gave anyone a reason to pay attention to us. One of the benefits of living in a city with a thriving nightlife is that no one questions neighbors who only come out at night.

My hunting experiences were still limited; however, I did know of a few areas in this quiet suburb that might offer some game.

I sucked in a deep breath and filled my lungs again with fresh air. I'd always loved the night, even before becoming a vampire. There was something calm and tranquil about the evening. Perhaps it was the cooling of the heat of the day, or maybe it was just the fact that night had always been my free time. No work or school to worry about, just time to relax. Whatever the reason, it seemed that now, as a vampire, the soothing effect had become more pronounced. The night welcomed me with open arms.

A faint hint of musk floated in the breeze.

Probably a stray dog. Humans have a sweeter smell, but it might be worth a look.

The scent, though weak, called out to me. My thoughts turned to blood as my mouth watered in anticipation. All it took was the faintest hint to draw my cravings out. Blood was a necessity—and so much more. Like alcohol to an addict, it was my vice—hard to resist. Even when satiated, the smells still enticed, begging me to take a second helping.

I wouldn't allow myself to make another mistake though. One had been more than enough. The crushing guilt was enough to make me want to seek my own end.

Time had not erased that horrible memory from my mind. One weak moment, giving in to my desires, had ended with the death of an innocent man whose only crime had been his attraction to me.

I'd worked hard in the last few months, learning to tame the beast within ... not an easy task.

Walking briskly down the street, I looked for the way out to the main road. Cookie-cutter houses of white stucco and pink Spanish tile roofs lined the street—a typical Vegas suburban housing development. The only differences were the variations of desert landscape in each front yard.

As I drew closer to the musky smell, my mouth watered. I absently licked at my fangs, until I spotted the thing it belonged to.

A skinny blur of dark, matted fur raced across the street.

Just a dog.

I sighed and continued on my path, rounding a corner. Finally, I found the outlet to the main road. Cars zoomed past, but no people were out walking on the street. I knew somewhere ahead would be a bike path that led down Pittman Wash, a small overflow creek bed. The news had recently run reports of gangs and vandalism down there, under the Pecos Street Bridge. If I could get someone alone down there, no one would see or suspect anything.

Other than the cars on the street, the main road was surprisingly quiet for this early hour of the evening. I headed down the street toward the bike path, wondering why no one was out riding bikes or taking a stroll. The scorching heat of the desert sun, during the day, usually kept more than just vampires at bay, but the cool of the evening hours normally drew them out.

I reached the mouth of the path that would lead me down into the wash. Closing my eyes, I sniffed at the air. A warm, sugary smell wafted up from under the bridge.

Perfect. I rubbed my hands in anticipation.

Someone was down there. From the strength of the smell wafting up to my nose I guessed there was at least one close by, but maybe more.

Closing my eyes, I centered myself, quieting my mind to sense if there were any other presence. This was not a place I normally visited, and I did not want to run into another vampire.

One more deep breath of the sweet smell, and my legs started moving of their own accord. I stepped onto the path, walking slowly, careful not to let myself be seen.

A man's voice, deep and husky, echoed under the bridge. There was another, too, but it sounded faint and distorted. It had an almost mechanical quality to it.

Odd, it doesn't sound like there are two people here. Where is the other voice coming from?

Not wanting to be seen yet, I kept to the side of the bridge as I closed in.

A short man came into view, though most of his face was hidden in the shadows. I stood, silently observing him as he paced the underside of the bridge, listening for any clue that would mark him as suitable prey. He was dressed in a white wife-beater tank top and khaki pants, sagging so low his boxer shots were visible. The cuffs of his pants dragged on the ground, making a soft scraping sound as he traipsed back under the bridge. I spotted a small black cell phone held to his ear.

Ahh that's where the second voice is coming from.

He spoke in a high-pitched, excited tone. His free hand waved a gun in the air, punctuating his words. An enchanting aroma, like sweet and tart lemon drops, hit me in waves as he meandered back and forth under the bridge. It leeched out of his pores. Anxiety and anticipation always sweetened the scent, but I could tell his was fueled more with the tangy hint of adrenaline. It had an enticing potency to it—stronger and richer. It took all my control not to rush in and take him.

"When you getting here, man?" He shouted into the small clamshell phone. "I can't be waiting all night. Let's do this."

A low mumbling, electronically-enhanced voice answered him, but I couldn't make out exactly what was said.

"Man, if you're not here in five, I'm going without you. That fool is dead. I don't care whose family he belongs to."

I didn't need to hear the rest of the conversation. That little bit was enough for me to sense the evil in him. He was excited and cocky, ready for this night's wicked schemes, whatever they might be.

Perfect. Dinner is served.

He snapped the phone shut and pocketed it. "Fucking douche bag. I don't know why I bother with his sorry ass." He turned and walked back into the shadow of the bridge.

I stepped onto the path and began walking toward him. My heart beat rapidly with anticipation. The beast inside me roared for blood.

Matching my pace with his steps, I was able to sneak up to him without his notice. I hovered behind him for a moment, savoring his perfume, contemplating my next move. Some nights I liked to prolong the moment, make them understand why they were going to die, watch the sorrow fill their eyes, and listen to them make their apologies to God. Tonight, however, I did not have time for that. I needed to be quick about it.

"Evening," I said, enjoying the slight jump he made at the sound of my voice.

He spun around, fist clenched and ready to attack. Wide brown eyes locked onto my face. "What, who…"

"Shhh," I whispered as I put a finger to his lips. I stared into his eyes, using my hypnotic power to hold him in place. Silently, I commanded him to drop his weapon.

I smiled, giving him a good view of my fangs. His eyes grew wide with shock and fear. I saw the mental wheels turning in his head as he realized exactly what I was. He shuddered, unable to move from where he stood, and the gun in his hand fell with a loud *clunk* onto the ground.

Vampires may be a thing of myth to most, but when those unmistakable fangs are mere inches from your neck, disbelief goes out the window.

I savored the fear leaching out of his pores. His scent intensified, hot and sweet, like pure honey. My body tingled with excitement, knowing I would soon have the blood I needed and desired.

"Try not to scream," I whispered.

He gulped and his face paled, turning a ghostly white.

Leaning forward, I wrapped my arms around his body and bent my head to his neck sinking my teeth into his soft, salty flesh.

His body tensed as my teeth broke the skin. A loud cry erupted from his mouth. He struggled against me, flailing his arms and beating them against my back in a pathetic, futile attempt to break free. He stomped at my feet and tried to push away from the wall to make me lose my balance. Finally, he tried to force his arms between our bodies. I let him have his feeble attempt to break free. His frantic movements caused me no real pain; they only served to make his heart pump faster, sending gushes of sweet blood into my awaiting mouth.

As his movements became weaker, I pushed against him, leaning him into the wall to keep him upright. He jerked and moaned as the blood loss caused him to go into shock. I sucked hard at the wound, drinking greedily, not wanting to waste time with this kill.

My body pulsed with energy. My heart sped faster, pumping his fresh blood through my veins, warming me. The dizzying head rush was like the high of a drug. The more I drank, the more I wanted. I could have drunk him forever, but as soon as the head rush hit me, his heart slowed. I knew that terrible fading rhythm as he edged closer to the last few moments before death. I stopped just before I heard the final beat of his heart.

Biting my tongue, I mixed my blood with saliva and licked the wound, sealing it and hiding my involvement with his death. I dropped him to the ground, still feeling the dizzy effects as my body flushed with energy.

I let the feeling run through me, placing a hand to the wall for support as I took deep calming breaths.

Just as soon as the ecstasy filled me, it left. I licked away the last few drops from my lips, savoring the sweet taste. His blood would sustain me for another day or two, but the immediate pleasurable effects faded quickly. That was what made it easy to give in to excess and hunt down another. Temptation is a powerful monster, and I worked hard to keep that monster at bay. I didn't like to kill, though the bloodlust made it easier. Unless there was a need, I wouldn't intentionally hunt down more than one.

Now to do something about this body.

I looked around, hoping to find a good place to dispose of the corpse lying in a heap at my feet.

A small, cold, prickling sensation tickled at the back of my neck. I knew this feeling all too well; I was being watched. Whoever it was, he (or she) was immortal. The sensation was unmistakable.

Closing my eyes, I sniffed at the air, searching for the scent of whoever was watching me.

Nothing.

I twisted left and right, trying to discern the direction this sensation came from, to no avail. Whoever it was didn't want me to know they were here.

The other vampires I'd had interactions with were all now dead, except for Lysander, the Peregrinus and of course, Santino. I wasn't quite sure what to expect from meeting one at random. An ominous sense of worry struck me.

What if it is Santino? No, he wouldn't be so close to my home.

Stepping out from under the bridge, I chanced a look around. The bike path was still empty.

The prickling feeling at my neck intensified. Adrenaline mixed with fresh energy from the blood I had drunk caused my heart to speed, pounding in my chest like a tribal drum. Intuition told me to run, but curiosity held me in place.

"You can come out," I whispered, knowing a vampire would hear me at a great distance without having to shout.

"We meet again, Alyssa," a low grumbling voice answered back.

My pounding heart stopped. I choked on a breath of air. I knew this voice.

Shit! Not again.

A raspy laugh came from the top of the street. "You young ones are so easy to track. Didn't your master teach you? Never hunt near your home."

He was right. I should have gone into the city. *But how does he know that I am so close to home?*

Dread struck me with the force of a Mack truck.

"Let's get down to business, shall we?" Santino said loudly.

He leapt from the top of the street, down into the wash, landing with a crack and a thud.

The loud crack was the unmistakable sound of bone. Santino had to have broken his ankle as he landed, but I knew that wouldn't stop him for long. A vampire can heal pretty quickly, especially when we have recently fed. His face contorted, wincing in pain for a moment before he stood upright. He limped a few steps, and then straightened, walking in a normal slow pace toward me.

His cold, cruel eyes fixed on me with a menacing gaze. A low, growling laugh rumbled out of him as he approached.

I knew there was no fighting him. He was much stronger, older, and deadlier than any other of my kind. I turned and ran, not looking back, down Pitman Wash. I wasn't going to stand there and let Santino or any of his hidden minions get me.

I needed to get far away and couldn't head back to the house. I was already too close to home. That would not only give Lysander away, but the rest of the Peregrinus clan too. I had to find some place to hide and get a message to them without Santino finding out.

I could tell he was still a little weak, but the fact that he recovered so fast from the fall told me he'd recently fed. His most likely source would have been another vampire. He would easily be able to keep up with me on foot. I needed something faster.

Vampires, though faster than mortals, are still limited by our own endurance. Like a cheetah, I might be able to reach high speeds quickly, but I can only maintain them for a short time. I needed fast transportation, and I needed it quickly.

I ran as fast as my legs would carry me, down the small canal that comprised Pittman Wash. It ended at the intersection of two busy streets.

Shit, where to go now?

I looked around for signs of Santino or his minions. There was no time to stop and try to sense anything or anyone in the area. If he was following me, he would be close behind. I needed to keep moving.

I walked toward the intersection, passing a bar. A car door slammed, catching my attention. I looked over and spotted the familiar yellow of a taxi cab.

In a superhuman blur of motion, I ran over to the car, stepping in front of it before the driver started to pull away. Slamming my hand on the hood of the car, I yelled at the driver, "Hey, I need a ride."

The driver, an obese, scruffy blob of a man, gave me an impatient glare. I flung open the door to the cab, almost ripping it off in my haste.

"Maryland and Harmon."

The cabbie turned to me, barking his words. "Lady, I got other calls to get to. What are you, a tourist? We don't pick up randoms. You need a cab, you call it in like everyone else."

I stared deeply into his eyes, willing him to relax, silently telling him to listen to me. I had no time to argue with him. Santino would be only steps behind me.

His eyes glossed over and his face softened, clearing of all expression. I could tell I was having an effect on him.

"Take me to Maryland and Harmon," I said again in a controlled monotone voice.

"Uh, yeah, sure thing, lady." He turned around and put the car into gear.

4

The cab pulled into the parking lot of a little strip mall directly across from the campus of the University of Nevada, Las Vegas. I knew I shouldn't have come here, but it was the first safe place I could think of. I needed to hide out in an obscure location, yet one that was filled with humans. Hiding in plain sight was the only way I could assure my safety until I could get a message to my clan. Santino protected humans from my kind. He wouldn't dare attack in the open and expose me, or the secret of vampires, to mortals.

My body hummed with nervous energy. I gulped a dry breath as I opened the cab door. Two hundred feet away stood my old mortal hang out, Café Copioh—a hole-in-the-wall, bohemian café. I had disappeared from here the night I was turned, and no one—not even my best friend—knew what had happened to me. I'd been forced to leave without saying goodbye to all things and people from my mortal life, reluctantly accepting, for the most part, that I would never see them again.

Reaching into my pocket, I grabbed a few bills and tossed them at the cabbie. "Keep the change."

He grunted and scooped the bills off the passenger seat.

I took a shaky step out into the parking lot, imagining the reaction I might get when I walked into the cafe. *What if they recognize me for what I am now? What can I say?*

Stopping short of the door, I looked through the front window. As usual, the café was filled to the walls. It drew a unique brand of clientele from the university and surrounding neighborhood: Goths, artists, musicians, and college kids. I knew most of the regulars, and that fact had me worried. They might ask me where I'd been. Months had passed since I'd last seen them. I needed to make up some kind of alibi, something simple that they might believe.

I looked down at my hands noticing how pale they appeared. A wave of cold realization came over me. My knees suddenly felt weak.

This is a bad idea. Before I could do the right thing— turn and walk away—the front door swung open, sending a rush of coffee- and incense-filled air into my face.

"Oh, God! Lyssa!" A blur of blonde hair and cream-colored skin rushed toward me. "It *is* you!" Arms wrapped around my neck, shocking me with their warmth. "I was so worried about you! You never answered your cell. You never came back to the café. When I saw your apartment had been broken into, I feared the worst. I'm so glad you're okay." Her words came out in a single breath. She squeezed me tight then abruptly jerked back. "Oh my God. You're freezing. Are you okay?"

"I'm fine, Fallon." *Yep! Coming here was a bad idea.* "Just had the AC up too high in the cab, that's all."

Her deep brown eyes grew wide as she pulled back to look at me. I'd seen this look so many times on my victims before I ended them. She knew something was wrong with me. She could see the differences: my pale skin, my light eyes, maybe even the tips of my fangs. I should have known she would. Fallon was my best friend. She'd known me all my life. She'd probably notice a new freckle on my face—if I had any.

A frown played across her small, heart-shaped face. "No. You're not fine. Alyssa, what happened to you? Where have you been?"

"Look, let's get inside. We can talk in there." I took a glance behind me, to see if I had been followed. The Goths were hanging around the café, as usual, but I didn't see anyone else nor feel the presence of any vampires. I'd be safe, for a little while, inside.

My stomach sank as she turned to open the glass door. I felt like I was betraying everything by coming here. Lysander had made it clear I was dead to this world and that I could never again see my friends. Now here I was walking straight back into my mortal life. There were bound to be consequences.

The door opened again, sending another pleasant rush of incense-filled smoke into my face. My heart stopped for a moment and emotion flooded to the surface. Café Copioh had always been like a second home—mortal home, that is. I fought against the tears welling in my eyes.

I miss this place.

I closed my eyes and savored the scent of espresso, chocolate, and cigarettes. I took slow, deep breaths, allowing each fragrance to bring back fond memories. Nostalgia did not last long though. The warm sugary smell of blood and people, surrounding me, tempted the beast inside me.

Thank God I just fed, or this would be unbearable.

Fallon reached out and grabbed my arm, jolting me from my thoughts.

"C'mon. Lets grab a table." She pulled me into the café. Soft lamplight filled the room in the bohemian coffee house. Copioh boasted its own unique flair. I felt wistful, noting each detail I had taken for granted in the past. Every wall had been painted in a different color: teal, brown, sage, and maroon. I spotted my favorite mural, a black light illuminated copy of Van Gogh's *Starry Night*. It covered the wall leading to the bar.

The hum of the patrons here was like music to my ears. Mindless chatter about parties, college exams, and who was dumping whom; it all reminded me that life went on even if I had been forced to leave it behind.

As we walked through the crowd, smiles greeted me from the regulars who had been acquaintances before I was turned. A few hands clapped me on the back. Old friends said their greetings and started to ask me where I had been, but Fallon pulled me away before I could answer.

We searched for an open table. The place was filled with a plethora of flea market style furnishings, no two pieces were alike, each one well used and showing its age. We found an open couch and table near the make-shift stage in the back corner.

"You want some coffee, Lyssa?" Fallon asked. The concerned look on her face tugged at my heart.

"No. I'm good." *Already had my drink for the night.*

"You look sick; you need something. Sit here." She pushed me down on the worn, cream-colored couch. "I'm getting something to warm you up."

"No, really, that's not necessary." I tried to protest, but Fallon was already walking back to the bar.

I sighed, wondering what, if anything, I should tell her. I was at a loss. I'd never been a very good liar and I knew my best friend would grill me until she was satisfied with the answers I gave her. I needed something to tell her. I needed to invent a plausible reason for my disappearance: vacation, sudden death in the family, natural disaster, something.

She came back sooner than I expected.

"Here, drink this." She handed me a Styrofoam cup filled with steaming black coffee.

The warmth from the cup felt good in my hands, making me aware of exactly how cold my skin must feel.

Fallon sat down in the chair across from me and lit a cigarette. "Spill it. What happened to you? I need details."

"Still smoking, I see," I said, trying desperately to change the subject.

She took a drag from her cigarette. "Yeah, well when my best friend disappeared off the face of the earth, what did you expect me to do? I haven't been sleeping or eating right either, thanks for asking." Her eyes narrowed at me.

"Dining on ashes isn't going to help the situation," I said, pointing to the cigarette in her hand. "You said you were quitting."

She took another long drag. Silvery-gray smoke rose from the tip, curling up to the ceiling. I watched it vanish, mingling with the rest of the haze that hung in the air.

"Listen, we're not here to talk about my bad habits." She exhaled, sending a cloud of smoke in my direction. "What the hell happened to you?"

"I… uh… look, that's not important right now. I'm here, right? That should be all that matters." I set the coffee down on a small table next to the couch.

"You're not getting off that easy." Her tone became sharp. "I've been worried sick. I didn't know what happened to you. I called the cops, filed missing person reports, and harassed them every week hoping to find out information about you. I need answers."

"Keep your voice down," I warned. I didn't need the entire café knowing my business.

"No! I want to know what happened to you." She clenched her jaw and tapped her sandaled foot on the floor.

"Okay. You want to know what happened?" Time to think fast. "I was on vacation, forgot my phone, and my apartment got broken into." I knew it was a lame excuse even as I said the words.

Fallon took another drag from her cigarette and blew a thick cloudy puff in my direction. "You expect me to believe that bullshit, Alyssa?" she asked indignantly. "What are you hiding from me?"

"Will you keep your voice down?"

My eyes met hers. I sensed the mix of anger and concern behind her cold stare. I sagged into the couch, my heart suddenly heavy and aching with sorrow. I didn't want to hide things from her. She was my best friend. But I didn't want to tell her the truth either.

Damn it. What do I tell her?

She stared me down with determination. I knew this look well: the narrow eyes, the slight wrinkle as her eyebrows pulled together, the pursed lips. It didn't take years of friendship to translate that look.

I don't want to have to do this. But you leave me no choice.

I looked deeply into her brown eyes. *Please let this go, Fallon.* I tried to call up the strength inside me, to will her to relax and drop the subject.

Fallon gasped. "Your eyes. They look funny."

The ache in my heart grew stronger. I let out a defeated sigh. "I can't do this."

"Can't do what? Lyssa, just talk to me. Tell me what's going on. You used to tell me everything. What happened to you?"

I fidgeted nervously in my seat, staring at the multicolored painted concrete floor.

What do I say? What can I tell her? Damn it. I shouldn't have come here.

"You wouldn't understand. Just please accept that I'm here now."

Fallon got up and sat next to me on the couch. She put an arm around me and pulled me in close to her.

"Whatever you've been through, I'll understand. Please, just tell me."

Her warmth radiated through my skin, reminding me of what it was like to feel the heat of the sun as a mortal. I took a slow deep breath; her sugary smell played at my nose, tempting me.

I jerked away. "No, please sit back over there." I pointed to the chair in front of me. I opened my mouth wide, gulping a breath of air, hoping to wash away the sweet smell that threatened to call out my hunger.

Fallon gasped. I realized she must have caught sight of my teeth.

Crap.

She jerked away quickly, falling off of the couch. "What the fuck!"

I reached down to help pick her up off the ground, but she recoiled.

"Yeah, I see how well you understand," I said, noting the horrified, wide-eyed look on her face. "I knew I shouldn't have come here."

Pushing myself up from the couch, I stood up and took a step toward the front door.

A warm hand grabbed me, and I looked back. Fallon still looked at me with horror, but something in her eyes told me to stay.

"Alyssa…" She looked like she was struggling with what to say. I wished I could read her thoughts. A rush of confused feelings vibrated from her. I felt each one as if they were my own. Anger, sadness, disgust, worry, and most of all, fear.

Against my better judgment, I accepted the pull of her hand, retreating back to the couch. She inched away to the edge as I sat back down.

"What… why… who…" She kept opening her mouth to speak and shutting it again as each sound escaped.

Do I tell her the truth? She knows, but she may not believe it until I say it. Is there some other explanation I can give her to calm her fears?

I took no pleasure in seeing how frightened she was. She wasn't my victim. It pained me to see the panic in her eyes. I recalled how it had felt when Lysander first told me what I was. I couldn't imagine being such a thing. I thought myself a monster. If Fallon made the connection—and the scared look on her face suggested she did—I had no doubt she would think of me as a monster too.

"I'm the same Alyssa you've always known. Please don't look at me like that."

Fallon reached up, trembling fingers pointed toward my face. "Your eyes, your skin, those teeth... What...What are you?"

"So I look a little different. I'm still me." I needed her to believe me. The terrified look on her face tore at my heart.

"What happened? You have to tell me." She pulled another cigarette from her pack.

I took a deep breath and searched for the right words. I needed to put this delicately. "What do you think I am? What do you think happened to me?" *Best to assess what she thinks before I go giving away too many secrets.*

"I... you're... This is crazy. I can't say it." She fidgeted unsuccessfully with her lighter.

Well, that settles it. She knows. She had the same knowing disbelief I had experienced the night I was turned. I had seen the truth staring back at me, but I hadn't wanted to believe it. "I am what you think I am." *Could I be more vague?* "But I'm not here to hurt you or anyone else."

I grabbed the lighter from her shaking hands and lit her cigarette for her.

"Thanks." She took a quick puff. "This is crazy. I'm not even going to say what I think you are. It's not possible."

"It is. And I am."

"How?"

How? That one word brought back flashes of memory: a fist slamming into my face, a knife thrust into my back, the cold, creepy oozing feeling of blood spilling out of my body onto the warm asphalt. I winced from the echoed pain, clenching my jaw.

"The night you ditched me," I said, a note of anger in my voice.

The cigarette dropped as Fallon's hand shot up to cover her mouth.

"I walked home alone that night and was attacked. Two men beat me. They tried …" The memory of the fat, ugly man holding me down as his friend unzipped his pants played before my eyes. "They tried to rape and kill me." My fist clenched at my side as I struggled to push the memories away. I spoke through gritted teeth, fighting to hold back the anger in my voice. "I almost died."

"I didn't know." Her voice cracked. "Lyssa, I'm so sorry."

I nodded and cleared my throat, taking a moment to calm myself. I wasn't angry at Fallon, but the memories of that brutal night were still very painful. "A man came to my rescue, and…" *How do I say this?* "Took care of them." I lowered my voice to a whisper. "He changed me because … otherwise I would have died."

"H-h-how?" She took a few heavy breaths.

"Calm down. Just breathe. Trust me. You don't really want the details." I had already told her too much. I didn't want to relive that night anymore, but my memory flashed again and I saw myself lying in Lysander's arms, drinking blood from his wrist. I writhed in pain as liquid fire surged through me, changing me—turning me into a vampire.

"You drink … blood … don't you?"

I groaned under my breath. This was the question I dreaded most of all. She couldn't possibly understand the need – the want. The desire.

I glanced down to the floor, not wanting to see the expression on her face when I quietly answered, "Yes."

Another sharp gasp came from Fallon's direction. I didn't want to look up; I knew the disgusted look was there, painted across her face. Who could blame her? What rational human being could understand drinking blood? I struggled with it myself in those first few weeks as a newborn vampire.

Though the café was filled with the continuous hum of conversations going on all around us, the silence between Fallon and me was all I could focus on. For what felt like a small eternity, I sat there, not speaking, not looking at her, as I awaited a response—any response.

She wasn't saying anything. Fear permeated her scent, intensifying it, making it more potent to my senses. She was in shock. I needed to snap her out of this.

I looked up and spotted the coffee Fallon offered me earlier. I grabbed it and handed it to her while stealing a glance at her face. She looked pale, her jaw trembled, and she stared blankly ahead, eyes blinking in a slow beat, as if in a trance.

I made my voice as soothing as possible. "Drink this, it will help."

Her limp, shaking hand grasped the cup. She brought it to her lips, taking a slow sip.

"I'm not going to hurt you."

She stared down intently at the coffee as she drank, refusing to meet my gaze.

"C'mon Fallon, why would I come here if that was my intention? I know where you live."

She shuddered and scooted further away from me.

"Ok, that didn't come out right. Look, you're still my best friend, and I need a friend right now."

Those words seemed to work. The tension in Fallon's shoulders relaxed. A little color started to return to her face. She took another sip from her coffee.

"So, what you're telling me is vampires are real and you're one of them?"

"Let's just try not to focus on that fact for right now, okay? I'm still Alyssa. No matter what has happened to me, I'm still your friend. Please... accept this."

She let out a loud sigh and fumbled with her cup. After a silent moment. she nodded and looked up at me. "I guess an undead friend is better than no friend at all." She set the coffee cup on the table.

"I'm not dead, or undead, whatever you want to call it." I held out my wrist. "Go on, check my pulse. My heart still beats."

Fallon recoiled again.

I groaned. "I'm not going to hurt you."

She hesitated for a second before reaching out to place her fingers on my wrist. "You're so cold."

"Poor circulation. Can you feel it?"

Her fingers rested over the blue vein pulsing slowly on my wrist. After a moment, a small smile spread across her lips. "I do feel it. But I thought..."

I shook my head. "Not all the myths are true."

"So are you... you know..." Her voice lowered and a spark of excitement glinted in her eyes. "Immortal?"

I giggled at how silly she sounded. "Yeah."

"Don't do that." She winced and leaned back in her chair.

"What?"

"Your smile, it's creepy. Just looking at those teeth." She made an exaggerated shivering motion. "How do you even talk with those things?"

I ran my tongue across my teeth. Fallon shuddered again.

"Will you stop that?"

"I guess I don't notice them anymore. Are they really that obvious?"

"When you smile they are. Just don't smile at me, okay?"

I bit back a laugh so she wouldn't have to see my fangs again. At least she was beginning to calm down about everything.

"So if I hadn't ditched you that night, you wouldn't be this…thing, huh?" There was a hint of sadness in her voice.

"Well, I wouldn't call myself a thing, but yeah, I probably wouldn't. Not that I blame you."

She fidgeted in her chair, grabbed her coffee cup, and rolled it back and forth between her hands. I awaited more questions.

"What's it like?"

"Uh, well…" *Not prepared for that one.* "Not much different from regular life. Diet kind of sucks, and I won't be getting a tan anytime soon, but it has its perks."

She cocked her head to the side. "So you can't go out in the daylight?"

"Nah." I frowned. "I tend to sunburn easily."

Her eyes darted around the room. I could tell she was avoiding looking directly at me. "Yeah, guess that's a downer."

"Wasn't much of a morning person anyway, so I don't miss it too much."

"So, what are the perks?" She seemed to be reaching to keep the conversation light.

"Well, my sire, Lysander. That's the guy who turned me. He is pretty hot."

"Oh?"

"Yeah, we're kind of a thing now."

She giggled. "Go on, describe."

I breathed a sigh of relief, feeling the anxiety was finally leaving her. She was right back to the old Fallon again. Girl talk trumped blood sucking any day, and I could sense she was okay with me, at least for the moment.

"Imagine the statue of David coming to life: tall, dark messy hair, perfect muscles, and gorgeous eyes."

She giggled again. "Oooh. Where can I find one?"

A sudden thought struck me. What if she wanted to be turned? I hoped that wasn't where the conversation was heading. "They aren't all hot guys." I shrugged, trying to look casual. "I just got lucky, I guess."

"I'd say. So any other perks?"

"You know, the usual," I said, flippantly waving my hand in the air. "Strength, speed, ability to leap tall buildings in a single bound… Oh, wait, that's Superman." I winked.

"Lyssa, stop playing."

"Okay, the strength and speed part are true."

"Really? Show me!"

"Not here. That's the thing." I leaned in closer to her, and thankfully she didn't back away. I dropped my voice to a whisper. "I kind of broke a rule by coming here."

"What do you mean?"

"I'm not supposed to tell anyone about what I am."

"Well, technically you didn't. I figured it out." She sat up tall in her seat, as if showing off how smart she felt.

"You'd never have known if I hadn't shown up."

"I see your point." She reached to her pack of smokes, grabbed one, and lit it. "So showing off is a no-no then?"

"Yeah."

"Gotcha. But, since I already know about you, can you tell me more?

The damage is already done. "I guess there's no harm in chatting. Let's just keep our voices low. Okay?"

"Yeah. So what else can you tell me? Oooh, weaknesses. Let's say I needed to kill you."

"Right." I laughed. "With that line of questioning, you think I'm going to tell you?"

"I was just joking. C'mon, I could never kill my best friend." She arched an eyebrow at me. "Just like she could never kill me, right?"

"I already told you, I'm not going to hurt you."

"Just checking. So what is it? Garlic, stakes through the heart, holy water?"

"None of the above."

"None? What the hell, you're just invincible?"

"Hardly. Those things aren't going to hurt me though. Stake through the heart might be really painful, but I doubt it would kill me. We regenerate really fast."

The fearful look crept back across her face.

"So what does kill you?"

I lowered my voice to a barely audible murmur. "Fire and dismemberment."

She cringed. "Well … at least there is something."

"Happy now?"

"For the moment."

Another awkward pause left us both fidgeting in our seats. I wished I were strong enough to read her mind. It would make this so much easier. I could sense her lingering fear rising back to the surface. I knew she wanted to know more, but the details we had yet to discuss were the ones that would scare her.

She nibbled at her thumbnail. "So, what about blood?"

"Do you really want these details?"

She took a deep breath and sighed. "Yeah, I think I have to know."

I groaned. "Before I answer this question, you have to know, I only do what I need to do to survive." *Please don't make me give details.*

"How often do you… drink?"

"Right now, every other night."

"Can you eat real food?"

"No." The answer came out faster than I wanted it to. My heart beat like a drum roll as I awaited the inevitable. *Here comes the bad question.*

"When did you last… have a drink?"

Not the one I expected; maybe she won't go into detail. Now, do I tell her I just fed, or do I tell her it's been a while? What will she be able to accept?

"I drank earlier this evening. I'm not thirsty, if that's what you're getting at."

She gave me a weak smile. "And how exactly do you get your bl… drinks?"

Crap, that's the one I was dreading. "Look, I've got plenty of sources all over the city. I told you, I have to drink it to survive."

"Hey, this isn't like choosing to be a vegan or something," she snapped at me. "You're drinking blood."

"Keep it down. I don't want the whole café hearing this."

"Fine. I'm just trying to figure out if I can accept this." Fallon's disgust was starting to show again.

Maybe if I keep her arguing with me, I can avoid the finer points of obtaining blood.

"Yeah, I get it, you're shocked. How do you think I felt? It's not like I had a choice in the matter." I shot her a cold stare. "I was dying. Cut me a little slack."

"Well this isn't easy for me either. I just found out my best friend is a blood sucking vampire."

A few people around us stopped their conversation and looked back giving me an odd look.

"Fallon, why did you have to ruin my secret?" I tried to fill my voice with sarcastic laughter. "Now what will I be for Halloween this year?" Thankfully with all the Goths frequenting this place, talk of vampires didn't draw too much attention.

Leaning in toward Fallon, I scowled. "Don't make me say this again. Keep your voice down. People are starting to look at us."

Her face reddened with embarrassment. "Sorry."

"Can you accept me for who I am now?"

"I'm trying to figure that out. I don't want you drinking my blood."

I rolled my eyes. "I'm not going to drink your blood. I already told you I'm not going to hurt you. Chill, okay?"

"Then where do you get your blood from?"

Damn, she just doesn't give up.

"I already told you, I have sources all over town. You don't need to worry. I'm not going to turn on my friends."

Please just drop this. I don't want to give you details.

My memory flashed. The faces of all my victims slowly came into view, one by one. I saw the terror in their wide eyes, seconds before I sank my teeth into their necks. My stomach turned and I felt sick as guilt washed over me, realizing I'd lost my humanity so quickly. In just a few short months, I had become accustomed to killing. I hadn't even given a second thought to those people I murdered. I couldn't blame Fallon for being scared. I would be too, sitting this close to a monster.

"Fine. Quit with the puppy dog eyes, I believe you. You just got to let me wrap my head around this, okay?"

I breathed a sigh of relief. "Thank you."

A few moments of silence passed between us. The strange, familiar prickling sensation tickled against the back of my neck. My head shot up. I scanned the windows, looking for signs of an immortal's presence.

I couldn't tell which direction the creepy prickling feeling came from. The hair on the back of my neck stood on end. Worry swam in my gut, but I figured I was safe, for the moment, in the company of humans. A hunter like Santino wouldn't dare attack in public. Hunters guarded our secret as well as they guarded the humans they protected us from.

5

itting in the café talking to Fallon was as good an insurance policy as any, but I knew it wouldn't last long. I couldn't stay here forever. I'd have to face the vampire stalking around outside sooner or later. Copioh didn't stay open all night, and even if it did, there was no way I could stay here past dawn—there were too many uncovered windows. I couldn't go home either and risk Santino or any of the Saints following me. I needed a Plan B.

I tried to blank my face of any worried expressions. I didn't need Fallon getting scared again. "Hey. You have your cell on you?"

Fallon fixed me with a narrow gaze before reaching into her small canvas purse. "Where's yours?" She pulled out a black clam-shell phone. "Guess that explains why you never answered my calls."

"Yeah. My phone's gone. It got smashed up pretty good the night I ... uh ... never mind. Besides, I wasn't supposed to tell anyone about myself, remember?" I took the phone from her and dialed Lysander's number. "You know, the whole secret thing."

"Well, the secret's out now. So I'll expect you to keep in touch."

I nodded as I pressed the send button. *Hmm, how do I explain this to Lysander?* It rang a few times before his deep voice greeted me.

I took a deep breath to gather my courage. This wasn't going to be a good conversation. I knew Lysander would be furious with me once I told him where I was and what I had been doing.

"It's me, Alyssa." I tried to sound casual. "I need you to listen for a second, okay?"

He cut me off before I could say another word. "Where are you?" His voice carried an urgent tone. "What's going on? Are you hurt? What is all that noise I hear in the background?"

I could just imagine the wide-eyed expression on his face.

"I'm fine. But none of us are really safe. I was right. I saw Santino while I was out…" Fallon's head turned just slightly to the side so her ear faced me. She was eaves-dropping. I knew I needed to choose my words carefully. I didn't want to say something that might spook her, but I needed to make sure that Lysander understood the warning I was trying to give. "… You know, when I left the house this evening."

"You saw him?" Worry strained his voice. "Where is he now? Are you safe?"

"Not sure. I got away. I'm at a café right now with a friend." I cringed. I knew he wouldn't be pleased with me.

"You're where?" His tone rose sharply.

"I'm at Copioh," I said sweetly, trying to act as inno-cent as I could. "I'm with my old friend Fallon." I bit my lip waiting for him to yell and scream. I knew I was in trouble.

His voice became unexpectedly monotone. "You told a mortal about us, didn't you?"

I gulped, and took a deep breath. "I had to do something. He won't bother me here. Too many people around."

"Who won't bother you?" Fallon asked.

I waved my hand to stop her from questioning me. I didn't need to hear it from both sides.

Fallon let out an impatient sigh and crossed her arms in front of her chest.

I mouthed the words, "I'll tell you in a second," before putting my finger to my lips.

"Stay where you are," Lysander said. It was more of an order than a request. "I'm going to discuss this with the rest of the clan. I will call you back at this phone number."

Wow, no screaming. He's taking this a little better than I expected.

I covered the receiver with my hand. "Fallon, can I use your phone for a bit tonight?"

Her deep brown eyes locked on me. "Yeah, sure, as long as you tell me what's going on."

I knew I wouldn't be able to escape the inquisition. This wasn't going to be a pleasant evening. Letting out an exasperated sigh, I took my hand off of the receiver. "Yeah, Lysander, call me back here."

"Okay. I will be back with you shortly. Alyssa, promise me you will stay where you are until I call. Do not do anything more to endanger yourself." The phone disconnected before I could say good-bye.

I placed the phone down on the table. "Great, he's pissed at me." Pissed for good reason, of course. Out of all the places I chose to hide, I had to pick one where I had mortal friends. There was nothing to be done about that now. I just hoped that Lysander would go easy on me when we did meet up again.

"What's going on?" Fallon still had her inquisitive eyes locked on me. "What else haven't you told me?"

Round two for the inquisition. Boy, am I getting myself in deep. I cleared my throat, while trying to find the right words to say. "Remember I said I wasn't supposed to tell people about my kind?"

She tapped her sandaled foot on the concrete and drummed her fingers against her folded arms. "Yeah. And…"

"Well, I'm kind of in trouble for that right now. Lysander is pissed." I lowered my voice to a whisper. "Oh, and I have someone after me."

Fallon blinked a few times and shook her head. "Did I just hear that? Someone is after you? Who's going to go after vampires?"

"Shhh." I leaned in closer.

"Sorry."

"Think about it. Who goes after …" —*How do I put this?*— "people like me?"

"You mean like…" I saw the proverbial light bulb go on in Fallon's eyes. "Vampire hunters?"

"Bingo! "I nodded.

Realization quickly turned to renewed fear in Fallon's expression. Her eyes grew wide, pupils dilating, her breath quickened. "Shit! Am I in trouble now too?" She pushed back in her chair. I heard her heart rate jump to a thundering drum beat in her chest.

"No, I don't think so." I shook my head. "If anyone sees you with me, they probably think you're my…um…

Well, you're probably in more danger from me than them."

Fallon stifled a gasp, covering her mouth with her hand. "They think I'm … your dinner, don't they?"

"Maybe." I shrugged and gave her a halfhearted smile. I wanted to look as casual as possible about it. I didn't want her freaking out about how true her assumption was. "Let them think that if it will keep you safe. Remember, they're after me, not you."

"So let me get this straight. Someone's after you, and you're out in the open, divulging your secret. Why?"

"As strange as it sounds, I'm safer here with you than out on the street."

She shook her head and waved her arms in front of her face. "Wait, this makes no sense."

"Okay, look." I scooted close to her and lowered my voice to a whisper. "They hunt my kind, but they also keep my kind a secret from your kind. Get it? They aren't going to attack me in the open, in front of lots of people."

She stiffened in her chair and reached for her cigarettes again. "What if you're wrong?"

"I'm not. Think about it, have you ever heard about us before? I mean really, not just books and stories?"

Fallon shook her head slowly.

"That's because both sides want to keep it that way. Trust me. No one will attack in the open."

The odd prickling sensation continued to nag at the back of my neck. I knew someone was close, and chances were, it wasn't anyone friendly to me. I glanced down at the phone, hoping it would ring. I needed some direction. I couldn't stay in the café all night. I needed a way out of here, past the immortal stalking around outside. My guess was that Santino had somehow tracked me here and was searching around the perimeter of the café, locating all of the potential exits, to prevent my escape.

Fallon sat quietly, across the table from me, sucking down her cigarette at record speed. I could tell she was having trouble processing all of this information. Not that I blamed her for that.

I scanned the area, looking around the café, searching through the front windows, watching people, looking for a sign, any sign, of who was out there.

"I need another coffee," Fallon said, finally breaking the silence between us. She snatched up her empty cup and headed toward the bar.

For a moment I wondered if she was using this as an excuse to leave. I wouldn't blame her for that either. I shouldn't have gotten her involved.

She stood at the bar, shooting nervous glances back in my direction as she waited for the barista to finish making her drink. Worry covered her face like an ugly mask.

The door opened and a few people walked inside. Fallon jumped as they got close to her at the bar.

What have I done? Look at her, she's on the verge of a nervous breakdown.

The cell phone buzzed on the table, snapping me back to the matter at hand. A wave of relief washed through me seeing Lysander's number on the caller ID. I snatched the phone and answered, "What's the plan?"

"We need you to stay out in the open until we can find a safe place to meet. How much longer can you stay at that café?" Hints of irritation still colored his tense voice, but I could tell he was more worried than angry.

"Uh … not much longer. I can feel someone close, and this café will start closing up in about an hour."

Silence filled the line, and then Lysander took a deep breath.

"Go to a casino. I don't know how long we will be. You can stay there safely all day if necessary. Just stay away from doors or any exits. When you get to a safe spot, call me and we will plan where to meet."

A casino. Why didn't I think of that?

"Is that your guy?" Fallon asked as she walked up behind me.

I nodded. "Got it, I'll call you when I get there."

I looked up to find Fallon gulping down her coffee.

"Hey, look, I'm sorry I dragged you into this. I'm going to get out of your hair."

Fallon breathed a sigh of relief, but something in her eyes told me she wasn't going to let me go.

I gave her a reassuring smile. "Don't worry, you should be just fine. I'm sure the hunter will be happy I left you alone."

"Where are you going now?"

"Nowhere really, I just need to hide out for a day or so until I can get back to my clan."

She hesitated, set the cup down on the table, and wrung her hands. "You...uh, need a ride?"

"Really?" I had expected her to run screaming back to her home after all I had told her. "No, I can't. I've dragged you in too far already."

Another sigh escaped her lips. I could tell she didn't want to be involved in anything I was doing, but she didn't want to betray her friendship to me.

"It's fine," she said, her voice trembling a little. "I'll drop you off and keep you company until your... people get there. It's the least I can do."

"Really, Fallon, you don't have to do this."

"I don't want to leave you all alone again, okay? Last time I did that, bad things happened." She bit her lower lip. "If you're in danger and having me around helps, I'm glad to do it. I just got my best friend back. I don't want to worry that anything else is going to take you away again."

The fact that she would support me, even though she was scared, warmed my heart. I shot up and threw my arms around her. "You're a true friend. Thanks."

She returned the gesture, patting me lightly on the back as she hugged me. "Just try not to get all vampy on me, okay?"

I pulled back; a smile stretched the corners of my lips. "Vampy? Is that even a word?"

Fallon cringed slightly. "There you go with those teeth   again."
The eerie prickling feeling intensified. A moment later, the door to the café opened and a dark figure, wearing a long, thick trench coat and heavy boots entered.

Shit! "Time to go," I said, almost knocking over a chair as I tried to move away from the table.

"Who is that?" The color drained from Fallon's face. She turned quickly toward the man who had just entered the café.

The odd sensation radiated from him like a wave. A wild mane of salt and pepper hair shadowed his face, but I knew exactly who he was… Santino. "Let's get out of here. Go ahead of me and get the car started. Meet me around back. I'll wait a few minutes before leaving to draw his attention."

"He's standing right in front of the door. How am I—"

"Just act like he's a normal person. Say 'Excuse me' and walk past. Remember, no one will hurt you. I'm the one he's after."

She hesitated for a moment before taking a few shaky steps forward. As I expected, he let her pass, but he kept an eye on her as she walked out the door. I used the distraction to make my escape. Ducking behind chairs and mixing in with the crowd, I tried my best to stay out of his direct line of vision as I headed back behind the makeshift stage to the emergency exit.

The back door led to a dark alley behind the building. I hoped Santino would still be looking around the café for me. This would give me a chance to get to Fallon's car without incident.

I kept to the shadows as I headed down the alley. A door banged closed behind me.

"You can't run forever, little one," Santino's grizzly voice echoed in the silence.

"Seems you're slow to keep up, Santino. Still a bit toasty from the fire?" I taunted, reminding him of the last battle my clan had fought with him. Anticipation hummed in my body.

Before I could make a move to run, a rush of air blew past me. A rough hand clenched around my neck before his face came into view. He was faster than I had anticipated. Santino slammed me into a cinder-block wall. The air rushed out of my chest with the impact. Stars danced in front of my eyes before the world momentarily faded to black.

"A smart mouth like that deserves to be shut. Forever," he growled.

I shook off the haze in my vision. "Not today," I choked out the words as I reached up to pry his hand from my throat.

Santino lifted me up with one hand. His other reached down. I knew from memory he carried a large knife in his belt. It was the one he'd used to behead Kallisto. The same knife that haunted my dreams.

I fought with all my strength, kicking my legs and throwing wild punches at Santino. My foot caught the crook of his right elbow. I shoved my sole down hard, knocking his arm back. He let out a muffled curse as he lost his grip on the knife. It flew into the darkness of the alley, landing with a loud *clank*. I thrashed even harder, trying to break his steel grip on my neck. Weapon or no, he was still a deadly warrior.

His fingers tightened, digging into my throat. I felt the pinch as his nails pierced my skin. His eyes narrowed, and he fixed me with a deadly stare.

I turned my head and squeezed my eyes closed, refusing to look at him. I knew the danger there. He was going to try to subdue me using only his mind, an old and very useful trick against young vampires like myself. I'd been warned many times by members of my clan to avoid eye contact for this reason. I would be just as weak and easily susceptible to his influence as a human was to mine.

With my back pressed to the wall for support, I lifted both legs and slammed my feet into Santino's chest. He was a solid wall of muscle. My heels ached from the impact. Santino grunted. His grip loosened just slightly around my neck, but not enough to allow me to break free.

A horn blared in the distance. I guessed it was Fallon, ready to make our escape. I heard the rumble of a car engine and the screech of tires near the outlet of the alley.

Chancing a look, I turned my head and opened my eyes. The alley opened up to a residential street, and there at the end was Fallon's old silver VW Bug.

She leaned out of the driver side window and yelled, "Put her down," then revved the car's engine. Fallon looked like she was ready to run us both down with the car. Guess she had been paying attention when I said it was only fire and dismemberment that killed us. I took a deep breath and braced for impact, wondering how much it was going to hurt.

Santino growled loudly, a sound of frustration, and shook me from my thoughts. "Perhaps today is not your day to die. We'll see each other soon."

The pressure at my neck was gone as if it had never been there. I fell to the ground in a heap.

Not chancing another look at Santino—not giving him another opportunity to destroy me—I took off at top speed, heading straight for the car. Fallon flung the passenger door open for me to climb in.

"Great job! Let's get out of here quick." I threw myself in and slammed the door shut.

My hands went to my throat, massaging the area where Santino had held me. I took a few deep breaths, trying to calm the pounding of my own heart.

With a loud squeal of rubber against pavement, Fallon took off, out of the alley. She barreled down Maryland, and then took Flamingo, all the way to the Strip.

"Geeze girl, remember you're not the immortal one here. Slow down before you get yourself killed," I yelled.

Fallon had a white-knuckle grip on the steering wheel. "What about that guy following you?"

"He's on foot. No way he is going to keep up with us." *Why did he let me go?*

"Was he the—"

"Yeah, he was the big bad-ass himself. Thanks for saving me back there."

A strange realization hit me. I shouldn't have been able to get away from him so easily. Santino never failed in his missions. *Why did he care that Fallon was around? He would know that she knew about us. Something is up. He's been near me twice. Near my home. He knew I was close to home when I was hunting. Why have I been able to get away from him so many times?*

"How are you going to hide from him?" Fallon's words shook me from my thoughts.

It took a moment for me to answer. "Take me to a casino. It's a perfect place to hide in plain sight. No natural light and an abundance of mortals... er... people."

Fallon turned the car on to the Strip. Traffic was slower here, as usual, so she was forced to drive at a more normal pace. "Okay, so which one?"

I looked out of the window. We were surrounded by the towering hotels of the Strip. Flashing lights, neon signs, and an endless sea of pedestrians crowded around us. "I don't care which one you pick. They're all going to have lots of people around."

A loud cannon blast accompanied a musical number as a fountain show started to my right. Large plumes of water shot up into the sky, and color-changing lights helped to set the mood. I watched the pedestrians swarming around the dancing water, trying to find the best vantage point to watch the show.

With so many people around, I should be safe from Santino. He wouldn't attempt to hunt me down in a casino, would he? Was he really hunting? Why did he just let me go? Something's definitely not right and, I need to figure out what he's up to.

6

I called Lysander as soon as we walked into the casino. He didn't sound particularly happy that Fallon was still with me, but told me to get a room and to keep her close until he and Nicholas showed up.

After wandering through the late-night crowd for half an hour, checking to see if we'd been followed, Fallon and I got a room as Lysander had instructed. I thought it odd that he wanted us away from the crowd, hidden in a hotel room. It was after all, the reason we chose a casino. Being surrounded by people would keep the Acta Sanctorum, and Santino in particular, at bay, but I was sure Lysander had his reasons, and I too was eager to have a little peace and quiet.

Fallon stretched her arms wide as we reached the room and let out a roaring yawn.

"I saw that," I teased. Her eyes looked tired and heavy. In the dim light of the hallway, the dark circles around them appeared like sagging bruises. "Why don't you try to get a little rest. You look exhausted."

I opened the door and flicked on the light. The room came alive. Standard for most hotels on the Strip, it had two queen beds, a TV armoire, a dresser, and a small table with chairs. Peaceful pictures of trees and streams hung on walls that had been painted in warm, earthy tones of brown and sage. It felt comfy and inviting. If I had been in a better mood, I might have given in to the urge to bounce on the beds and test out the fluffiness of the pillows.

Fallon cupped her mouth to stifle another loud yawn. "I'm not a night owl like you."

"You used to be. What happened?"

She shot me a cold glance and flopped down on the bed. "Try a couple months of worrying yourself sick about a friend. You know the cops weren't any help. I called them after I went to your apartment." She reached into her purse and pulled out a crumpled photograph. I knew it before she unfolded it. It was the one of us on the beach. The one I'd left her to find in my apartment. "When I saw this, I knew you were gone."

Her words cut me like a knife. Tears welled in the corners of my eyes. I hated that I'd made her worry so much. I turned to look out of the window. We had a beautiful view of the Strip below. It was a sea of rainbow-colored neon and people, moving all around as far as my eyes could see. Humans, completely unaware of the secret world that I lived in. "You understand now why I had to leave everything behind, right?"

"Yeah. I get it now. But then, I was a mess. The cops let me put in a missing persons report, but they never looked for you. I checked back with them every week, hoping to hear something. I haven't had a good night's sleep in a long time."

"I'm so sorry, Fallon," I said, drawing the curtains closed, using it as an excuse to not have to look at her and see the sadness on her face. "Just crash here for a bit. Lysander should be here soon." I admired the weight of the curtains, running my hands over the material, thankful that the hotel used very thick black-out curtains on their windows. That would come in handy once the sun rose.

"He's nice, right?" Fallon asked sleepily. "This Lysander guy?"

"Yeah. No worries about him. Trust me." I turned and smiled innocently. I knew Lysander would be upset that I had broken the rules. "He won't hurt you. It's my head he's going to bite off." I was more worried about his anger towards me than his reaction to Fallon. "But yeah, he's a good guy."

Fallon seemed to be past any real caring. She flopped backward on the bed and curled up with the pillows and blankets. She was snoring in moments. I took the opportunity to relax a little myself. I settled into one of the chairs and grabbed the TV remote to flip through channels, hoping for a little distraction. Again, I wondered why it had been so easy to escape from Santino. It was strange. It wasn't like a great warrior of his stature to leave survivors, let alone allow a young vampire like me, to get away. *Fallon's presence wouldn't have been enough to stop him from trying to kill me. Why did he let me go?*

The news report caught my interest. It was a replay from an earlier broadcast. The anchor, a handsome, well-dressed man in his early thirties, spoke about gang-related violence in North Town. A woman had been brutally killed and her dismembered body left in pieces all over the street. Witnesses clamored around the reporter to get their five minutes of fame and give their report. People of all kinds smiled and waved to the camera from behind the news reporter as he interviewed an eyewitness.

"He was on something," a middle-aged woman commented. "All messed up. On drugs. And he had bloodshot eyes. He was swearing and cursing and falling all over himself. When he saw that woman he just lost it." The lady on the television put her hand over her mouth. "He ran after her." The woman's voice rose sharply, giving away the true extent of the horror she'd witnessed.

A tall, emaciated woman with stringy hair spoke up, pushing the first woman out of the camera view. "He chased that poor girl." Her arms waved wildly as she tried to describe the scene. "Damn near ripped her hair out trying to catch her. As soon as I saw that, I was on the phone dialing 9-1-1-"

The reporter came back on screen, continuing to describe the scene as paramedics wheeled the dead body—or what was left of it—zippered in a black body bag, into the back of an ambulance.

A flash of anger burned through me. *Santino chases us down and calls us monsters. Humans are monsters too. Look at what they're reporting on the news. A vampire wouldn't have done that. Who's the real monster?*

***

I was beginning to worry, wondering if Santino had found Lysander or the others. Time was again mocking me. Anticipation knotted my stomach. I found myself constantly checking the time on Fallon's phone.

An eerie feeling crawled up the back of my neck, and my hair stood on end. A vampire was close. I flinched when I heard a knock at the door, and then a warm soothing feeling washed through me, erasing my fear.

I knew without a doubt that Lysander was here. We were bonded not only as master and fledgling, but also as lovers. I felt his strength and presence like a beacon even before I heard his voice on the other side of the door. "Open the door ,Alyssa."

I ran to it and almost tore it off the hinges in my haste to see him. Lysander's face gave away his anger before he had the chance to speak to me. There was an unusual and cruel slash to his mouth. As he entered the room, his sharp eyes moved from me to Fallon's sleeping body and back, but he didn't say a word.

Wanting to diffuse his anger, I threw my arms around his neck. "I'm so glad to see you. I've been so worried." I planted a small kiss on his cheek before pulling back to look into his eyes. They were narrow and cold as he returned my gaze. His jaw looked tight, as if he were clenching his teeth to avoid speaking.

I sighed and resigned myself to getting an earful about how foolishly I'd acted. At least he was here and safe. That was all that mattered for the moment.

Nicholas strolled into the room, a smug smile plastered across his face. He chuckled as he caught my forlorn expression. "Trouble loves you, doesn't it?"

I shrugged. "I guess it does."

Fallon stirred under the covers.

I shot Nicholas a cold look, putting my finger to my lips. "Keep it down, she's really burned out."

Lysander finally spoke, his voice low and monotone. "You knew better, Alyssa."

"I had no choice. Santino was following me. I needed to go somewhere populated. It was the only place I could think of." The words came out in a single breath. I felt anger radiating in waves from Lysander's silent stare.

Nicholas strutted over to the bed and hovered above Fallon. "You live in a tourist town and some silly little hole-in-the-wall café is the only place you could think of with people?"

Heat rose to my face, flushing my cheeks. "Look, it was a snap decision. Would you rather I had just let him kill me?" I stepped closer to the bed, hoping to put myself between Fallon and Nicholas. I didn't like him being so close to her.

"You need to be more careful in your choices," Lysander said, his voice still eerily monotone. "There are repercussions when you bring mortals into our world."

I jerked my head in Lysander's direction. My heart skipped a beat. I knew he was mad. I was prepared for yelling and screaming, but his unnatural calm and talk of repercussions had me worried. What if I was wrong in thinking Fallon was safe with us? "Wait, what do you mean 'repercussions'?"

Fallon woke with a start and shot bolt upright in bed. She recoiled at the sight of Nicholas next to her and tried to pull the sheet over her head. She squealed, "What's going on? Who are they?"

I held my hands up hoping to stop her from bolting from the bed. "It's okay. Don't worry, Fallon. This is Lysander and Nicholas."

Fallon inched herself away from Nicholas. She fell off the bed, hitting the floor with a *thud*, and then quickly scrambled to her feet and backed against the wall.

I turned to Lysander. "You never said anything about repercussions. What do you mean?"

"Is something else wrong now?" Fallon asked, her voice shaking.

"I'm sorry, Alyssa, but you brought this upon yourself and your friend," Lysander's tone was somber. He raked a hand through his dark hair and exhaled a deep sigh. "She knows too much, and I cannot allow her to leave us."

"What do you mean?" I slowly came to a terrifying realization. My hands clenched into tight fists at my side. "No. Lysander, she's my friend. You can't do this."

Fallon took another half-step backward, plastering herself against the wall; her already large brown eyes widened more as she listened to our conversation. She looked like a deer caught in headlights. Her body shook with fear. I guessed she had come to the same realization I had.

"I'll take care of this. You'll be fine." I needed to calm her down, but inside I wasn't sure I could. Lysander and Nicholas meant business. The serious and deadly looks on their faces were hard to ignore.

Lysander frowned. "Alyssa, our laws are put in place to keep our kind protected. We have to—"

"We can trust her," I pleaded, grabbing ahold of his shoulders and gazing deep into his eyes. I'd never forgive them if they killed her. I had to find some way to smooth things over. I wanted him to let her go. I willed him to feel the fear I felt for her, sending out all my mental anguish in a wave toward him. He couldn't do this. He couldn't end her life because I broke a rule.

Fallon took advantage of the momentary silence. I saw the flash of her shadow as she sprinted toward the door. Nicholas made quick work of preventing her escape. In a superhuman blur, he caught her by the door and took hold of her wrists.

She struggled against his grip. "Damn it! Ouch … you're hurting me. Let me go." Leaning as far away as she could manage, she turned her pleading eyes to me. "Alyssa … help."

"Nicholas, stop," I yelled as I saw him twist her around and wrench her arm up behind her back.

He walked her back to Lysander, ignoring her whimpers of protest. "Don't take that tone with me," he growled at me. "You do not command me, little one. Lysander has made up his mind, and we will follow his orders."

I turned back to Lysander. "Please, don't do this." Tears formed in my eyes making it hard to see, casting the room in a blood-red haze. I wiped at my face, seeing the tinged traces of bloody tears staining my pale skin. "You can't do this to her. She's the only reason I'm alive. She helped me escape from Santino."

"Alyssa, this is for the best. You will understand this in time." Lysander's voice was soft, but hardly reassuring. "If it will make you feel better, you can be the one to do it."

"What?" Both Fallon and I shrieked at the same moment.

"I will allow you to turn her," Lysander answered. "I cannot let her remain mortal."

I breathed a momentary sigh of relief. *Oh, thank god he doesn't want me to kill her.*

"Hey. Don't I get a say in this? I don't want to be one of you," Fallon said, still struggling to fight against Nicholas's grip. She was no match for his strength though. He wrapped an arm around her waist and pulled her back against his body.

"It's better than the alternative," Nicholas spoke into her ear. A wicked sneer covered his face.

Lysander's head cocked to the side, he arched an eyebrow at her. "Miss Fallon," he said reaching out to take her hand and pulled her toward him. "Please understand this is for the best." He covered her hand with his—a gesture I assumed was meant to be comforting. "Think of this as a gift."

The effect was lost on Fallon. There was no relief in her eyes. She stood stiff as a board, biting her bottom lip. The thundering drumbeat of her heart gave away her fear, even though she tried to hide it with a blank stare.

"Please, it's not that I don't appreciate what you offer, I just don't want it."

Lysander was silent for a moment. His lips pinched together and his nostrils flared as he breathed. "We cannot allow our secret out." His low, controlled tone sent a shiver down my spine. "The Saints are just one group among many who wish to see our kind and others of the supernatural world destroyed. Secrecy is our first line of defense."

Fallon's eyes glossed with tears, she lowered her head and focused on the floor. My heart ached. She looked so defeated.

Lysander guided her in front of me. "Since you trust Alyssa, I will let her be the one to take your blood. You can rest assured she will not kill you. I hope that will be of some comfort to you."

Fallon's body shook, trembling with fear. The intoxicating scent of it would have normally sent me into a ravenous frenzy, but not this time. I did not want to taste her blood. I did not want to do anything to harm her. Guilt churned in the pit of my stomach.

"I should have never gone to you. I should have never told you what happened. I'm so sorry, Fallon."

She whimpered, still looking at the ground.

"Please forgive me. Say something."

She looked up. Tears were streaming from her puffy eyes. "Will it hurt?" Fallon sniffled. She was a wreck, but trying to be brave.

What do I tell her? Yeah, this is going to hurt, quite a bit actually. She's already a mess.

I remembered back to the excruciating pain I had felt as the blood—the liquid fire Lysander had fed me—rushed through my veins: the head splitting ache of my skull as my jaw shifted to accommodate my new teeth, and the sharp stabbing pains as my internal organs died off. I winced at the memory of that pain.

I chose my words carefully. "I'll do my best not to hurt you."

She gasped, probably realizing the hidden meaning behind my half-truth.

I took a deep breath and held out my arms to embrace her. "Come closer, please."

Part of me waited with anticipation for the hot rush of blood once I opened her vein. Instincts are hard to quiet; however, a larger part of me felt pure sympathy for her. I knew how hard this was for Fallon. The uncertainly, the fear, the anticipation. My psychic abilities, though very limited, allowed me feel the swarm of emotions tearing through her. She put on a brave face. Her eyes, though glassy, were stubbornly locked on mine.

"Just be calm and relax," I whispered, calling forth the strength inside me. I matched her stare, sending a wave of calm toward her, willing her to be still, numb, and accepting. "This will all be over soon."

Taking her neck into my left hand, I leaned in, my mouth salivating in anticipation.

A small, almost unrecognizable sound rang through my head. A voice. High pitched, yet sounding as if it were a great distance away. I hesitated for a moment.

Alyssa, please don't do this to me, the voice said.

It was Fallon, but she wasn't speaking. I was hearing her thoughts. I had never been able to hear another's inner monologue before. As a young vampire, I had yet to develop that ability as the other, ancients had. She must have been screaming the words in her head. I closed my eyes and silenced my mind, trying to listen again.

Please don't, please. Alyssa, please let me go.

My stomach sank, a new rush of guilt made me feel queasy.

I can't do this to her.

I released my hold on Fallon and turned around, looking imploringly at Lysander.

"It will not be as bad as you fear, Miss Fallon," Lysander said. I had no doubt he could hear her frantic thoughts.

"I don't want this. I don't want to be like you," she blurted between sobs. "I don't want to drink blood. I like the sun. I want to grow old. Have children. And not have to hide from my friends."

"Please reconsider, Lysander. You can trust her to keep our secret," I begged. "I can't do this to her if she doesn't want it."

Nicholas stepped in. He wrapped an arm around her preventing her from flailing. Taking hold of Fallon's head, he bent it sideways, exposing her jugular. "This shouldn't be that complicated. Be happy you are being given the option to live. In my time there was no such choice." He opened his mouth wide, fangs bared to strike.

"I don't want this," she whimpered.

"Nicholas, stop," Lysander commanded.

Nicholas let out a growl of disappointment and raised his head.

Lysander turned to me.

Please let her go, I silently begged as I locked eyes with Lysander. *We can trust her. I would bet my life on it.*

His stern look softened as he stared into my pleading eyes. He glanced back at Fallon, then to Nicholas, and back again to me. "This goes against my better judgment, but I will let her remain human."

I breathed a sigh of relief.

Nicholas let Fallon go with a slight push, causing her to stumble a few steps. He glared menacingly at Lysander but did not speak his protest.

"Don't make me regret this decision, Miss Fallon," Lysander said. "I'll kill you myself if you cause us trouble." He stared straight into Fallon's eyes as he made his warning. "There will not be another offer for immortality. Do you understand?"

I knew this look, and I knew the tone in his voice well enough to know Lysander was as serious as death.

Fallon nodded quickly, and wiped her eyes with her hands. "Thank you," she squeaked. "I won't cause any problems. I promise. I'll never even utter the word 'vampire' again."

I reached out to Fallon. "Sorry about all of this."

She refused to look at me. She wiped her eyes once more, then turned quickly and rushed out of the door.

"Fallon," I yelled after her, but she did not answer. The door slammed shut behind her with a loud *bang*.

Nicholas caught me by the arm. "You too, should be held accountable for Fallon's actions," he said. "If she lets the word out about us, it will be your fault. You could have just turned her."

"She's my friend, Nicholas." I snapped at him and pulled my arm from his grasp. "I couldn't hurt her."

"She *was* your friend. I doubt she is anymore," he said coldly.

"You know, you're an asshole."

"Someone has to be. This isn't a fairytale."

"That's enough, you two," Lysander interrupted. "We have other business to deal with. The rest of the clan should be here soon. We will stay in this casino today and we will all..." he gave me a cold stare, "leave together tomorrow evening."

Nicholas pivoted on his heel and walked to the door. "I'll be at the poker tables to pass some time. Come find me if you need me."

Lysander grabbed me by my shoulder, stopping me before I too walked out of the room.

"Know this, Alyssa... you may be my treasure, but I will hold you accountable if anything happens." His eyes bore into me with an icy harshness.

"What?"

"We cannot let our secret out. Our secret is our protection. I cannot risk more of our kind for one human."

"You're starting to sound like Kallisto." I twisted out of his grasp.

He winced at the mention of her name. "If I were anything like Kallisto, your friend would be dead now." His hands balled to fists. "There is a lot more to leading a clan than just getting your way. I have others to consider, not just you or myself. I would be selfish to risk the lives of my clan mates over one person who could have been turned." His words were cold and unfeeling, his upper lip curled into a sneer as he spoke, revealing his fangs.

"She didn't want this, and I don't blame her." I matched his hard stare. "Given the choice, I wouldn't have either."

Lysander's jaw clenched. His hand reached out and twisted the door knob, yanking the door open. "She had better not betray us," he said as he walked out of the room, slamming the door behind him.

I stood there for a few moments, in silence. I didn't want Lysander to be angry with me, and I didn't want to lose my best friend.

"I'm so sorry," I said to the empty room as I slid down the wall, to the floor. "I've really fucked things up this time."

7

Sulking wasn't going to do me any good, nor was going stir crazy in the empty hotel room. I needed to try to fix what little I could, starting with finding Fallon.

I wandered through the casino amid the constant ear-splitting chimes of slot machines ringing out all around me. Even in the late hours of early morning, people sat glued to the machines, hoping to win their fortune. Various colored lights flashed on my left, followed by the tinkle of coins. A man let out a triumphant cheer.

Someone must have won a big jackpot, I mused.

I weaved my way through the table games, stopping briefly in the Poker Room. Nicholas and Rozaline were inside, seated side by side at a crowded table. Both of them had chip stacks almost double those of the rest of the ten players at the table.

I watched for a moment as Nicholas laid his cards out on the table with a smile. His pair of eights held up over another player's busted straight draw. After looking at the cards, I could tell Nicholas had been using his mental abilities to force his opponent to keep betting even after he had no chance of winning.

Rozaline spotted me and beamed a smile. She indicated the spot at the table where the man Nicholas had just busted was leaving.

Vampires don't have regular jobs. We make our money in whatever way we can. Being a Vegas native, I was already well versed in the game of Texas Hold'em. And being a vampire, with the ability to mentally influence the other players, made the game so much more fun. That handy little ability made sure I would never have to worry about money again.

Under normal circumstances, I'd have joined them, but I still wanted to look for Fallon. I mouthed the word "Later" and continued on, searching the casino.

In the back of my mind, I doubted I'd find Fallon. Knowing her, she was probably driving, pedal to the floor, down the 95 freeway in an effort to put as much distance as she could between us. I would have, if I'd been in her shoes. I hoped, at the very least, if I couldn't find her, that she'd try to contact me in a few days, after she calmed down.

The Sports Book was next door to the Poker Room. I wandered inside, eyeing all of the TV monitors replaying various sporting events of the day. Lysander was sitting at one of the small cubicle booths, scribbling notes onto a pad of paper. I knew he could sense me, but he didn't look up. I turned on my heels and walked out of the dark, cave-like lounge. It was probably for the best. After my comment about him being just like Kallisto. I'd be surprised if he wanted to talk to me at all. Kallisto may have been dead, but I knew some piece of him couldn't let go of her dreadful memory. She had been a cruel mistress, ruling him for a thousand years, and then had haunted him for another thousand when he tried to escape her. Not something easily forgotten.

Crystal and Drew found me as I was heading toward the heavily-tinted front doors. "Too late to go out there. Dawn is approaching," Crystal warned.

"Great, we're trapped inside of the casino for the day," I sighed.

Casinos are a haven from natural light. It's part of their trap. They don't want tourists knowing how long they have been gambling. No sunlight and no clocks to give time away masked the hours one could spend inside, wasting money. If Lysander was right, and he usually was, this would be the safest place for us all to hide out until nightfall. But it wasn't where I wanted to be stuck.

"You could keep us company to pass the time." Crystal pulled me into a comforting hug. "I heard you had quite the evening. Care to share?"

I nodded. I needed that hug. Crystal was like that, always there to comfort someone. Since my turning, she'd been there for me, helping me along the way, making me feel more at ease with all the changes. As terrible as I had felt all night, it was good to know not everyone was mad at me.

I pulled back from the hug and smiled. "I'm surprised Lysander hasn't told you all about my screw-up."

We wandered together toward the shopping corridor of the hotel.

"He told us enough," Drew said casually. He was a man of unusual height, towering over everyone we passed. His tall, muscular frame was hard to ignore. People gawked and moved out of his way. I had to laugh at their reaction. I'd always thought of him as more of a gentle giant. Vampire or not, he was the most easy-going of the men in the clan.

His sandy-colored hair fell in front of his eyes as he looked down at me. "I'm not saying you made the worst decision possible. You did what you felt was right. I just think there could have been other ways to avoid divulging our secrets."

I craned my neck, looking up at him. "I couldn't think of another option at the time. I was winging it."

Crystal reached upwards to pat her mate on the back. "Go easy on her, love. I'm quite sure Lysander has given her enough grief."

"Yeah." *That's an understatement. They didn't hear his warning to me.* I smiled innocently. *At least Crystal is on my side.*

"What of this friend of yours, Alyssa?" Crystal brushed her long, wavy brown hair away from her face as she walked. At five foot one, she seemed so short, walking next to her giant-sized mate. Her petite frame was dwarfed by her large muscular man. They held hands as we strolled by various shops. "Do you know where she ran off to? I'm sure Lysander will want you to keep tabs on her."

Dropping my gaze, I shook my head. "She's a mess right now. I'm not sure where she's gone. Maybe she ran back home. I dunno. I've got her cell phone number, though, so I can give her a call in a few days, after she's had a chance to calm down. I doubt if she wants to talk to me after Nicholas and Lysander scared her."

Crystal patted me on the back. "If she is as good a friend as you've said, she'll be okay."

I turned to her and let out a loud sigh.

She gave my shoulder a small squeeze. "Remember how hard it was for you to accept this life?"

"Yeah." I gave a halfhearted nod. I remembered sitting under the stars, bawling my eyes out, saddened by the changes my life had taken. I had been mourning the loss of my life and friends, and Crystal had been my shoulder to cry on, telling me it would all work itself out.

I really couldn't blame Fallon for her reaction.

"Give her time. What's done is done," Crystal said, bringing me back to the present. "Right now, we must concentrate on getting out of here."

"And lying low for a little while," Drew added.

"I'm all for that," I said. "So what's the plan? What will we do once night falls?"

Drew looked puzzled for a moment; his eyebrows arched high before he opened his mouth to speak. "We will leave town."

"I know that, but where are we going? Are we finally going to take that trip to Boston to pick up Lysander's old memoirs?" After he had been told where to look for them, Lysander had been excited to go, but he wanted to wait until I was fully comfortable with my new life as a vampire. His passion had always been the "documenting of living history," as he called it. Leaving town would provide the perfect opportunity to make that trip and pick up his old writings.

"That's best decided once we're on the road," Crystal said in a whisper. "We don't want to discuss our plans openly, for obvious reasons."

For a second I didn't understand what she was saying, and then it suddenly became clear. *What if someone was listening in on our conversations?* "Ahh, I got it." Heat rose to my face. I was already in trouble for divulging secrets, and in my eagerness to plan our next move I was about to broadcast more information that could potentially harm the clan. "So what do we do until then?" I asked, looking down to the marble-tiled ground.

"Good question." Drew looked around at the variety of slot machines. "What is there to do in a casino, other than gambling?"

I shrugged. "Sadly, not much. At night there would be shows we could see, but they're all closed now. Vegas isn't really a morning place."

Crystal and Drew both chuckled.

"I think this casino has a movie theater. We could probably go see something once they open," I said.

***

The hours passed slowly. We'd paced the shopping corridor enough times to memorize the patterns in each marble tile decorating the floor. Finally, it was 11AM, and the movie theater was open. Standing in front of the box office, we read through the listing of available films.

"Sorry, but I'm not in a dramatic mood," Drew said, with a sigh. "I'd prefer something a bit lighthearted, maybe a comedy."

"What's this one?" Crystal asked. "*Bonded by Blood.*"

"That's a vampire flick, not a comedy," I said. I didn't want to admit that I had been waiting to see this movie before I'd been turned. I had almost forgotten about it. Vampires had always been a favorite Hollywood monster of mine, before I knew they were real and had become one myself. In my youth, I'd read all the popular books and seen every movie ever made. The reality of my transformation had made me lose track of the things I had wanted to do in my mortal life.

Drew laughed. "They may not be comedy to you, but I find it hilarious how Hollywood portrays our kind."

"Okay. *Bonded by Blood* it is then," I said with a smirk. "Sound good to you, Crystal?"

She pulled her long hair into a loose ponytail at her neck and secured it with a small rubber band. "Sure. It sounds better than these other lost universe and date my sister movies."

We purchased our tickets and walked inside. The scent of buttered popcorn permeated the air, assaulting my senses. My stomached turned and my nose wrinkled. What once had been such a pleasing smell now seemed revolting. I used to gorge myself on popcorn, not so long ago. It used to be my favorite movie treat. I could remember getting the largest popcorn offered and enjoyed it soaked with butter and sprinkled with enough salt to kill a person. Fallon always said I would die of a heart attack if I kept eating that way. A brief feeling of sadness tugged at my heart. *I hope I see Fallon again.*

We passed the concession stand, and a pleasing scent teased my nose: the musky perfume of the attendant behind the counter making the popcorn. His satisfying aroma called out to me. I stopped for a moment, taking in a deep breath, savoring his smell. Humans generally had a sweeter fragrance compared to the musk of animals. He was no different. His scent was like warm sugar, vanilla, and spice.

"Can I get anything for you, Miss?" He smiled, a wide toothy grin while holding up an empty soda cup.

"Oh. No. Nothing for me." I returned his smile, making sure my fangs were hidden behind my lips. "I'm on a diet."

"Come on, Alyssa," Crystal said. She waved at me to follow.

We walked into the theater. Being the first show of the day, it was completely empty, a fact I was very thankful for.

"Do you know what this movie is about?" Drew asked.

"Yeah. It's one of those 'What if vampires lived in regular society' stories."

"Ah, so it really is a comedy then?" he said with a laugh.

Crystal giggled, settling herself into one of the seats and propping her sandal-clad feet on the chair in front of her.

"Maybe someday we could try to live among people. You know, let's all get along," I said.

"That will never happen." Drew kicked his feet up on the chairs.

"Why not?"

"Let me put it to you simply. I saw what you did back there. You were smelling that poor kid. You probably wanted a taste of him."

Heat rose to my face. I tried to hide my guilty expression.

"You think you could get along around people all day, every day?" Drew asked. "Have you forgotten that we kill our food?"

"Only because we can't take sips without letting our secret out. I bet there are tons of people out there who wouldn't mind being donors, if they knew they wouldn't die." I turned to Crystal. "Back me up on this."

"Sorry, hun. I have to agree with him."

Drew draped his arm around Crystal, pulling her close. "If more people were willing to donate blood, the Red Cross wouldn't have to beg for it all the time."

I groaned loudly. I knew there was no way to win this fight. These older vampires were all set in their ways. Vampire law forbids letting our secret out.

The lights dimmed as the previews started. I gave up the fight.

***

I felt a little sleepy after sitting in the theater for over two hours. It seemed even Hollywood was against my theory of vampires and humans co-existing. The vampires in the movie all ended up moving to a secluded island by the end, shunned by human society after a bloody war.

So much for my hopes of using this movie as an example.

"Why do they always have to show us having the ability to fly?" Drew complained.

"Honey, what did you expect? It's not like they know what we can and can't do," Crystal said.

I laughed at Drew. "Jealous?"

"Maybe I am," he said with a smirk.

Crystal grabbed a hold of her mate's hand. "Let's go check on the rest of the group."

"You guys should go on ahead. Lysander is still probably mad. I doubt he wants to talk. I'll just go up to the room for a bit. I'm a little tired."

"Are you sure?" Crystal asked.

"Yeah, I could use a little sleep."

"Okay, we'll be up to check on you later then. Sleep well."

We parted ways and I headed for the elevators. By the time I reached the room, drowsiness had set in. My eyes felt heavy, and I longed for the comfort of the soft bed.

As I reached the door, I heard a cell phone ringing from inside the room. I opened the door and flipped on the lights. Immediately, I spotted a small bag sitting on the bed.

Crap, Fallon left her purse.

I ran to it and pulled out the ringing cell phone and answered it. "Fallon?"

"To whom do I have the pleasure of speaking?" a strange male voice asked. The formality of his speech was too odd to have been a friend of Fallon's, but it didn't sound like Santino's voice either.

"Who's this? You called me," I snapped.

Whimpering came from the background of the phone.

"Now's not the time for games, monster. I know what you are. Your little friend told me all about you."

My stomach sank. *Shit, this is bad.* "Where's Fallon?" I roared the words.

"She's safe, for now. I want to have a little chat with you. If you cooperate, she will go free, unharmed."

Whoever this man was, he had to be Acta Sanctorum. No one else would have grabbed Fallon. "She's human, you can't hurt her. You're supposed to protect humans."

"You are laboring under the impression that I play by the rules," he laughed.

Anger built up inside me. Blood rushed to my face. My heart thundered in my chest. I wanted to reach through the phone and strangle the life out of this man and silence his taunting voice.

"If you are willing to risk her life, then by all means, ignore this call and go about your day. However, if you do ignore me, rest assured, she will die."

I gulped. My brain jumbled with fear, anger, and anxiety. *Lysander was right. Why did I have to get her involved?*

"Now. Do I have your full attention?"

I took a few moments to calm the anger and make my voice sound normal.

"What do you want?"

"Just a chat, that's all." There was laughter mixed in with his voice. He was baiting me, mocking me.

He gave me an address and told me to meet him just after sunset, warning me that I was to come alone or he would kill her.

He hung up before I could say anything more than, "Okay," leaving me with nothing but silence.

Visions of Fallon enduring horrible tortures crept into my mind. "Why did I have to get her involved?" I whined to the empty room. "Would he really hurt her? He has to be Acta Sanctorum. But they protect humans, they don't harm them! What if he isn't one of the Saints?" I paced the room, my mind running a mile a minute trying to figure out what to do. "It's some kid of trap, obviously, but would they really hurt Fallon if I didn't show up?" Sunset was still hours away; I was trapped, powerless to stop whatever it was they were doing to her. "I can't leave her life to chance. I brought her into this. I have to go… alone. But how will I get away from the clan?"

Crystal and Drew would soon be coming to check on me. "I have to hide out. That's it. I have to get out of here and keep myself hidden until sunset." Splashing a bit of water on my face, I cleaned myself up. "I have to save her. This is all my fault," I said to my reflection in the mirror.

I took Fallon's purse and phone and left the room.

8

I managed to hide out for a few hours, waiting in the stairwell of the hotel tower. My mind swam with guilt for bringing Fallon into this mess. Lysander was right; I should have never gone to her. Divulging our secrets had only brought trouble. *How could I be so stupid?* I cursed myself for ever going back to the café.

Lysander's warning weighed heavily on my heart as well. He wouldn't go after her. He wouldn't want to save her. In fact, he'd probably be glad to be rid of the problem her knowledge caused. Hell, he'd said he would kill her himself if she became a nuisance. I knew my only choice was to clean up the mess I'd made. I had to go after her. Alone.

Time moved slowly, as it always does when you're waiting for something important to happen. I counted down the minutes as they changed on the phone's display. I was relieved when the green LED told me it was 8 pm, late enough to be dark. I could finally leave and go after my friend.

I took a cab to the address the caller had given me, an old warehouse in the industrial district. I knew the area well, having attended many parties and raves there when I was younger. The years hadn't been kind to this place. The whole area had been neglected. Buildings carried rust and chipping paint. Broken liquor bottles and shredded newspapers lined the streets. The stench of rancid garbage hung in the air and the pitter-patter of rodents scurrying in and out of storm drains filled the otherwise silent night.

A familiar shiver ran up my spine, spreading to all my nerves as I walked close to the old building. The hair on the back of my neck prickled. I had the distinct feeling I was being watched, but it wasn't the same sensation that accompanied a vampire's presence. Though different, it was no less creepy. If I hadn't known I was walking into a trap, I wouldn't have had a reason to fear. The Acta Sanctorum employed strange methods of destroying my kind. They were the only humans a vampire need fear.

Trap or no trap, I have to at least try to save Fallon. I took a deep, calming breath and picked up a faint hint of sweetness in the air: a human smell. Immediately, I thought of Fallon.

"I'm here now. Let Fallon go," I shouted, hoping the volume of my voice would mask the fear speeding my heart. It beat like a drum roll preceding my impending doom.

"But we haven't had our little chat yet," a male voice answered. I recognized the arrogant tone. It was the man who'd called earlier.

"Why hide in the shadows?" Turning left and right, I tried to discern the direction the voice had come from. I fought to keep fear from leaching out into my voice. "Are you too afraid to face me, coward? Where is my friend?"

"Now, now. Let's not resort to petty name calling." His voice was tinged with laughter. "She's safe ... for the moment."

A weapon discharged. The loud *bang* sounded mere milliseconds before I felt the sting. My ears rang from the blast, which blocked out everything but the pain. The bullet tore through my body, searing my insides. It burst through my back, taking with it flesh and bone. As if time had slowed, I felt every excruciating sensation. My eyes watered. I bit back a scream and fell to my knees.

"Stings a bit, doesn't it?" the man said with a mocking laugh. "I'll bet it does. But, as I can't have you trying to fight me for your friend, I must ensure you are not a threat."

I couldn't tell where the voice came from; pain flooded every cell of my body, overcoming all of my other senses. Hunching over, I looked down to see the gaping wound in my stomach, and fought back the urge to scream. No ordinary handgun would have made an entry wound that big. It had to have been some kind of high-caliber round. Blood gushed from the wound like a fountain. I felt as if I were deflating, emptying out onto the street, as the darkened pool spread out beneath me. My vision faded in and out. My eyelids started to droop. As if from a great distance, I again heard a shot. I felt a second white-hot sting, this time whipping through my shoulder. I swayed and dropped down hard on my hands, crying out in agony.

I'd lost too much blood. I'd failed before I could even attempt the rescue. I was at the mercy of whoever it was hunting me, having foolishly played right into their hands.

A third shot rang out, but I was too far gone to feel it. Weakness took over. I collapsed on to the hot asphalt as my vision faded to black.

***

Surprised to be alive, I awoke, finding myself laid out on a cold flat surface. Even in my groggy and disoriented state, I knew this wasn't good. The Acta Sanctorum didn't take vampires as prisoners. They were killers, plain and simple.

An odor of stale blood, mixed with the tang of metal and bleach, hung in the air. I tried to fight against the heavy weight of my eyelids, needing to see where I was, but the strain caused stabbing pains to streak through my head like lightning.

I tried to get up, but thick, unyielding straps at my wrists and feet kept me in place. My stomach and shoulder ached as I tried to move. My clothes pulled against fresh scabs, ripping open my tender skin, reminding me of the gunshots that had taken me down. I moaned in pain, but the sound was muffled by a gag.

I was really screwed!

"You see how easy it was to get her here," an arrogant male voice said. "You spend all this time chasing down the monsters and for what? It's a waste of energy when you can make them come to you."

"I do not put innocents in harm's way with *my* methods… Sir," I heard Santino reply.

Finally cracking open my eyes, I fought against the blurriness to examine my surroundings. A light hung directly over my head, its brightness blinding, causing my eyes to water with pain. I struggled to keep them open and turned away from the light. Once my eyes adjusted to the bright room, I was able to focus and see cabinets lining the walls surrounding me. I had the feeling this room was some form of makeshift laboratory.

I spotted the familiar form of Santino standing over me. His arms were crossed in front of his chest and his jaw was tight as if he were grinding his teeth. Disdain narrowed his eyes, yet he made no motion to act on his contempt.

Feebly, I struggled once more against my restraints. I needed to break free, but they didn't budge. My chest felt heavy, as if a weight sat on it, holding me down. Neither of the two men paid me any attention as they continued their conversation.

"No innocent was harmed to capture this beastly creature," the arrogant voice said. I craned my neck to see who was speaking: a man with dark eyes, framed by a pair of silver reading glasses. His neatly cropped, raven-black hair was cut in the same fashion as Julius Caesar's. He dressed all in black with the tell-tale white collar of a Catholic priest.

His domineering manner was a shock to me. He showed no trepidation at all in front of the warrior Santino. Everyone I had met since my turning had regarded Santino with a certain level of respectful fear, yet this man seemed to be openly sniping at him. And more surprising than that, Santino was subserviently taking this treatment. I guessed he must be Quentin, the one Nicholas spoke of. I shuddered at the thought that there might actually be someone out there worse than Santino, and I was at the mercy of them both.

But why am I here? And why did they leave me alive? It didn't make sense.

"Perhaps not injured, Quentin, but the covenant of secrecy was broken," Santino growled.

"Not by us. You reported to me yourself that this ..." Quentin pointed a chubby finger at me, "monster was divulging her secrets long before we took the girl as bait."

"That does not excuse our putting a mortal woman in danger." Santino finally turned his head to look at Quentin.

"Santino, you cannot see things as always black or white. This young human woman is a sympathizer. She would allow these monsters to run around unchecked. Her life is insignificant in the grand scheme of things. But we can still use her to help us take down the entire nest of those creatures you've been hunting." A sparkle of excitement glinted in his eyes as he spoke of killing off my clan.

Santino turned away again. His jaw clenched. He took a deep breath before speaking. "I am not comfortable operating under these methods. Humans are to be protected. Not used as bait."

"Some humans can be very useful to our cause. You will see in time. You will adjust." He smiled wickedly.

The irony of his words was not lost on me. Nor Santino, it seemed. A human telling a vampire what he would learn in time. Ridiculous.

Santino's lip curled and his eyes narrowed. "Do not deign to lecture me about time, Quentin."

"Someone should." Quentin chortled. "After all your centuries, you are still nothing but a petty enforcer. One would think you would have been promoted to something more prestigious by now, with all of that age and experience you have."

Santino's body stiffened. His hand balled into a fist at his side. "My position in our organization is not in question. Your methods are. This is not our way."

For once, I agreed with him. I hoped that he might persuade Quentin to let Fallon go. She would be no use as bait for my clan and, in some weird way, it was his job to protect her.

Quentin waved a dismissive hand at Santino. "Do not let yourself get too set in those old ways. One must move with time and adapt with the changes. To fight against the *Unnatural* one must employ many unconventional methods."

Santino grunted his disapproval and turned his angry glare at me.

I gulped as my heart jumped into my throat.

"Shall I finish her now?" Santino asked as his fingertips danced on the hilt of the knife sheathed in his belt.

"No, I don't think I'm done with her yet," Quentin said. He adjusted his glasses, pushing them up on his nose. "I may be able to use her to bring in others."

Santino let out an exasperated sigh. "You have the human girl. There is nothing more to do with this vampire. She is a monster to be put down."

His words were cold and emotionless. Another streak of fear shot through me. My death was imminent. Again I tried to struggle against the restraints. Biting at the gag in my mouth, pushing at it with my tongue, I tried everything I could to dislodge it. I stretched and pulled against the ties at my hands, feeling my wounds tear open with the struggle. For all my preternatural strength, I couldn't break my bonds. I was too weak. I wished I had not lost so much blood. With a groan of frustration, I gave up the fight and focused on Quentin, wondering what he wanted to do with me.

"I have my plans. Leave us." Without a second glance, he waved Santino off.

Santino's nostrils flared and another growl rumbled through his chest. "As you wish, Sir." He turned and stalked to the door.

Quentin gave a snort of a laugh. "I've left a dog in your room. In case you need a bedtime snack," he said with a mocking smile. "Good work tonight. I'll make my report to our superiors of your accomplishment."

The door slammed shut behind Santino, and Quentin's smile turned to a scowl. "I'm getting tired of his insubordination. Perhaps it's time I get rid of him. I'm sure I can come up with a reason for his death. Something to tell the superiors without raising suspicion." He punched his fist into his palm as he paced the room.

I tried struggling again, moaning as the straps bit into my skin.

The sound of my struggle caught Quentin's attention.

"Don't worry, I haven't forgotten about you." He gave me a sinister smile. "You're going to help me with a little experiment." He leisurely walked toward me.

Experiment? What the hell!

Quentin reached above me to a shelf. My eyes trailed up his arm to see what he was reaching for. He pulled down a strange-looking needle with plastic wings. There was a tiny tube-like line attached to it on one side, ending with a collection bag.

His eyes lit up. "Ahh yes, this is what I need."

I'd given blood enough times to recognize this setup as some form of fluid collection. But I couldn't fathom what he would want to do with my blood.

"Maybe if I find you useful, I'll keep you around." He chuckled as he started prepping my restrained arm. "Hmmm, where is the best place to stick you?"

Don't you touch me! I jerked, trying to avoid his touch. The restraints bit into my skin. I pulled against them with all my might, but it was no use.

"Now, now. We can do this the easy way, or the hard way."

My nostrils flared as I sucked in quick, deep breaths. I bit down as hard as I could on my gag.

"Seems like you want to do this the hard way." He laughed. "More fun for me."

Fuck you!

"Such language. Perhaps I should let Santino put you down."

What the hell, how did he hear me? Curiosity momentarily stole my focus. I had never met anyone other than a vampire with clairvoyant abilities. Not real ones, anyway. Psychics and mentalists were usually the focus of late-night infomercials and scams. A mortal, a human, with such abilities was a shock.

He jabbed the needle into my arm, and I winced at the sharp prick.

Quentin grinned and laughed at me. "You're not the only one with special abilities. Yes, I can hear everything you are thinking. A useful little skill when dealing with your kind."

I growled in anger.

"Tell me, how does it feel to take someone's blood? Do you enjoy it?"

Anger and hatred flushed through my body. I wanted to rip him to shreds. I wouldn't have any regrets ending his life.

"Does it make you feel powerful?" He laughed, mocking me. "Because I certainly feel it. Look at you. You're a pathetic excuse for a vampire. Subdued by a human with a gun. I should just kill you to put you out of your shame."

I felt the loss of my blood as it slowly drained out of my arm, making it limp. Pangs of hunger nagged at me, adding fuel to my rage. But I had no strength to act on it. The slow healing of my wounds was proof of how weak I was becoming. I wondered how much more blood he was going to take.

"This was far too easy; but then again, you are merely a child, aren't you? I do hope your master will put up more of a fight. I see no need for antiquated warriors like Santino if your kind are so easily taken down."

Rage enveloped me. I needed to be free. I needed to destroy this man. He was more than just a fanatical religious killer—he was evil, pure and simple. He took way too much pleasure from this. Still, I wondered why he left me alive. What use was my blood to him?

Coward! Release me and we will see how much of a child I am. You wouldn't be so cocky with my teeth in your throat.

"Well, if that is the attitude you're going to take, perhaps I have no further use for you."

Dizziness started to take hold. I blinked a few times, struggling to remain conscious.

He held up the collection bag. Inside it was filled to the seams with my blood.

"Ahh, yes, this should be plenty."

My body cried out for it as he held it above me. I shrieked in need of it, but the gag muffled my cry.

"Oh, now don't be a baby, it's only a pint. I could have drained you dry."

Untie me, you asshole. I'll enjoy ending you, you Acta Sanctorum piece of shit!

"I think I've had about enough of you for one evening. Perhaps after a little time to think, you will be more agreeable."

Closing my eyes, I turned away so I didn't have to look at him. I wanted to rip him to shreds, but there was nothing I could do about it at the moment.

"Look at me when I talk to you."

Something hit me. A sharp stinging sensation started at my cheek and throbbed through my jaw. I opened my eyes to see his hand raised and cocked for another strike.

I refused to give him the pleasure of another pain filled moan. I shot him a deadly stare, calling up all the power I could muster.

He didn't flinch or show any sign that my influence was having any effect on him. He laughed a deep, loud belly laugh. "Got a little fight left, have you? Your mind tricks have no effect on me. I'm going to have a fun time with you. Learn some respect and you might have a place with us, creating new recruits." He patted me on the head like one would a dog. Carefully standing up, cradling the bag to his chest as if it were a precious little child, he turned away and left the room.

The door slammed behind him.

What the hell is he doing? Is he trying to create a new set of Saints? I've got to figure a way out of here.

My limp arms barely had the strength to move against the leather straps holding me.

Why didn't I have an effect on him?

The lightheadedness increased, and my vision blurred. My body felt heavy, but I managed to lift my head a little. I looked at my arm. The needle was still there and the plastic tube attached was left open at the end. A slow drizzle of cherry-red liquid dripped to the floor.

The creak of the door echoed oddly in my ears. My hearing was becoming distorted. Sound reverberated off the walls.

A sweet scent, like honeysuckle, hit my nose before I could turn to see the blur of a body being tossed into the room with me.

Whatever it was, it was human, and it was bleeding. The unmistakable honeyed scent of fresh blood awakened the monster inside of me. It roared to life, demanding fresh blood. I frenzied with strength. I needed it.

Fighting harder against my restraints, I twisted and jerked, not caring about the pain wracking my body as old wounds ripped open again. My only thought was blood. The needle fell from my arm, but I could not budge the restraints. A loud, angry growl erupted from me, shaking the walls. Fresh blood. The aroma was so intoxicating. Every ounce of my being cried out for it.

The human, a female, by the high pitched sound of her whimper, stood somewhere on the other side of the room. Probably scared. I would have been too, trapped in a room with a hungry, blood-deprived vampire.

Oh, please come closer and let me have you. I moaned through the gag. *It's not personal. I just need your blood.* The monster inside of me was ravenous and demanding.

The human girl moved. Out of the corner of my eye, I saw her stand up.

I took a long, deep inhale, savoring the smell. Fresh blood must have been dripping from an open wound to cause the scent to be so strong. It teased at my nose. I sucked in a deep breath filling my lungs with the sweet air, dying for just one little taste.

The ache in my body nagged at me. It would not be denied.

Maybe I can make her come here and untie me. Then I could have her.

I turned my head to see my soon-to-be victim.

My vision, still a little fuzzy, distorted the room, but I could easily make out the features of my once and longtime best friend. *Crap. Well, of course it's her.* She was the reason I was in this predicament.

My heart slammed painfully in my chest and my stomach somersaulted. I fought back against the monster demanding its prize. I couldn't let myself harm her, no matter what my need. I was the reason for all of this. Guilt flooded me, momentarily silencing the dangerous beast crying for her blood.

Her wide brown eyes were filled with fear. She backed herself into the farthest corner of the room, plastering herself against the wall. Her right hand clutched her left, and I could see that it was the source of the blood. A line of red trailed down it and was slowly dripping on the floor.

Quentin is a sadistic fuck, isn't he?

Fallon shuddered under my hungry glare. She gripped her arm tighter.

He wants to torture me and see if I will eventually feed on her.

Every cell in my body cried for blood—her blood— but I had made Fallon a promise. I wouldn't hurt her— and I wasn't about to go back on my word.

I opened my mouth, trying to breathe through the gag, hoping to avoid the tempting smell threatening to send me into insanity.

I still need her to help untie me. Focus, Alyssa! C'mon, you can do this.

I tried to look as innocent as I could as I attempted to make eye contact with her.

Look at me Fallon. I moaned through the gag. *Look at me, dammit!*

She avoided my gaze at first. A smart instinct on her part, considering I hadn't warned her about our ability to control the minds of humans. As the old saying goes, the eyes are the window to the soul. It's a fairly accurate statement. But where vampires were concerned, the eyes were more like the welcome mat to the mind.

I moaned again, this time more pitifully. *Look at me please.*

She looked up, meeting my eyes.

Perfect.

Reaching out with my mind, I sent out a silent request for her to come closer.

She blinked a few times. I could feel her trying to fight me. She had a strong mind, for a human, and I wasn't at my best, considering all the blood I had lost this evening.

I concentrated and sent the mental request again.

Slowly, she took a step forward.

Good, Fallon. Come here, untie me. I won't hurt you. She took another step, then another.

That's it, keep coming. Fallon reached the table where I lay. The smell of her blood overpowered me. I lost concentration. My body instinctively arched toward her. Her hand hesitated on the leather strap holding down one of my wrists.

I fought against my needs, moaning as I tried to regain focus.

Please...Fallon... Untie me.

I lost the connection with her, but she still responded. Her hands wavered, but she reached out and undid one of the leather straps.

The pressure released. My arm came free.

"Please don't hurt me," Fallon said, her voice shaky and fearful.

The next strap came loose, and both my hands were free. I sat up, removing the gag from my mouth. "Get away from me," I croaked.

Fallon jerked backward, slipping on the pool of blood below the table. She fell to the ground with a loud thud. Her hands slapped at the floor, smearing blood as she scrambled to get up. She slid across the floor leaving a red, smeared trail in her wake.

I groaned in frustration. *How much temptation can one take?* Thankfully, I was still partially strapped down, preventing me from lunging toward her struggling form.

Covered now in a mix of her blood and my own, Fallon got up. Sliding all the way, she crossed the room, plastering herself against the wall again.

I made quick work of the straps at my legs and feet and freed myself from the table. A low, feral growl rumbled in my chest as I turned to see Fallon, cowering in the corner.

"Don't hurt me, Alyssa." Fallon squeaked. "We're friends ... remember?"

9

Fallon trembled violently in the corner of the room. The frightened look on her face—wide eyes, quivering lips, and stuttering gasps of breath—enticed my hunger. The sweet smell of her blood permeated the room. Every synapse in my brain called out for it.

Absently licking at my fangs, I let myself imagine, for a moment, the sweet taste and soothing effect her blood would have on my poor starved body.

It would be too easy to take her.

"Don't hurt me." Fear leaked out in her squeaking voice.

I must have looked crazed as I fought to control the need, the urge to kill. Looking down at the floor, I inched backward, toward the far wall. Each movement took all of my concentration. I wanted—no, I needed blood. I didn't know how much self-control I had left. I could snap at any moment. Quentin's plan was working too well. He knew I would need to feed. He set the trap and baited it perfectly. No doubt he expected me to kill her, and he could then use that knowledge to further his cause somehow, whatever that was. Only a monster would devour her own friend.

"Alyssa," Fallon murmured.

I heard her shuffling, sensed her getting closer but refused to look up and confirm my suspicions, fearing I would lose control.

"Stay where you are." My voice came out as a monstrous growl.

She let out a gasp. Her body thudded back against the wall.

"Don't trust me, Fallon," I said through my teeth. "I don't know how long I can hold out." I covered my nose with my hand. The smell of her sweet blood in the room threatened to push me to insanity.

The sounds of her fear echoed in my ears. Short staccato breaths came in symphony with the erratic drumming of her heart. Crouching down into my own corner, I pulled my knees to my chest and wrapped my arms tightly around them.

"No matter what I say, don't look at me, don't talk to me. Don't ... come ... near me." I lowered my head to my knees and took in slow, controlled breaths, trying to calm my inner beast.

Visions played in my mind. I saw my teeth ripping into the tender skin of her neck; her dark cherry-red blood, flooding my mouth, the sweet taste of it, bathing my tongue in ecstasy.

I groaned in desperation and bit my lip, piercing through the soft flesh. Liquid pooled and I sucked it away, pulling my bottom lip slightly into my mouth.

The craving—the need intensified. The taste of my own blood coated my tongue, but there was no satisfying rush of energy; no sweet, sugary taste. I needed more. I needed fresh. I needed Fallon's blood.

I cried out in agony.

She flinched against the wall.

"Alyssa, you're scaring me."

"You should be scared." I barely recognized my own voice.

"No, I'm not scared *of* you." She was lying. I could feel the fear, the repulsion coming from her. "I'm scared *for* you." Her voice found a small measure of strength. "You're hurt. You're in pain. I don't like seeing you like this."

"I'm immortal, I'll heal," I lied. I knew I would soon have to answer to the effects of my blood loss. The gunshot wounds, the blood Quentin took—it would take its toll on my starved body soon enough. Paralysis would come, and that would leave me completely helpless. My death would be certain after that, either at Quentin's or Santino's hands.

Soft footsteps, rubber squeaking against linoleum, caught my attention. I looked up to find Fallon inching gradually toward me. "Stay away," I barked the words, giving her an icy stare.

Her eyes met mine. *Such a bad idea.* I lost control of my willpower. The monster inside took over. My will to live and my need for sustaining blood pushed aside thoughts of friends or promises of protection.

Come to me. Come and let me drink you. I reached out with my desire, reeling her in like a fish on a line.

Fallon was no match for me. Like countless other mortals, she gave in to my mental control. Her face slacked, blanking of all emotions. The trembling of her body lessened. She lumbered forward in a slow steady step. Her eyes remained locked on mine as she mindlessly walked toward me.

She was putty in my hands. *She is your friend*, a tiny voice, the distant echo of my conscience, whispered. I blinked, breaking eye contact. *Don't do this.* I fought with the last shred of control I could muster.

Fallon hesitated, wavering where she stood.

"I told you not to look at me." I roared. "I told you not to talk to me. Do you have a death wish?" Surprisingly, she didn't retreat. She knelt down next to me and extended a shaky hand.

"You won't hurt me, Alyssa." Her words were confident, but the weak voice behind them said otherwise.

"Don't tempt me," I growled and scooted back. "You don't know what I'm capable of."

"I know you don't want to hurt me. You're my best friend."

"Then why make it harder on me? You know what I am." I found myself shouting at her. The need for blood was almost too much to handle. "Why would you stand there, bleeding right in front of me?"

"Well, what am I supposed to do?" Her voice gained a little strength. "We're trapped here. I was trying to help untie you so maybe we could get out."

The thought of escape hadn't even crossed my mind. All I could focus on was blood. Her blood. It would taste so good on my lips.

"I'm not going to be much help here. You would have been better off leaving me tied up. I'm as dangerous as a rabid animal right now."

"It's a risk I have to take. We have to get out of here, Lyssa. That Quentin guy is nuts. He was talking all crazy about creating an army of Saints."

That must be why he took my blood. He wants to turn others.

"What the hell are the Saints anyway? Aren't Saints supposed to be religious good guys or something?"

I felt her hand at my back, gently patting me. I didn't dare look up. I kept my eyes locked on the ground. I couldn't trust myself to look in her direction.

"Keep your distance, Fallon. I'm trying hard not to hurt you. Don't touch me."

The hand on my back vanished.

"I'm sorry. I don't know what this must be like for you."

"You would have, if you had let me turn you back at the hotel."

"I didn't…" Her tone changed sharply. "I don't want to be a vampire. I don't want to drink blood."

"Lysander was right. Mortals are a liability," I growled.

"What?"

Immediately I wished I hadn't said that out loud. My control was hanging by a thread. I took a deep breath and tried to soften my tone. "If you had let me turn you, we wouldn't be in this mess. They used you as bait."

"Hey lady, you're not blaming this on me. You were the one who came to me about all of this … this craziness. I didn't ask to be given a back stage pass to the world of the supernatural, so you can just quit with the guilt trip."

"Excuse me for visiting an old friend."

"Don't sugar coat it, sister. You needed a place to hide. You would have never come back to see me if you hadn't gotten yourself into trouble."

"Pissing off a hungry vampire isn't the smartest thing to do, Fallon." Anger was only fueling the demon inside of me, yet it seemed to be anchoring me to consciousness. Every instinct I had screamed at me to attack and drink my fill. I knew it was only a matter of time before exhaustion would take over and my body would go limp from lack of blood. If I could last that long without harming Fallon, maybe she would be okay.

"Is that supposed to be a threat?"

"It's a warning. Take it how you want." *Please just get away from me, Fallon. Run, go escape while you can.*

"Some friend you are."

"Yeah, some friend. I'm doing all I can to keep you alive, and you want to piss me off and make me lose my self-control."

"Oh? And what self-control is that?"

"If you were anyone else you would be dead now. I can smell every tiny bit of blood oozing out of that cut on your arm. I'm starving, Fallon." My throat dried, making my voice hoarse and raspy. "I've lost a lot of blood, and I'm at the edge of sanity being here in this room with you. I'd say I'm using a lot of self-control right now, and you should appreciate that."

I was reaching the limit of what my vampire body could do with so little blood. My head started to feel fuzzy. Soon I would pass out, and Fallon would be safe, or at least safe from my hunger.

"So, Quentin was right. You do kill people."

I sighed loudly. I didn't want to have to admit this to her, but there was no hiding it now.

"I have."

"And you will again too, huh?"

I didn't appreciate her condescending tone. "Proba-bly… Yes, definitely." *If we ever get out of here.*

I chanced a look up at Fallon. As expected, she didn't look happy. Her lips were pursed together. She stared at me with narrow, accusing eyes.

"So all that talk back at the café about sources all over town, that just meant you were using the city as a hunting ground?"

"You have to understand, Fallon." It was becoming harder to speak. I felt like a drunk person, slurring my words. "It's how we live. We need the blood to survive."

"Drink cow's blood," Fallon snapped at me. "Go to a butcher shop."

"I have."

"And?" Fallon's voice echoed oddly in my ears, sounding as if she were at the far end of a tunnel.

"It's horrible." I mumbled. I didn't have the energy left to explain the finer points of drinking blood. The difference between live, fresh blood, flowing from a beating heart, and the stale, coppery tasting, sludge that was old, dead blood. Blood from anything dead would do nothing to sustain me. Without the life force in living blood, I would get no energy to fuel my body. I would lose the ability to function and become nothing more than an immortal vegetable.

"That's no excuse."

"I have to drink live blood." I struggled to find the right words. I needed to tell Fallon, to make her understand if I could. "It sounds bad. You wouldn't understand unless you had to. Look, I only hunt criminals if that makes a difference. And I only hunt a couple times a week."

"How many people have you killed?"

I felt a spike of anger hearing the accusatory tone in her voice. It gave me a momentary rush of energy. She wasn't even trying to understand my situation.

"I'm not answering that. That's a loaded question, like when a chick asks her boyfriend how many girls he's slept with."

"Don't try to deflect."

"I've already warned you, Fallon; don't make me lose the last bit of self-control I've got right now."

"Fine, don't answer. But don't expect me to just accept this. You're nothing but a cold-blooded killer."

My stomach sank hearing those words. My best friend thought me no more than a common murderer. Not that I could blame her, but that didn't stop me from feeling the gut-wrenching guilt that threatened to consume me.

The room went quiet. Neither Fallon nor I spoke.

I sat still, breathing through my mouth, staring off into the distance, fighting against unconsciousness, wishing I could read Fallon's mind. I knew she must be deep in thought. I wanted to know all of the horrible things she must have been thinking about me.

Weakness settled into my limbs. I knew this feeling. I relaxed onto my back, lying down on the floor with an arm bent behind my head. Soon, I would be immobile, just like when Kallisto had drained me and left me as bait to draw out Lysander.

"What are you doing?" Fallon snapped at me, breaking the silence.

"I'm weak…" I struggled to get the words out. "I'll be immobile soon. You won't have to worry about me after that."

"I thought you said you would heal. You're immortal, right?"

"Immortal. Yes. Invincible … indestructible, no. I'm going to… pass out soon."

A look of panic crossed her face.

"What can I do?"

"Nothing. Just try to figure out a way to get yourself out of here."

"Wait, what about you?"

"Don't worry. Just get yourself out."

"I'm not just going to leave you here. There has to be something I can do."

"I need blood."

"What if I…" Her voice weakened. "I could, maybe…"

"No … I can't … I won't. I've just spent all this time trying to stop myself."

"But, if it's the only way to help you." She cringed as she spoke the words.

"No. Fallon, I'm not going to pretend the idea isn't enticing. I've already killed you several times in my mind."

She gasped. I guess she wasn't ready for blunt honesty.

"The fact is this. I'm not a cold-blooded killer. I'm still your friend. I need blood so much that I doubt I could stop myself once I started. And I won't put you in that kind of danger. I've already done enough of that."

"But-"

"Just get yourself out."

Fallon scooted across the ground. Her warmth closed in next to my body.

"I'm not leaving without you."

Footsteps echoed outside of the door to our room. A jingling of keys preceded a loud creaking sound, and then the door burst open.

10

Fear renewed my weakened energy. The haze receded from my vision. I struggled to lift my head and found the cold, twilight eyes of Santino, staring back at me. His large body filled the doorway.

"Isn't this an interesting sight?" He laughed and turned toward Fallon. "I wouldn't get too close to her, young lady. She looks like she's ready to feed."

I groaned. "I'm not a killer." *How many times am I going to have to explain myself tonight?*

"Not a very good one, no." His nostrils flared and his eyes narrowed as they locked on me. "But you are a killer, none-the-less."

"Let us go," Fallon yelled. She stood up, putting her body between me and Santino.

"Why haven't you killed her?" Confusion flashed across Santino's face. "You need blood, and here it is, fresh and hot, just waiting for you to take it."

"I'm not going to kill my friend. I don't harm innocents."

"Interesting." He laughed again. "You like to hand pick your victims, then?"

Oh, he's just trying to make it sound worse. "If I must kill to survive, I will only do it to those who deserve it."

"So you think you are judge and jury for mortals? You feel you are qualified to decide who lives and dies?"

"Maybe more than some." I rolled onto my side to get a better view. Fallon still stood in front of me, her hands balled into trembling fists.

Santino took a step forward and Fallon flinched. "Enlighten me then," he said, sarcasm dripping from his words.

"If it weren't for criminals, I wouldn't be a vampire." I glared at him. "So yeah, I think I have grounds to judge some of the evil in society."

"Fascinating," Santino huffed. "So you think by killing criminals, you absolve yourself of the crime of murder. Or is it your own personal vendetta? Kill others to make up for crimes committed against you?"

"Things aren't always so black and white. You know I have to feed—"

"How is murder anything but black or white?"

"You kill your own kind because you feel it is the right thing to do. Is that not murder?"

He looked away. "This is not about me."

"Oh, but it is. You kill too, you can't deny that." I thought I saw a hint of guilt in his eyes. I took the opportunity to press my small advantage. "Your reasons though are to protect humans, right? Well, I kill because I have to, and I choose the dregs of society as my prey, because they would do harm to others. We are not that different, you and I. Our base goal is the same. We both stop criminal elements from harming mortals."

He gazed down at me with contempt. "You accuse me of being black and white, yet you reduce things to such simplistic terms. I am on a mission; I answer to a higher power. I'm not a monster giving into my urge to feed."

"I'm not a monster, and I don't deserve to die," I yelled.

Santino cracked his knuckles one by one on each hand. The loud *popping* echoed through the room. "That remains to be seen."

Fallon whimpered. I had almost forgotten she was still there.

"Look, kill me or do whatever it is you're going to do. I have no strength left to fight you. Quentin bled me out. Just let her go."

Santino's eyebrows pulled together, and his lips thinned in a frown. "What did Quentin do?"

"He took my blood."

His head cocked to the side. "Did he try to drink it?"

"I don't know what he was doing with it. He used a syringe or something. He had a collection bag."

"He said he was going to make an army," Fallon added.

Santino's hand shot to his forehead. He stepped into the room and paced its length, muttering to himself.

Fallon and I exchanged worried glances. It was clear Santino wasn't completely aware of Quentin's plans.

"This is distressing news." He stopped pacing and turned to me. "How long ago did he leave you?"

"I don't know," I said with an exasperated sigh. "I've been a little out of it."

"And did you hear him say he was going to make an army?"

"I did," Fallon said raising her hand slightly like a child wanting to get a teacher's attention. "He was asking me if I knew where Alyssa was and said he wanted to create an army to destroy the monsters. He said the Acta

Sanctorum was outdated and vampires were becoming too much of a threat."

Santino pinched the bridge of his nose. "And I brought a vampire here and gave Quentin a fresh supply of blood. Lord, please forgive me for my ignorance." His voice was no more than a mumble, but I was still able to pick up what he said.

"What's going on, Santino?" I asked.

"I should have known when he didn't have me kill you that he was after blood. Exactly how much of it did he take?"

"I don't know. Whatever fit into that bag. A pint, I think he said." *Guess he's not completely ignorant of Quentin's plans.* "What's he doing with my blood?"

"Can you get up?" His words were more like an order than a request.

I clenched my muscles, trying to lift myself. Groaning from the strain, I managed to push myself up to a sitting position.

"I'm not going to make it very far without blood. I told you already. Do what you want. Just let Fallon go. She's an innocent."

"Quentin never planned to let her go. That is obvious by the fact he brought her in here with you. He wanted you to feed on her, so you would replenish your blood. Which he could then harvest and use for his own means. Get up. We're leaving."

"What?" Fallon asked.

My thoughts ran all over the place. I didn't want death, but I couldn't figure out why Santino would be offering to take us out of harm's way. Unless, perhaps, he was planning to take us to some obscure place and finish us off. It was obvious he didn't want Quentin getting any more of my blood.

"We have to get away from here," Santino said sharply. "Quentin will expect you to have killed her by now. He'll be back soon, for more blood."

I groaned. My muscles were weak and unresponsive. I tried again to push myself up. My legs gave out and I collapsed back to the ground. "I'm not going anywhere without blood."

"You have a donor," Santino said, pointing at Fallon.

Fallon gasped. The color drained from her face.

As tempting as it was, I hadn't fought all this time just to use her for blood to escape. "I'm not harming her," I said, determined, though the monster inside of me was begging for a taste.

One of Santino's eyebrows rose sharply. "What?"

A pained expression crossed Fallon's face. "Can you do it without killing me?"

"That's not the point. I have to make you—" I looked at Fallon, then Santino. "Both of you understand I'm not evil. I'm not feeding from Fallon. I'll die before I do that. I'm not a monster."

"I know you aren't," Fallon said as she knelt down beside me. "I don't understand all of this, but I know you're still Alyssa, my friend." She placed a reassuring hand on my shoulder.

"No." I shook my head. It was so hard to fight when she was right there offering it to me. "I won't drink from you. You might say you understand, but things would never be the same afterwards."

"You don't have a choice. Quentin will just use you if I leave you here. Now feed!" Santino demanded.

"No! I'm not feeding off my friend."

Santino growled and squatted down, eye level with me. "We don't have time for this." He pushed Fallon aside and held out his wrist in offering. "I don't need you falling behind. Drink, damn it."

My eyes grew wide. "What the hell? Why are you doing this?"

"We don't have time. Drink." Santino barked the words at me.

A hate-filed expression marked his face. Stone cold eyes met mine, confirming how much he despised me. I never expected my survival to rest in the hands of my worst enemy, but here he was, offering me his blood. He must have really wanted us to get away to be making this kind of an offer. I struggled to lift my arms and take his wrist.

Shutting out my thoughts, I bared my fangs and sank them deep into his arm. Santino neither flinched nor made any sound of pain. He knelt there, rigid as a statue, as I fed. His blood flooded my mouth: sweet, tingling, and intense. I drew hard at the wound, swallowing gulps of the refreshing liquid. Pure energy surged through me as I drank. His blood was powerful, like drinking from Lysander. I could taste his age and strength.

"That's enough." Santino shook me off of his arm, sending me crashing back to the floor. "Get up."

Euphoria momentarily disoriented me. My heart pumped hard and fast, renewed by the powerful blood circulating in my system. It rushed through my veins, rejuvenating me, strengthening me.

I wobbled getting up, my head buzzing as if I were high from a drug. Wiping the blood off my face, I let out a sigh of pure pleasure. It took a moment to recover from the initial rush.

Fallon cowered and backed away from me.

"Sorry," I said, trying to calm her fear. I could see my recent feeding had frightened her. Not that I blamed her. It must be a terrible sight. "You see now why I couldn't do this to you?"

Fallon didn't respond. She covered her mouth with her hand as if trying to hide her repulsion.

"Move, you two," Santino ordered as he walked to the door.

He held it open and looked out into the hallway. "Stay close and listen to what I say. Don't fall behind."

"Where are we going?" I asked.

"Out of here; that is all you need know. We need to leave undetected. Quentin is a special human. He can sense things, like we can. Listen and do exactly as I say."

He stepped through the doorway, into the hall, holding up his hand in a military fashion, as if to tell us to stop. I listened carefully. My preternatural hearing, just like Santino's, would be able to pick up the sounds of people from far away. Fallon, on the other hand, would be limited by her human senses.

Santino's blood coursed through my veins, building up an energy inside me, ready to be called on if the time were right. I hoped we wouldn't need to fight our way out, but I was ready if we did.

Fallon stood rigidly still, keeping a noticeable distance from me. I had tried to make her understand, and even thought she had, but apparently the sight of my feeding had been too much for her. She was back to acting as if I were a monster. I'd reassure her later. Now, escape was the most important thing.

I inched closer to her and the doorway, ready to move at Santino's signal. The hallway was quiet now. No sound of anyone; guards, soldiers, or Saints.

Thank goodness. Quentin must be pretty sure of himself to have not placed guards at the door.

"Move out," Santino whispered. He waved his hand toward the hallway.

We moved silently, darting out into the hall, staying close to the wall. I kept my steps in time with Santino's to mask the sound. The old building was suspiciously empty; nothing more than barren, drab, concrete hallways with locked doors. There wasn't a guard in sight.

"Where is everyone?" I whispered.

"I'm not sure. Quentin has been having secret meetings lately. Perhaps he is having one now."

"Why aren't you there?"

"I'm not a favorite anymore," he said curtly.

I was starting to wonder what was going on in the ranks of the Acta Sanctorum, if the most feared hunter in history was being excluded from secret organization meetings.

We stopped at the intersection of two hallways. Santino closed his eyes, inhaling slowly. I copied him, breathing in the air, searching for unfamiliar scents. A mortal was nearby, but it wasn't Fallon I smelled. I detected the aroma of a male. His scent was odd: a thick, caramel-like odor that wafted in from my left.

"This way," Santino ordered, taking off down the hall to our right.

I followed close behind.

"Ugh," Fallon groaned.

A soft *thud* hit the ground. I turned in time to see her scrambling back up to her feet. Behind her, further down the hallway, a man in a dark uniform turned and spotted us.

My enhanced sight picked up on strange details, telling me there was something wrong with him. His eyes had a bloody, veiny appearance. His face was thick and bloated. He let out a scream as loud as a banshee and moved clumsily toward us.

Fallon screamed and tripped over her feet as she passed me at a sprint to catch up to Santino.

I stood, dumfounded. The man yelled incoherent insults, flailing his arms as he ran toward us. A line of drool dripped from the corner of his mouth. Elongated fangs poked out from behind his lips.

"Is he one of yours, Santino?" I asked.

Something was off about this guy. His scent was human. His skin was dark, and his eyes were a bloody red, not the faded blue-grey of a vampire; but he had fangs. Long ones. I'd never met anything like him before. I'd run into Saints before. That was the code name for the vampires employed by the Acta Sanctorum. But they were never this crazed. Like Santino, they were brainwashed to be perfect killing machines, for vampires. But they never attacked humans. The way this man advanced on both me and Fallon was a serious red flag, going against everything I understood about this organization.

Before I had the chance to turn and run, the strange man shrieked again and barreled straight at me tackling me to the ground. He slammed punches into my torso. I grunted with each painful impact. Throwing my arms up in defense, I did my best to block his assault, but he was fast, like a vampire. I could barely keep up. He pummeled me with rock-hard fists as if I were a speed bag. As soon as I blocked a punch, he delivered another and another to my head and chest. I twisted and thrashed beneath him, trying desperately to find a way to get him off me.

He screamed unidentifiable words at me like a man on the verge of a complete mental breakdown giving in to the insanity. Saliva dripped from his mouth and his red eyes dilated, looking like black holes surrounded with red spider web veins.

Santino appeared above us. He ripped the man off me, sending him crashing into a nearby wall.

"Go on ahead. I'll take care of him. Just keep running straight down the hallway. I'll meet you outside." I caught a hint of worry in his voice.

The crazed man recovered quickly and lunged at Santino.

"Run," Santino barked.

Loud cries erupted from the man—the thing—locked in battle with Santino. The two creatures were a blur of motion, wrestling in the empty hall. I could barely make out their motions as they clawed and bit into each other's flesh.

Turning on my heel, I sprinted after Fallon.

"Let's go." I pulled her along with me.

We made it outside. I scanned the area, quickly taking in the surroundings. Thankfully, there were no other members of the Acta Sanctorum waiting for us.

Santino was only moments behind. He jingled a set of keys and pointed to a dark Jeep Liberty parked on the side of the road.

"We need a safe spot. A place where they won't come looking for us." He was almost breathless as he spoke. A line of blood trailed out of the corner of his mouth. "I need to sort this out and come up with a plan."

"What the hell was that thing?" I asked.

"That was your blood in action."

"What the fuck? *My* blood? What the hell is that supposed to mean? I need some answers here. That thing ..." I pointed back toward the building. "Whatever it was, it wasn't human or vampire."

Santino's hand moved faster than expected. He smacked me hard, leaving a stinging welt on my cheek.

"Listen to me," he said. "We need to get out of here. That is not the only one of those things out there. I'll explain when we are safe."

"I don't think so. You tell me what the fuck is going on now."

"Do you wish to stay here and have another one of those things come after us?"

"Well, —"

"And while we are on that subject... you're welcome. I could have let you die back there."

"I'm not thanking you. You brought me here to die."

"I could just kill you now. Take my blood back and then some. Lord knows I need it."

"Stop it! Stop it! Both of you," Fallon shrieked. "We need to get the hell out of here."

"Your friend is right," Santino said. "Let's go. We will continue our fight later."

"Fine," I groaned.

We all jumped into the car and Santino tore out of the parking area.

"Where are we going?" Fallon asked.

"We need to go somewhere populated," I said. *Somewhere with reinforcements, the hotel maybe.*

"Why don't we go back to the café?" Fallon suggested. "It's dark, it's populated, and it's friendly territory."

"Friendly to whom?" Santino asked.

"To us, obviously. We aren't going somewhere friendly to the Acta Sanctorum," I said, not bothering to hide my disgust for his organization.

Santino fell silent, probably weighing out his options. I wished I could have read his mind.

I had no doubt he knew my intentions. Lysander knew of the café, and if Lysander—mad at me or not—was looking for me, that was one of the first places he would go. Lysander could handle Santino better than I could. He was much older and very strong.

"We will go to your café," he said, not sounding very pleased at the idea. "I need to think of what my next move will be."

11

For the second time that week, I walked through the doors of Café Copioh, my old hang-out, only this time I wasn't alone. Santino and Fallon trailed behind me, moving more slowly now that the immediate danger had passed.

The smells of chocolate and coffee greeted me. They were enticing, but not as much as the multitude of human smells all around. I sucked in the sweet air, enjoying the tempting aroma before changing to breathing through my mouth. Keeping company with a mortal, I wasn't about to show any signs of bloodlust. Fallon had already shown her unease at my dietary needs.

Even though we had stopped off at a gas station to clean up, we looked a mess. I hoped we wouldn't draw too much attention. Santino let me borrow his large duster jacket to help cover my shredded and blood-stained clothes. It was so long it fell almost to my ankles, but at least buttoned, it covered the gaping hole in the center of my shirt.

Fallon didn't look much better: dried blood caked the edges of her short blonde hair, frosting the tips in reddish brown. Her jeans would have to be tossed after tonight—there would be no way to wash the blood out of them.

We took seats in a dark corner, by the makeshift stage. Thankfully, poetry readings were over for the night, so we would not be subjected to the barrage of nonsensical ramblings of the local Goths.

Even though I didn't feel another immortal's presence, I looked around, wishing I could see Lysander. I wondered what he must be thinking, if he was worried or happy to be rid of me. After our last fight, I wasn't too sure what to expect if or when I saw him again. A pang of guilt struck me, remembering the harsh words I'd spoken. I should have never compared him to Kallisto. I knew there was a good chance that he and the rest of the Peregrinus had left as planned. They could be halfway to Phoenix by now.

"I'm going to go make a phone call," Santino said, a rough edge to his voice. "You two stay here. I'll have my eye on you."

We both nodded. There was nowhere for us to go at that moment anyway. Our gritty and beaten appearance was already getting us strange looks from some of the café regulars. Thankfully, none of them chanced the opportunity to come talk with us. Santino's presence might have had something to do with that. His grizzly appearance carried a menacing air that said plainly, "Stay away."

The effect wasn't lost on Mike, the thirty-something beatnik café manager. He had a frightened look in his eyes as Santino approached him. After a few quick words, he nodded and shakily nudged a cordless phone across the bar to Santino. I could only imagine what he must be thinking. Santino didn't look as bad as me or

Fallon, but he still looked pretty rough after the run-in with the zombie-like creature back at the warehouse.

Fallon's eyes darted from my face to Santino and back.

"You okay, Fallon?" I asked cautiously.

"No. Not really." she mumbled, chewing her bottom lip.

I reached out and grabbed a hold of her hand. "It's okay. We'll get through this."

Thankfully, she didn't recoil. Fallon turned to me and let out a sigh. I smiled and gave her hand a small squeeze before releasing it.

A strange prickling sensation crawled up the back of my neck, accompanied by a familiar warmth. I recognized it immediately. A flame of hope ignited inside me. The bond that was created when Lysander turned me made it easy for us to sense each other. The feeling of his presence was akin to that of a nice, warm blanket in the middle of winter. I welcomed the sensation, excited that he would be able to rescue me and Fallon from Santino. Glancing around the room, I noticed Santino seemed to be doing the same. All vampires can sense another's presence, I knew he would assume it was Lysander or another one of my clan.

Santino scowled and turned his head toward the door as he handed the phone back to the manager. He stalked over to where Fallon and I sat.

The front door opened and my heart skipped a beat.

Lysander strolled in, tall, dark, and handsome as ever. He turned toward us and a relieved smile played across his lips.

Oh thank God, he's here.

I shot up from my seat to walk toward the door when Santino's hand caught my wrist.

He fixed his cold eyes on me. "Where do you think you're going?"

"Where do you think?" I shot back at him.

"He will come to us. Sit down." Santino jerked my arm backward, causing me to lose my balance and fall back onto the couch.

Lysander approached Santino, a snarl curling his lips.

"Greetings, my old nemesis," Santino said without turning around to face Lysander.

He threw his shoulder into Santino as he passed him and bent to help pick me up.

"Are you okay?" Lysander asked me.

"I'm fine." I looked deep into his eyes, willing him to hear my thoughts. *The Acta Sanctorum stole my blood and are planning on using it for experiments for some kind of an army.*

"I've no doubt you can glean the nature of our predicament from your fledgling's mind," Santino said, lowering himself into a chair. "So, let's not play any games."

Lysander lifted me to my feet and wrapped his arms around me in a tight embrace. "We have much to discuss about your recent behavior," he whispered into my ear.

My stomach sank. Relieved as he may be to see me at that moment, Lysander was still mad. The calm in his voice did not mask the anger behind his words. He had made his warning clear back at the hotel. If any more trouble was to come from Fallon's presence, he would hold me accountable. I knew if we got out of all of this alive, I would still have his anger to deal with. I wasn't looking forward to that discussion or any potential punishments that might follow.

"Can we talk about this later?" I asked as he released me. This wasn't the time to fight with him. He nodded, and we both took seats on the couch.

Fallon sat frozen in place; fear radiated off her in waves. The presence of Lysander seemed to be disturbing her. Not that I blamed her. She too had been given a warning about what would happen if she caused any trouble. Her hand fisted at her side and I heard the telltale thundering of her frantic heart. I sensed that she wanted to run and get as far away as she could.

I leaned over and whispered. "It's okay, Fallon. Breathe."

"I think I need a coffee," she said. "Maybe a pack of smokes too."

I nodded. "Yeah. You look like you need something. Just please don't try to run. You're in too deep for that now."

She gulped, stood, and walked stiffly to the bar.

Running would be of no use to her. My clan wanted to turn her for the knowledge she possessed, and her knowledge of vampires made her a pawn in the Acta Sanctorum's fight to destroy us.

"We are in an interesting situation, you and I," Santino said.

"We?" Lysander asked. One of his eyebrows arched sharply. "I don't see what is so interesting. There is no 'we' here. There is you, and there is me, Alyssa, and the mortal. You are outnumbered. I will be taking the girls with me now."

"If you do, I'll just hunt you down."

"No need for that. You are alone. Your order has abandoned you for a better soldier. You are no threat to me or my clan. It would be futile to come after us."

I smiled, feeling a little relieved at hearing Lysander's words. He was right; Santino alone should be no match for the clan.

Santino made a noise that sounded like a hoarse laugh. "Never underestimate a lone hunter. I can get in where an army cannot."

"I could kill you myself right now, if you like." Lysander's eyes narrowed. "That would put an end to this annoying posturing you are doing."

"Temper, temper, old friend."

"I'm no friend of yours."

"I beg to differ. How does that saying go? The enemy of my enemy is my friend... right?" Santino smirked.

Lysander looked more annoyed than amused by his remark. He stood and motioned toward the door. "Come, Alyssa, grab your friend. We are leaving."

I shot up from my seat and waved to Fallon who was staring blankly at the black-light mural of *Starry Night*.

"I can't let you leave," Santino said. "Without me."

"What? Why would we take you with us?" I asked.

"He needs us, it seems," Lysander answered with a hint of boredom in his voice.

"He is right, I do need you." Santino looked at me. "Why do you think I agreed to come here? I knew Lysander would find you. Please, sit."

"No." Lysander took my hand. "We are going now."

"They are a threat to us all," Santino shouted, his voice overcoming the din of noise in the cafe.

The room suddenly fell silent. All eyes of the café patrons were trained on Santino.

He lowered his voice to a whisper. "Stay. Hear me out. If after, you still want to leave, then I'll let you."

Lysander let out an exasperated sigh, and returned to the couch. After a few moments of awkward silence, the people in the café returned to their own conversations.

Santino leaned forward, focusing on Lysander. "Quentin has been working on new methods of hunting down vampires."

"That is old news. The Acta Sanctorum has always tried to stay one step ahead of the game."

"Yes, I know." Santino smiled. "I would not have been turned if it weren't for their attempts at shifting the balance. This time, though, they go too far. Quentin has been feeding humans our blood to make them stronger."

Fallon returned and took a spot on the couch next to me. "Mike says its last call. He's closing up shop soon." She pulled a cigarette from a fresh pack and lit it.

Neither Lysander nor Santino seemed to acknowledge her. Their focus was on each other, staring intently as if having some silent contest of egos. Tension hung heavy in the air between them.

"Feeding humans our blood. I don't see the problem," Lysander said after a few silent moments. "They will die."

Fallon gasped hearing this. She coughed and sputtered, puffs of smoke escaping her mouth like old Indian smoke signals.

"Vampire blood and human blood don't mix," Lysander said. "I'm surprised your order is even considering doing this foolish experiment. They will most likely kill more humans than they save."

"Now you understand some of my misgivings about this experiment."

"I fail to see the threat here," Lysander said.

Santino leaned in closer, dropping his voice. "What if the humans didn't die? What if they lived on? Our blood would make them strong. Strong enough to fight a vampire, but not held back by limitations of sunlight."

The café became eerily quiet. Only the sound of the door opening and closing as the patrons left broke this sudden silence.

Lysander's hands folded together in front of his mouth. His lips pursed and his eyebrows lowered in deep concentration. "That is impossible. There is no middle ground," he said after a few moments pause. "You are either vampire or human. What you are proposing would kill a mortal."

"Wait, why would they die?" I asked. "Isn't that how you turned me? You fed me your blood. I remember it. I don't understand. Wouldn't it just make a human super strong?"

Lysander turned to me. "Do you remember me saying that sometimes it doesn't work?"

My memory shot back to the night I had been turned. I remembered the terrible searing sensation of Lysander's blood streaming through my veins. After blacking out, I had woken up confused and disoriented in a cold shower. The water had been refreshing as it poured down on me. I remembered Lysander's voice speaking from behind a white shower curtain.

He did say something like that. 'It doesn't always work.'

I nodded.

"Vampire blood is—for lack of a better term—poisonous to the human body. It uses human blood as fuel. That is why we must drink it to maintain our immortal bodies. When vampire blood enters a human body, it takes over, changing the organs. The more human blood there is in your body, the more damage is done in the transition. If the transition is not done just right, the body is destroyed rather than changed. That is why we drain our potential children to the point of death before attempting the transfusion."

Fallon stamped out her cigarette then turned to her coffee and gulped down the contents of her cup.

Lysander continued, "The human body holds approximately ten pints of blood. A human's blood pressure will bottom out and the heart will stop when about half of that is removed. It is just before that point we introduce our blood. The right mix must be found to ensure the transition. If there is too much human blood in the body, that blood will boil, organs will deteriorate, and the heart will be destroyed. The heart is the most crucial organ. That is one of the few that remain functioning after the transition. Without it to circulate blood, the human would die, rather than turn."

Fallon gasped. No doubt the matter of fact way Lysander spoke of human death bothered her. She fidgeted in her seat and brought a hand up to cover her mouth.

Still, Lysander continued without missing a beat. "If the right balance is struck, the vampire blood can circulate through the body, changing everything in its path quickly. The key is keeping the temperature low and removing most of the fuel that is the human blood." He looked at me. "That is why I put you in a cold shower afterwards. I needed to keep your core temperature down to help facilitate the change."

"So what happens when Quentin gives humans our blood?" I asked. "They would burn from the inside out and die, right?"

The café manager wandered around us, setting chairs on top of tables, loudly performing his closing routine.

Lysander turned to Santino. He spoke in almost a whisper. "That is what should happen. How is he prolonging their life?"

"I'm not completely sure. After I refused him my blood, he stonewalled me from the project. He sent me on errands while he bled the rest of my men dry, using their blood for his experiments."

"Why not just kill you?" I asked.

I expected Santino to be put off, or at least react in some way to my casual comment about his death, but he didn't give me the satisfaction. He smiled at me as he spoke.

"I'm too well-known in Rome. My death would be put under a microscope by the organization, and Quentin would loose his freedom to operate."

"I see. So why not just kill Quentin?" Lysander asked.

"Don't think I haven't considered that. I cannot kill a human, Lysander. I am honor-bound to protect them. I pledged an oath. I will answer to God eventually, and I must have a clean slate. He needs to be brought to justice, though."

"Still a man of the cloth, eh? Even if that cloth is stained with innocent blood?" Lysander asked.

"Why do you think I sought you out?"

"Just kill him and be done with it. I am sure your God will forgive you," Lysander said.

"It's not so simple to kill him. He is telepathic, like we are. He knows things before I do them. I know he has been able to read my mind for some time now. Also, he is immune to our influence. He's some special breed of human with real mental capabilities. I've tried, unsuccessfully, to contact Rome on many occasions. He has found ways to stop me each time." Santino looked agitated. His lip twitched nervously. "The superiors of our order must be the ones to administer his punishment."

"What else do you know of this project?" Lysander asked.

"Based on what I could gather, he uses a combination of drugs in his injections of vampire blood: something to slow the blood pressure, an opiate to numb the pain, and vitamin supplements. I don't know what else might be mixed in. He never allowed me to get close to his notes. I don't know what prolongs their lives."

"Interesting, but they are still on limited time. Once vampire blood is introduced into their system, it will eventually burn through all of their human blood. It will change them, their organs will cease to function, and their bodies will stop making blood. How long can they be expected to live?"

"I don't know. He only just started running his most recent test. I'm assuming as long as he keeps feeding them our blood, they will continue to function on some level."

"And how strong are they?" Lysander leaned in, resting his elbows on his knees and his chin on folded hands.

"Strong enough to fight me, and drugged enough not to care what happens to them. They become completely mindless, like aggressive zombies."

Lysander pinched the bridge of his nose and shook his head slowly.

The sudden sound of smashing glass stole our attention. Our heads all spun in unison to face the shattered window. A large hulking creature of a man climbed through. His hair was matted and stuck to his face. A line of drool dripped from the corner of his mouth.

Fallon screamed. Lysander and Santino both shot out of their seats in an instant, blocking us from this new threat.

"You trapped us, Santino." Lysander snarled, throwing his shoulder into Santino's chest. "Very clever."

Santino didn't budge. "I assure you, he is not mine. Quentin must have sent him. He knows Alyssa has escaped."

The hulking creature stopped and looked straight at our group. Though his eyes were bloodshot and fierce, he looked at Santino as if he recognized him.

Opening his mouth wide, the zombie-like creature let out a shrill cry. Fangs stuck out at odd angles from his mouth.

"This one is only recently... infected. He still has some of his mind left," Santino said cautiously. "These things have been terrorizing the city when they are let out. I've had a mess of a time cleaning up after them. Leave now. I'll deal with it."

"No. I will take care of this one myself," Lysander growled, lunging forward at the creature.

A screeching sound filled my ears as the two bodies hit the floor together. Lysander moaned as the creature raked its clawed hands across his face, ripping open his skin. I cringed and took a step toward the fight. Santino caught me and held me back.

"We need to help him," I shrieked.

"No. He's right. He needs to handle this one. It's the only way he will understand."

Lysander grasped the creature and chucked him across the room, sending him crashing into an old wooden coffee table. Lysander barely had time to catch his breath. The creature was back up on its feet in seconds. He grabbed an old rocking chair and flung it at Lysander. In a blur of motion, Lysander ducked. The chair flew across the room, barely missing him and then shattering as it hit the commercial stainless steel espresso machine.

The café manager stuck his head out from behind the back kitchen door. "Holy shit. What the fuck is going on here?" Mike's eyes were wide. He walked over, joining us, watching the scene as Lysander and the creature fought, trying to rip each other to shreds. They were a blur of motion and splattered blood.

Santino turned to Mike and punched him, knocking him down to the floor with a dull thud.

"I thought you said you didn't harm mortals," I yelled, taking a swipe at Santino. He grabbed my hand and held it still, as if I were a child and had no strength of my own.

"I said I don't kill them. I have to protect our secret just as you do. He'll be fine when he wakes up."

I jerked my arm out of his grip. "*If* he wakes up," I corrected.

The unmistakable sound of bone cracking caught my attention. I turned just in time to see Lysander snapping the creature's neck. He stood over the now lifeless body. Four bleeding scratches on his face began to heal, the skin knitted itself together, and in a few moments looked smooth and unmarred as if nothing had happened. He brushed his blood-soaked hair away from his face and returned to us.

"Imagine one of those breaking into your home during daylight," Santino said calmly as he surveyed the scene. "Not affected by the sun, no need to feed to keep up their strength, only one thing on their mind. For their limited time, they are the perfect killing machines."

"Why are you so opposed to them? Isn't it your job to kill our kind?" Lysander asked, a little out of breath.

"Yes, but not at the expense of other mortals." Santino walked over to the corpse and looked down. Disgust played across his face. "If they go willingly to their death in battle, that is one thing, but they aren't even told they are signing their death certificate when they are given the blood. I don't wish to say this any more than you wish to hear it. I'll need help to destroy all of them and bring Quentin to justice."

Lysander let out a loud sigh. "I will bring this news to my clan, and we will decide what to do. If you will excuse us, we will go now."

"I would rather go with you and present it to your clan myself."

"I'm sure you would, but I am not about to divulge our safe home to you. You and I are still enemies, no matter who else we may fight. I will meet you back here, tomorrow night. You will have our decision then."

12

Lysander drove us back toward home in the quiet suburb of Henderson. Although his SUV was large and comfortable, the silence and anger swirling around inside the vehicle made it feel small and oppressive. I sat in the passenger seat, shooting glances between Lysander and Fallon who sat in the back seat, picking her nails.

Lysander's face was an implacable mask, but he couldn't hide his seething anger from my vampire senses. Though I could feel it, I couldn't tell if it was the encounter with Santino and the knowledge he had just learned that fueled his anger, or if it was the situation with me and Fallon that sat at the forefront of his mind.

He stared straight ahead at the road, jaw clenched, nostrils flared, fingers wrapped around the leather steering wheel.

I wanted to say something to him, but I was afraid of what he might say in return.

Fallon was the one who finally spoke up, breaking the silence. "Thank you for coming to get us," she said pleasantly.

"No offense, Miss Fallon." Lysander's voice was calm and monotone. "But my concern is for Alyssa, not you."

"Well, that's pretty rude, Lysander," I said.

"Again, no offense meant." He didn't turn his head to acknowledge me, but kept his eyes firmly locked on the road. "I am sure Fallon is a wonderful person, but she is just that—human. Which makes her a liability to our clan."

"I resent that remark." Fallon's voice rose to a sharp pitch. "I've done nothing to you guys."

"She's my friend—"

"Yes, you've said that many times, Alyssa." Lysander turned his piercing gaze to me for a brief moment. "But you have yet to grasp the point that vampires and humans cannot be friends. The sooner you understand that, the better."

"I don't care about vampire law," I huffed.

"This isn't about laws; it's a fact." Lysander's voice remained calm and emotionless. It infuriated me, the casual way he spoke of terminating my friendship. "Tell me, Alyssa, what do you eat?"

I groaned. I knew he was going to bring this up. "Blood. But we—"

"And, what flows through her veins?" he asked.

"Blood." I crossed my arms in front of my chest and leaned back into the seat.

"Can you deny craving her blood?"

"No." I sighed. "But it's not like that. I won't feed from her." My stomach knotted with worry. *He's making me sound like a monster again.*

Fallon remained quiet in the back seat. I turned around giving her a pleading look. "You know I would never hurt you, right?"

"You cannot be a real friend," Lysander continued, "if you wish to do her harm. Your need for blood would be a constant threat to her. Good intentions aside, it is in your nature now to feed from humans."

"But I don't wish to harm her. I've already said I won't feed from her. I didn't do it back there when Quentin had bled me out." I sighed in frustration, knowing nothing I was going to say would really change his opinion. I still had to try, though, futile as it might be. "Can't you see I want to protect her?"

Lysander's lip quirked. "And what will you protect her from? Death?"

"Yes. Exactly."

"She's mortal. By definition, her death is assured. It does not matter if you save her today or tomorrow. Her life will eventually end. It is inevitable."

"But she doesn't have to die now."

"No one knows when death will claim them. However, your foolish act of bringing her into our world has no doubt shortened her already limited lifespan."

Fallon cleared her throat.

Lysander's eyes shot up to the rear-view mirror. "Do not think that I don't hold you partially accountable, Miss Fallon. You were too foolish to accept the gift I offered. You wouldn't have to worry so much about death if you had let me turn you. I offered a way to remain friends with Alyssa."

"She didn't— " I tried to say, but Fallon interrupted me.

"I don't want to be a vampire. Quit fighting over my mortality. We're friends, Lysander. Alyssa and I have been friends since we were kids. I've known her longer than you have. She's just trying to help me."

"I'm sorry, Fallon, but unless you wish to become one of us, you are beyond our help."

"I won't. I don't want to be a vampire," Fallon insisted.

"It's really not that bad, Fallon," I said in my most convincing voice. "We could be friends forever."

She crossed her arms in front of her chest and fixed me with one of those 'I-don't-think-so' glares that said quite plainly, "Drop it."

I sighed, shaking my head.

"Both of you must accept the truth," Lysander said. "When this threat has ended, so will your friendship. Our two worlds cannot co-exist."

"Sure they can," I said; though somewhere, in the back of my mind, I knew Lysander had a point. I remembered the look on Fallon's face, seeing me feed from Santino. She had looked at me like I was a monster.

"You are not mortal anymore," Lysander said, glancing at me from the corner of his eyes. "You cannot live in the human world, just as she is not a vampire and could not survive in our world. It is too dangerous."

"No one from our clan would hurt her," I grumbled.

"That is not the point. There is more than just our clan out there. We don't all follow the same… dietary restrictions that you do. Some of our kind do hunt beautiful blonde women. Do you think she is safe from them?"

I hadn't given thought to others outside our clan. I looked out the window, hiding my face so Lysander wouldn't see me struggle for an answer.

His words were cold and void of all emotion. "What are you going to do if she is fed on by our kind? Would you deny our race the only food we can consume, because you are friends? Would you condemn and fight your own kind over a meal?"

Turning around, I glanced back to Fallon. She covered her mouth with her hands, but her wide eyes still gave away her horror. I felt the fear she was trying to hide. No doubt Lysander did too.

"I'm not going to let anyone hurt you, okay?"

Lysander's tone softened slightly. "I'm sorry to have to be so blunt, but you must understand the differences here. Alyssa is no longer a human; she is no longer a mortal. She is a vampire. She belongs with us, not with humans."

Tears welled up in my eyes. "She's my friend. I won't give her up. Haven't you ever had friends, Lysander?"

"You fail to see the very basic point I am making here. Already you have caused problems by bringing a mortal into our world. If you had never said anything about us to Fallon, she would have never been in danger. Just the knowledge of our kind has threatened not only her life, but yours; and by extension, our clan's lives."

I didn't know what to say. Lysander made some good points, but I couldn't just let her go again. The damage had already been done.

Fallon remained silent in the back seat. I did the same, turning to look out the window into the silence of the night. The streetlights we passed and the other cars on the road held no answers, but they at least did not condemn me for the problems I had caused.

*****

When we arrived at the house, Lysander curtly ordered us to get out of the car, then told us to wait in the living room while he called in the rest of the clan.

"We will have this human staying with us for a few days," Lysander said with a hint of unease as the clan slowly began to congregate in the living room. "I want you all to promise not to harm her while she is a guest in this house."

Animosity ran thick in the air. Heads shook and whispered voices mumbled their displeasure. I knew a few members of the clan would not be happy with this situation, but I hoped I might have at least a couple of people on my side.

Nicholas got up from his seat on the couch. "Weren't we going to turn her?" His voice hinted at his annoyance.

Crystal's smiling face appeared from behind us as she entered the room from the kitchen. "Is this the friend you told us about, Alyssa?" she asked, brushing the wild strands of hair away from her face. She tilted her head to the side as her eyes trailed from Fallon's head down to her feet. A small grin turned the corners of Crystal's mouth up and the tip of her fangs became visible.

Fallon gnawed on her bottom lip. Standing rigid, she folded her arms across her chest.

"No and yes," I answered them both putting as much authority as I could in my tone. "Fallon doesn't want to be turned, so she is to remain mortal."

"Oh," Crystal said with a pout. She turned and gracefully walked toward the couch.

"Why is she here, then?" Nicholas's eyes narrowed as his gaze shifted from me to Fallon and back.

"The Saints know that she has knowledge about us." Lysander answered. "She's linked to us until we can take care of this issue."

"What!"

"Get rid of her."

"No!"

"She's a danger to us."

"She can't stay here. They'll use her against us."

Everyone in the room had something to say.

"They already have." Lysander's voice boomed over the crowd. "That's why Alyssa disappeared." He turned and stared coldly at me. "She went to rescue Fallon."

"Alyssa, that was very foolish. You had us all worried." Rozaline walked into the room. Her long, multicolored gypsy skirt flowed to the floor, hiding her tiny feet and making it appear as if she were walking on air. She took a spot next to her mate. "You should have come to us first. We might have been able to help you." Her words were calm, but the serious expression on her face told me otherwise.

"How long are we going to have to babysit this little mortal?" Nicholas asked.

Rozaline smacked his arm. Her eyes narrowed, giving him a warning glance. "She's fine to stay here if necessary." She turned to smile at Fallon. "It's okay, dear. No one here will harm you."

"Thank you Roz," I said loudly, hoping to make a point to the others. "I knew at least someone would be on my side."

"It seems there is no choice. You've already left us once to go save her," she said sternly. "We would end up losing you if we sent her away." She leaned in close to my ear. "And Lysander will be a complete monster to deal with, if that happens."

I tried to stifle a giggle.

"I'm not so sure about having a mortal around," Drew said from the hallway. He walked into the living room to join the rest of us. "It's dangerous, for her. We have needs that might put her in harm's way."

"We'll go feed before sunrise, honey," Crystal said. She walked to her mate and circled her arm around his waist.

Drew looked down at Crystal. His eyebrows pulled together and his lips pursed as if he were fighting to hold back what he really wanted to say.

Now more than ever, I wished I could read their minds. Drew was normally as easygoing as his mate.

"Well, we cannot watch her during the day," Drew said in a whispered breath. "She's going to have to fend for herself while we sleep."

Crystal stood on tip toes, placing her lips next to his ear and whispered, "Don't worry so much, love."

"Drew is right. What about daytime?" Nicholas picked up on the opportunity to argue more.

"She's not a child," I snapped at him. "She'll be fine here while we sleep."

"She's just as much a child as you are, little one," Nicholas said with a sneer.

"That's quite enough," Rozaline cautioned, before I could respond. "Lysander has told her she can stay here. It is his home; we must honor his wishes."

I gave Nicholas a spiteful look. "She'll be fine here, okay?"

Fallon stood stiffly, almost trembling, next to me. I reached over and put my hand on her shoulder. "Really, Fallon. It's okay. You're safer here with these people than you are out on the street, or even in your own home. Even Nicholas, with all his barking and growling, is safe to be around." I leaned in close whispering into her ear. "And his bark is worse than his bite."

The corner of Fallon's lip rose in a small grin. It was a tiny sign, but I could feel a hint of acceptance. "Thank you all," she said meekly. "I don't want to be a bother. I understand you guys are… different. I don't want to cause any more problems."

"Then let us turn you," Nicholas said. "It's easier to deal with a newbie here like Sparky—" He shot a menacing glance at me. "—than to deal with a mortal."

Fallon's eyebrow arched. She turned to me. "Why did he call you Sparky?"

Heat rushed to my face. I looked down at the ground. "Accidentally set his mate on fire," I mumbled. "It's a long story. I'll tell you later."

Her hands fell from clutching her chest. She laced her fingers together in front of her. "Look, it's not that I don't appreciate what you are offering me." She took a deep breath. "I just don't want to become a… uh…"

"Go on, say it. You think we are monsters," Nicholas said with a taunting smile.

"No." Fallon jumped at the sight of Nicholas' toothy grin. "Not monsters … just, well … I don't want to have to drink blood. It's fine for you, just, um, I don't want to—"

"It's okay, Fallon," Rozaline said softly. She reached down and grabbed Nicholas's hand and guided him behind her, a clear sign that she wanted Fallon to feel safe. Nicholas grumbled, but didn't fight his mate's pull. "No one here will force you into anything you do not wish." Rozaline looked over her shoulder to her mate. "Right?"

The room agreed in unison.

Like Lysander, Rozaline carried a certain power in her words, and she was rarely opposed. Even her mate, who was much older than she, had never challenged her in public. It was a good sign to me that she was openly supportive of Fallon's decision.

Fallon reacted well to Rozaline's display of acceptance and protection. A faint smile crossed her face, and she let out a deep breath, dropping her shoulders.

"Good. Now that this business is finished, there is one more matter to discuss." Lysander's words grabbed the attention of the room. "Santino Vitale is alive."

A collective gasp sounded in the room.

"And he needs our help."

"What?"

"That has to be a joke."

"You're kidding, right?"

The room burst into chatter.

"Apparently," Lysander's voice rose over the others in the room, "Quentin has begun to experiment with our blood. He's been working to create a serum that will enhance mortals long enough to send them after us...while we sleep."

"Is the serum done?" Drew asked. "Is it already being used?"

"According to Santino, he's close and has been running trials on humans. And these tests have had some interesting results. I've seen myself the effects of this new experiment. I've also spoken with Santino. He has told me of the problems he has encountered keeping these...'things' at bay."

"Why doesn't he just destroy them all?" Nicholas asked. "He's a hunter. This makes no sense."

Lysander nodded in agreement. "That was my question too. He seems to have no trouble killing these... things, these hybrid creatures. But, for some reason he cannot kill—"

"Refuses to kill," I added.

"He claims he cannot kill Quentin because of his oath to the church." Lysander shot me an angry glance.

"Santino's issues aside, these experiments are getting out of hand, and they threaten our way of life. If Quentin succeeds in his plan, we will have more than just hunters like Santino to worry about."

"That might explain the strange news reports I've been seeing." Nicholas lifted his hand to his chin to stroke at his stubble. "For the last few weeks there have been strange and brutal murders reported on the local news. I assumed it was a young vampire without a master, hunting the city, leaving a messy trail."

Lysander shook his head. "No, not a true vampire. His creations are more like crazed zombies: mindless, drugged, and extremely volatile. I've seen them firsthand. One showed itself at the café where I found Alyssa."

"Quentin called them 'Frenzy Soldiers,'" Fallon added. "He said he wanted to create an army."

"And Quentin has my blood. He took it while he held me captive." I looked to the floor, hiding my shame.

Lysander sighed. "With a fresh supply of vampire blood, he has the ability to create many more of these things. Santino has asked for our help in destroying Quentin and his operation. If we do this, we could effectively shut down the Acta Sanctorum's presence here in Nevada. I'm not going to force anyone, but if you want to, we are to meet in a small café tomorrow night to discuss plans."

"Well, I'm all for destroying the Saints," Nicholas said loudly. "I don't need any secondary reasons, but we need to be on guard with Santino. We cannot trust him. He's a hunter. All he cares about is killing us."

"Agreed," Lysander said. "We should be prepared to eliminate him if the need arises."

"We will assist you with whatever you decide to do," Drew added. He looked down at his mate. Crystal nodded.

"As always, you have my support, Lysander," Rozaline said.

"Wonderful." Lysander clapped his hands together. A proud smile crossed his face. No doubt the instant support of the clan pleased him. "Tonight, rest up, feed, do whatever you need. Tomorrow, we begin."

The meeting broke up. Everyone began returning to what they'd been doing before we arrived.

I shot Lysander a cold stare. "Can I leave now?" I asked.

"Where do you think you are going?" There was a strange, unexpected sadness in his voice.

"I need some alone time. I don't want to be around you right now."

I looked over to Fallon. She appeared much calmer now. Rozaline walked toward her and struck up a conversation. Crystal joined them both. Fallon smiled and admired one of Rozaline's many crystal point necklaces. Being a pagan, Fallon would find Rozaline intriguing. I listened in for a moment and heard Rozaline mention the healing power in quartz crystals and knew there would be nothing to worry about. Fallon was at ease.

"I'll be back in a bit," I said to Fallon and took off down the hallway toward the master bedroom.

"Alyssa, we still need to talk." Lysander's words trailed after me.

13

I stormed into the master bedroom, slamming the door behind me. I needed some alone time, and a hot shower to help wash away the stress of the day. The shower had always been a place where I could relax and be at peace with my thoughts—something I desperately needed at that moment. Between the near-death experience with Quentin and Lysander's stubborn anger about Fallon, my nerves were on edge.

Why does he have to hate my best friend?

I walked into the bathroom and found my reflection in the vanity mirror. Mimicking

Lysander's monotone voice I repeated, "Then accept that your friendship is over. Our two worlds cannot co-exist."

I rolled my eyes and turned away to start the shower. A high-pressure cascade of water shot out of the showerhead as I twisted the brushed nickel knob.

"Just because it hasn't happened, doesn't mean that it can't. Who's to say we can't remain good friends? I mean, she already knows about us." I shrugged off my coat and unbuttoned my jeans.

"Thank goodness for Rozaline. At least she seems to be on my side."

I slid the jeans down around my ankles and stepped out, and then made quick work of my top and bra.

"How do I get him to understand? We're not that different, Fallon and I. We can remain friends when this mess is all over."

Standing in front of the bathroom mirror, naked, I studied myself.

"Okay, maybe we are a little different."

No sign of the previous fights marked my perfect, smooth skin. Amazed, I fingered the spots where I remembered the bullets tearing though me. I noticed how closely my skin matched the vanilla ice cream-colored walls. I almost blended in like camouflage. Only the pink of my nipples, the blue of my eyes, and the red of my hair made me stand out. It still surprised me, even after months of life as a vampire, how different I was. As a human, I should have been dead, or at the very least, scarred and mutilated from all of the action I had seen. But my immortal body always returned to its original state of perfection, healing with no trace of injuries.

"Well." I turned away from my reflection. "Even if we are a little different, I'm not losing my best friend again."

Steam flowed from the shower, telling me the water had reached the perfect scalding temperature. I loved the heat. My poor circulation and slow beating heart left me in a constant state of chill—especially in places like my toes and fingertips. I loved to be around any form of warmth.

I stepped into the shower, enjoying the momentary shock, the initial hot sting from the temperature change. It quickly turned into a sensual, full, heat that warmed my entire body. I felt some of my stress melt and slide away, disappearing down the drain. Facing the water, I let it hit my face and run down my neck and breasts, washing away whatever grime might be left from the day.

The door opened, and from the corner of my eye I saw the dark hair and athletic figure of Lysander. There went my relaxing shower.

"I don't want to talk to you right now," I shouted.

I turned around and let the water run down my back and busied myself by opening a bottle of citrus-scented shampoo. I didn't feel like being lectured by him anymore and hoped he'd take the not-so-subtle hint to go away.

"I do not wish to fight with you. But you must understand my position." His voice carried that annoying hit of authority he used when he wanted things done his way.

I ignored him, spreading the shampoo into my long hair, massaging it into my scalp, creating a foamy mountain of lather on top of my head.

"Alyssa, stop acting childish and listen to me."

His choice of words were far from endearing and had the opposite effect on me. I turned my back, facing the water, letting it wash away the bubbles. The rushing cascade muffled Lysander's words.

The shower door opened and Lysander stepped inside. His hand grasped mine, pulling it from my hair. With one twirling motion, he forced me around to look at him.

"You will not ignore me," he said, a note of frustration in his voice. He stood naked before me, holding me, crushing me against his hard body.

"I have nothing to say to you."

I didn't need another lecture. I had done what I thought best at the time, for better or worse. There was no way to go back and change those actions. Harping on me wasn't going to solve anything. I tried wedging my hands between our bodies, but he wouldn't allow it.

"You endangered us all. Don't you see that?"

"No. I endangered myself," I snapped at him. "Do you think I would have willingly done things to hurt the clan?" I pushed again at his body, trying to free myself from his grasp. "You think I'm so naive, that I have no sense at all, don't you?"

He looked down, locking his eyes on mine. I felt the odd press of his mind, trying to delve into my own. I knew he was trying to use his power to subdue my anger, and I didn't want that. I had every reason to be angry with him, and that anger helped me focus enough to break his stare. I turned my head away from him—the only real defense I had. I was no match to play mental games with a two-thousand year old vampire, and I knew it.

A low growl rumbled in his throat. I could feel the rage like an electric current, vibrating inside of him. A small voice in the back of my head told me to just be quiet and let him say his piece, but anger consumed my better judgment.

"I left you at the hotel. I went after Fallon, alone. I never once involved you or the clan in my attempt to save her. When we escaped, I brought Santino to a neutral spot. Never once did I contact you or give you or the clan's location away. So you tell me, how the fuck I endangered anyone but myself?" I slammed my fist into his chest, punctuating the anger in my words.

He stood silent for a moment. Against my better judgment, I looked up, intending to demand his answers and apology. Our eyes met, but I didn't see anger there. Pain was etched across his face. My rage faltered. The hypnotic pull of his twilight eyes caught me in my momentary weakness. His voice whispered in my mind. *I thought I had lost you.*

My head began to swim, feeling heavy as his power invaded. Fear crept into my mind—not a fear of Lysander or of death, but of the all-consuming emptiness of a broken heart.

I never want to lose you, Alyssa. He whispered in my head. *I was so afraid for you. You are my reason to continue living. You ended my loneliness. Be angry with me for acting as a leader and reprimanding you, but please do not endanger yourself. I could not bear that loss. I need you at my side.*

He wanted me to feel everything: the fear, the pain, the sadness, the loss. He wanted me to feel how hurt he had been when I left him there in the hotel. And I did. The crushing weight of those devastating emotions enveloped me. For a brief moment my own heart ached as if it were being slowly ripped from my chest. A lump formed in my throat, and tears welled in my eyes. It felt like my world had fallen apart.

He released me from his mental hold, and I collapsed into him.

"Please do not make me worry like that again." His tone gave away the emotions he felt. He sounded so wounded. So lonely.

My head cleared and the tidal wave of heartache receded. I understood his anger and pain, and felt terrible for causing him to feel that way; but he needed to understand my motivations. "I'm sorry, but I had to. You wouldn't have let me save my friend."

"Alyssa, you will always bring trouble, won't you?" He reached a hand up and stroked my hair.

I buried my head into his hard, muscular chest, unsure how to take his words. Did that mean he understood? It certainly didn't refute the fact that he wouldn't have saved her.

"I don't know," I whispered. "Probably. Trouble loves me, right?"

Lysander wrapped his arms around me. "It seems you live only to attract danger. You are my heart, Alyssa. You allowed me to feel for someone again. You could have been killed. I don't know that I could survive that."

"It was my life at risk, and it was a risk I was willing to take. I couldn't let them harm my friend."

"Your life is not something I want to risk. You are young, and though immortal, you are not invincible. I do not want to lose you."

"But I brought her into this. I had to save her." I felt like I would have to drill the point into his head to get him to understand.

"You did not have to bring her into this."

"What's done is done. I can't change what's already happened, and you have harped on me long enough for this."

"You are right. I know your intentions were good. As the leader of this clan, I cannot condone your actions, but as your mate, I'm glad that you did what you felt you had to in order to survive, even if that meant bringing a mortal into this."

I smiled, my face still buried in his chest.

He's never called me his mate before. "You consider me your mate?"

His hand trailed up my back. Long soft fingers twisted into the hair at the base of my neck. I breathed a deep sigh, enjoying the gentle caress of his touch.

He slowly pulled me away from his chest, urging me to look up at him.

"Yes, Alyssa, how could you think we were anything less? I love you. I want us to share immortality as mates, like Crystal and Drew, or Nicholas and Rozaline. You are my heart."

I melted as his words sunk in. He loved me. He cherished me. Underneath that hard, aloof exterior his heart beat for me.

"I love you too, Lysander," my voice was barely a whisper, but I saw the acknowledgement in his eyes.

He bent his head to me, his lips crushed into mine. The connection was like a strike of lightening, fusing our love. My heart jumped in response.

You are my heart. His voice whispered in my mind.

Lysander's mouth opened and his tongue traced my mouth, requesting entrance. I let out a slight moan as our tongues met and danced together.

As sweet as the moment was, I still had a lingering nag in the back of my mind. I tried to push rational thoughts away and enjoy the slow tango of Lysander's tongue and the gentle pressure of his massaging hands at the nape of my neck.

He loved me and I him; but what about my friend? I pulled away and looked up at him. He seemed taken aback by my sudden withdrawal.

"What about my friend?" The words flew from my mouth in a rush. "What about Fallon? I'm not losing my friend … I've dragged her into all of this."

His jaw tightened, and he let out an impatient sigh. "Let us get through this mess with Santino first. Then we will figure out what to do about your human friend."

"That's not much of a reassuring answer."

"It is the best answer I can give you. We have never dealt with human acquaintances. It is just not done."

"But that doesn't mean it can't be."

Lysander looked on me with pleading eyes. "Alyssa, please. I've already assured her safety in our home. I am trying to show you I care. Let that gesture be enough for now."

I knew better than to press too hard about this. It was obvious that Lysander was trying, even if it was only to ensure I didn't run off again. I leaned into him and wrapped my arms around his waist. "Okay," I sighed. "For now."

We stood under the soft cascade of warm water without speaking for a few moments. Through the glass shower door, the room became hazy as the bathroom filled with a thick cloud of steam.

Lysander finally broke the silence. "Do we forgive each other then? Can we try to be happy, my love?"

His hands caressed my back; feather-soft touches of his fingertips traced swirls and shapes on my skin.

"Mmm-hmm," I mumbled. It was so hard to remain mad at Lysander when he was so adept at smoothing things over. I couldn't resist the soothing feel of his hands. My muscles, still tense from stress, melted under his gentle strokes.

His hands sank lower down my back, applying more pressure, still tracing the random patterns into my skin.

"I can't stay mad at you forever," I said.

Warmth radiated between my thighs as his fingers traced around my hips. I reached out, taking one of Lysander's hands, and guided it between my legs.

"Someone is impatient tonight." He laughed.

I smiled seductively and batted my eyelashes at him.

A growl tore its way up his chest, rumbling out of him like the call of a hungry beast. His mouth again found mine. Lysander pushed me roughly up against the wall. His hands ran down my back and cupped my ass, kneading my skin. He ground his body into mine, pressing his already thickening member against me.

The warm pulsing between my legs intensified. Reaching down, I took his hard length into my hands. I broke from our kiss, looking up into his large dusky-grey eyes and gave him a mischievous smile.

I focused on Lysander's eyes, willing him to see the erotic images playing in my head.

I squeezed a little, enjoying his weight and girth, teasing him with slow strokes, and was rewarded with a loud moan of approval.

His hands left my ass, tracing the curves of my hips, inching his magic fingers around slowly to the pulsing warmth between my legs. As his fingers neared their target, they changed direction, moving back to the outside of my thigh.

I groaned in frustration.

He leaned in and whispered into my ear. "I should punish you for leaving the way you did." The heat from his breath sent a shiver down my spine.

"Not fair."

He bit at my earlobe, not hard enough to break the skin, but enough to send another streak of pleasure straight to my sex.

He nipped at my skin, creating a trail down my neck, all the while heating my blood with need. His fangs scraped over the thundering pulse in my neck. His fingers again traced my legs, moving closer to the hot, needy flesh between them. My breath hitched in my chest, anticipation threatening to drive me to insanity. If he wouldn't give me what I wanted soon, I'd have to force his hand.

Finally his finger found the spot, and at the same time, his fangs penetrated my skin. I gasped as his finger delved deep into me, sending pleasurable waves through my body.

The sensual pull of his mouth as he fed from my neck was like a euphoric drug coupled with his capable hands exploring my folds. I was paralyzed with ecstasy, enjoying every sensation, every pleasure he lavished on me.

My hand still firmly grasped his cock. In my euphoria, I had momentarily forgotten what I was doing. I caressed his thick length, wringing a loud moan from him. He released my neck, throwing his head backward. I stroked him hard, enjoying the look of bliss on his face.

"Who is teasing who here?" he said between moans of pleasure.

His free hand reached and covered mine as I stroked him. He rested there, holding my hand, guiding my strokes as his eyes rolled into his head. The right corner of is mouth rose in a crooked smile and he moaned again.

Suddenly, his hand gripped mine, stopping me. He pulled my hand away. "Not yet." He sighed. "I've not properly taken care of you."

He leaned in for a gentle kiss. His lips touched mine, light as a feather, but he didn't linger long. Slowly, he kissed a path from my mouth to my neck. From my neck, he blazed a trail of light kisses to my breast, stopping to nip playfully at each one. From my breast he moved down, stopping briefly at my navel, before traveling lower.

I leaned my head back against the wall as his tongue worked its magic, writing invisible words of ecstasy onto my clit.

I mumbled unintelligible words of pleasure, calling his name between moans and gasps. He was an expert at the art of love, and used his skills to command my body.

I cried out as the cresting wave of pleasure washed over me. The pulses of ecstasy making my knees weak. I buckled against the wall, almost falling on top of Lysander.

He stood up, smiling wide, clearly proud of the pleasure he had given me. I wrapped my arms around his neck, and stood on tip toes to kiss him.

His arms encircled me, lifting me up. I wrapped my legs around him and felt the tip of his thick head graze my folds. He leaned me against the wall again and with a powerful thrust, impaled me onto his hard length.

"Oh God," I moaned, as full length of his shaft filled me. He waited a second, allowing my body adjust to his thickness.

Through our connection, I felt the torture of that momentary pause. Lysander struggled to hold back; he wanted to charge into my ready and willing body, though that conflicted with his desire to draw out the pleasure.

He started slowly, gently thrusting, pressing my back into the wall as he drove into me.

I gripped his shoulders and thrust my hips in return to meet his charge, ensuring every inch of his thickness would fill me.

The slow rhythm soon became a fevered rush as together, through our bond, we shared every blissful, toe-curling sensation.

I held on tightly as he plunged harder and deeper into me, finding that secret spot inside that caused stars to dance in my vision. I dug my nails into his skin, and my breath came in short staccato bursts as I rode high onto the cresting wave of ecstasy. Closing my eyes, I threw my head back, screaming out Lysander's name. He too let out his own primal growl as we came together.

Out of breath and completely spent, we remained motionless for a few moments, enjoying the aftershocks of our pleasure.

14

I had a sneaking suspicion that Fallon would try to make a break for it while we all slept, but I was wrong. After having slept all day, thankfully with no nightmares, I awoke to find her eating a pizza in the dining room.

"You look surprised to see me," she said in a cheery voice.

"And you look surprisingly comfortable here," I replied.

Fallon took a big bite from a slice of supreme pizza before replying. "Yeah, well, I figure I'm pretty safe here … during the day."

The smell wafted to my nose: cooked tomatoes, mushrooms, cheese, and black olives. It turned my stomach. "You didn't have that delivered, did you?" I covered my nose with my hand.

"Nah." She shook her head. "Give me a little credit, will ya? I'm not completely stupid. You guys had no food, so I stepped out for a minute and found a grocery store nearby. Oh, and by the way. Thanks for leaving me with the vamps while you went off and fucked your boyfriend."

Heat spread across my face. I was glad I was partially hidden by my hand, still covering my nose. "Sorry about that. We got kind of carried away."

"Yeah, the whole house heard." She winked at me and took another bite from her pizza. "Sounded like you had a good—"

"I get it, I'm sorry." I was willing to bet my face was as red as the pizza sauce. Sheepishly, I looked away, quickly thinking of a change of subject. "So... I'm guessing the clan was nice to you, while I was ... uh ... occupied?"

"Oh, yeah. Crystal was really nice. I chatted with her and Rozaline too for a while. They really have some neat stories to tell. How long have they been around?"

I had to think for a second before answering. I knew Rozaline was turned by Lysander after he escaped from Kallisto's coven. "Roz has been around since, about the 1300's, I believe. And Crystal's a few hundred years younger, I think. Never really asked them their ages." I chuckled. "You know, it's not polite."

"I seriously doubt vampire women have the same issue with age as us mortals," Fallon said as she brought her hands to her face and stretched the skin in a mock facial.

"Yes, immortality is better than any anti-wrinkle cream." Crystal's voice shocked us both. "And for the record, I'm five hundred and twenty-six years old." She stood in the archway to the hall, looking like a statue of a Greek goddess. She wore an old fashioned cream-colored night dress that hung delicately off her shoulders. Her hair had been pulled away from her face into a tight braid, holding back her natural wild, curly locks.

"Good evening, Crystal," I said as cheerfully as I could, feeling a bit embarrassed that she had walked in on us chatting about her. "Sorry, we were just—"

"Curiosity is natural, Alyssa. Don't be ashamed. I'm sure Fallon has lots more questions about us, and I'd be happy to answer." She walked gracefully toward us and took a seat at the table.

"You're awesome, Crystal," I said.

Fallon swallowed a final bite of pizza and wiped her face with a napkin before speaking. "Really, I don't want to pry. I just can't imagine all of the history you've gotten to experience."

"Well, if it's history you're after, you should talk to Lysander. He's the true historian of our group." She pointed toward the other room. "He's filled the library in the living room with all of the things he's experienced."

Fallon frowned and looked down at her hands. "I don't think he likes me much."

"He's protective of us all, and the fact that a mortal …" Crystal nodded at Fallon. "…knows about us is unsettling to him."

"No, I think he hates me because Alyssa and I are close."

"He doesn't hate you, dear," Crystal said. "This situation is not a normal one. Your friendship with Alyssa isn't the issue. It's your mortality. The liability that comes with that is a potential problem."

"Yeah, I get it." Fallon stood, grabbed her plate, and then walked into the kitchen. Her voice trailed behind her. "Things would be easier if I were a vampire."

The faucet turned on. I assumed she must be washing her dish. *How thoughtful.*

"I just don't want to be one," Fallen called out from the kitchen. "I want to get older. I want a family. I want to have kids some day and see them have kids. It's not that I don't appreciate what's being offered. It's just, if given a choice… " The sound of running water stopped and Fallon walked back into the dining room, drying her hands on a red dishtowel. "I want to remain human."

Crystal beamed at Fallon. "And I will respect that choice along with Alyssa. I'll admit I have been saddened in the past that I couldn't bear a child. It is a beautiful thing to be able to create life. I have a feeling you'll make a wonderful mother some day."

Fallon breathed a sigh of relief and sat next to Crystal.

Drew's voice called from the hallway. "Alyssa, a word, if you please."

His tone bothered me. Normally, Drew was the easygoing one, like his mate. The stiff way he asked to talk to me now hinted otherwise. I tried to force away the frown etching its way across my face. I didn't want to alarm Fallon with any unnecessary worry. "Be right back," I said in a breath and hopped out of my seat.

Drew's large frame filled the hallway. He stood just past the arched opening so that Crystal and Fallon wouldn't be able to see him from the table. His lips formed a tight line across his face. I knew whatever it was he was about to say wasn't going to be happy.

"A word of warning," He cleared his throat, and bent down low to speak in my ear. "You do understand that we cannot guarantee to protect your human friend. If we choose to assist Santino and take out the Acta Sanctorum, that will be our focus, not her safety. Your friend is no match for a vampire or for the Saints. I suggest you send her away. Now."

"What? We can't do that to her. She has nowhere else to go." I tried to keep my voice down, but my anger and worry turned the volume up.

Drew crossed his arms over his chest. "You must make her understand. If she is not one of us, she is vulnerable. As a mortal she is easy to kill, and as your friend, she will be a target. I'm not forcing you to do anything; this is just a warning." He walked away before I could respond.

"I'll protect her," I mumbled, "If you guys won't."

Peeking around the corner, I watched Drew greet his mate with a loving kiss, acting as if we had not just had this unpleasant conversation.

A loud succession of pounding fists drummed against the front door. The sudden sound startled me, breaking my smoldering thoughts.

The pounding continued. Rozaline strolled out of her bedroom, her brow furrowed. "Were we expecting company?"

Another bedroom door opened behind me. "No," Lysander growled, and stalked past me. "Damn him. I should have known."

I followed him out to the foyer.

Lysander ripped the door open, almost pulling it off the hinges. "You!" he barked the word.

Only one person would have elicited that kind of a response. Everyone in the house was up and crowding the foyer behind me. My memory flashed back to an earlier meeting with Santino. I remembered him saying he knew I was close to home. I shuddered, thinking of how easy it would have been for him to attack us. Lysander had always warned me about keeping a low profile so our home could remain inconspicuous. I guessed we hadn't been inconspicuous enough.

In a flash, Lysander whipped Santino through the doorway and threw him hard on the tile floor at our feet. "How dare you come here!" He gripped his hands tight around Santino's neck.

"Take your hands off me before I remove them," Santino choked out the words. He threw himself sideways, breaking Lysander's hold and knocking him off balance.

Before Lysander had time to grab him again, Santino jumped, cocked back, and threw a punch.

I stifled a gasp, and my eyes grew wide upon hearing the impact of Santino's fist with Lysander's jaw.

Lysander grunted and turned his head, but remained standing and unmoved from his spot.

Fallon tensed at my side. She grabbed hold of my arm. "It'll be okay," I whispered. "These two have fought before."

Lysander took a step closer to Santino, raising himself to his full height, and leaned in close, leaving only a fraction of an inch between their faces. "Give me one good reason why I shouldn't end you right here and now."

The two men stood equal in height and stature. Neither one had the advantage of mass over the other.

Santino narrowed his eyes and matched Lysander's menacing posture. They appeared ready to rip each other apart as they postured before striking their next blows. "I think you have it backward, old friend." He pushed Lysander with a quick thrust of his arms.

Lysander teetered back, off balance, thumping into the wall, and let out a groaning breath of air. Bouncing back quickly, he dove at Santino's chest with a roar.

Fallon and I jumped out of the way as the two men tumbled to the ground together, a mass of flailing arms and snarls.

Nicholas lunged forward, but Rozaline held out a hand to stop him. "Lysander has this under control," she whispered.

A growl rumbled in Nicholas' chest. I turned to look at him. I could see the eagerness in his eyes. He wanted to be in the fray. His lip curled into a sneer. He balled up his fists, but made no further attempt to assist.

Lysander slammed Santino's head into the ground. The force of the impact cracked the tile floor. He looked up, hatred painted across his face, flames dancing in his eyes. "Get me a knife. I'm ending this now," he shouted at us while holding his palm over Santino's mouth.

Drew, who stood closest to the kitchen, nodded and walked away.

Santino flailed his arms out, raking Lysander's face with each swipe of his sharp nails. He thrust his hips up and twisted sideways.

Lysander appeared to lose balance. He leaned over, preventing a fall with his outstretched hand.

"Watch out," I yelled as Santino wriggled out from under him and delivered a sharp kick into Lysander's hip, knocking him sideways.

Santino jumped to his feet, fist raised and ready for action. "I came here in truce, but if this is how you want to handle things, so be it."

Lysander wiped a streak of blood from his cheek. "We agreed to meet elsewhere. How long have you been stalking around my home?" He stood, raising himself back to full height and started side-stepping slowly, putting himself between us and Santino.

Santino's muscles tensed. His mouth ticked at the corner, and his eyes darted to Drew, who was returning with a large butcher knife. "After the events of the last evening, it would be foolish to show up at your little café again. The human barista might remember," Santino said slowly, as if choosing each word carefully. "This place seemed more fitting for our chat."

"This is our home. Our sanctuary." The words rumbled from Lysander's throat.

"There was no time to call ahead." Santino's eyes roamed the faces of my clan members looking at him, taking particular interest in Drew, who was tapping the knife lightly in his hand.

Santino loosened his fist and held his hands palm out in surrender. "I've come here alone and unarmed. I meant for us to have a truce. We need each other. You need my knowledge to help you destroy Quentin's operation, and I need your numbers to help me do it."

Nicholas's voice was a low rumbling growl. "How do we know you're not sending us unwittingly into a trap?"

"I've no doubt that death is a possibility," Santino rasped.

Nicholas's eyes narrowed; the sneer never left his face.

Santino matched the cold stare. He spoke through his teeth. "We could all die."

"There is no 'we.' There is us and you." Nicholas folded his arms across his chest.

Lysander's jaw tightened and he locked eyes with Santino. An ominous silence filled the room as the two stared at each other.

Santino cleared his throat, breaking the silence. "Perhaps I have been too, what is the term, black and white, in my hunt. I see the human is still alive." He turned, looking in my direction, and gave me a slight nod.

Fallon took a deep breath behind me.

"That fact alone," Santino continued, "says quite a bit to me about your particular clan. I have labored under the impression that all of… our kind are monsters."

A pained expression crossed his face as he referred to "our kind." It must have taken him a lot to admit that.

"I see now that there are those out there who do not kill indiscriminately." Santino continued. "We may never be friends, but in this case, I think we would do well to be allies."

"You are in no position to offer us anything," Nicholas snapped.

Lysander's eyes met mine for an instant before he turned to Santino. "He did bring Alyssa back to me."

"Yeah. He helped Fallon and me escape, as well as saving us from one of those things," I added. "That has to be worth something."

Santino lowered his hands to his side and allowed his shoulders to relax. If I wasn't mistaken, I could have sworn I saw the hint of a smile quirking up the corner of his lips.

Nicholas shook his head and huffed. "Alyssa, you are always in need of some kind of saving. It is getting rather tiresome."

Rozaline grabbed ahold of Nicholas' shoulder. "Really, Honey. That's enough."

"My point is this." He pointed a finger at Santino while looking straight at Lysander. "That is not enough to calm my fears about this man being in our home."

"I understand your concern, old friend," Lysander said solemnly. "But the damage has already been done.

He is here now. Let us at least hear his proposition. If we, as a group, feel it is not in our best interest to aid him"—he shot Santino a cold sneer—"we can dispose of him and continue with our original plans."

"Agreed. Let's hear what he has to say," Rozaline said. She squeezed Nicholas's shoulder.

He glared at Santino. "If I must."

"Don't think I am happy about this either," Santino said gruffly. "But it seems a necessary evil."

Lysander extended his arm, gesturing to the living room. "Go. Have a seat and let us discuss this ... truce."

The rest of the group walked behind Santino into the living room. Nicholas stayed behind with Lysander in the foyer. I hung back, staying close to Lysander, hoping to hear what was being said. Nicholas and Lysander spoke in low voices.

Nicholas' hand covered his face, muffling his words, but I could still hear everything he said. "I do not wish to go against you, but I do not like this man here in our home. He could have led Quentin straight to us. This could all be an elaborate trap."

"I know your intentions are good, old friend, but as I said before, the damage is done. We are already mixed into this deadly game. He holds information that we may need to defeat our enemies—Santino included. Do not think that I am, in any way, trusting of this man. Let us glean what information we can and prepare for battle."

"Agreed; but for safety's sake, we do not stay here for daylight sleep. I suggest we go back to a hotel, someplace highly populated, for our rest today. Our home has been compromised."

"Agreed."

"You can stop eavesdropping now, Alyssa," Nicholas said, pushing past me as he walked into the living room.

Lysander squeezed my shoulder. "Come, let's go see how much of an ally he will be."

15

Lysander and I sat together on the loveseat in the living room. The air was thick with nervous energy. I gulped back a lump in my throat and silently prayed this meeting would go well. Lysander's hand came to rest on my knee. It was probably meant as a soothing gesture, but the effect was lost on me.

The others had claimed spots on the large leather couch, leaving Fallon to sit in the only space remaining, next to Santino, on the other loveseat. He whispered something to her that I didn't quite catch. She gasped and covered her mouth. Tears formed in her eyes, threatening to run down her face.

I shot a menacing glance at Santino, who sat stiffly next to Fallon. "What did you say to her? Why is she crying?"

Santino ignored my angry stare and turned his head toward Fallon. "I don't see why you are so upset. The barista is alive."

"How could you?" She pointed a shaky hand at him. "He burned it down, Lyssa! Copioh. It's gone. Destroyed."

I understood now her sadness. She loved Copioh as much as I did. It was more than just some coffee shop. Now, apparently, it was gone.

"Fire?" I spoke through gritted teeth, glaring at Santino, hoping he could feel my anger. "That's how you cleaned up the mess from last night?"

Santino seemed unaffected; perhaps he just didn't care at all. Neither his actions nor our emotional outburst registered any emotion on his blank face.

"Fire cleans a lot of trouble away," he said.

I had no words. I didn't know what to say. The Café. Copioh. It had been a home for most of my life—my mortal life. Even if I hadn't been able to return as a vampire, I was still happy it was there, filled with my friends. This was like losing one of them—an old welcoming friend. A tear welled in the corner of my eye. I wiped it away quickly with the back of my hand. I wouldn't let him see me cry. Besides, there was too much else going on for me to start bawling over my old home. We had bigger issues to deal with.

Tension hung thickly in the air. Friend, enemy, or something else, no one wanted Santino here, and it showed plainly on each of the scowling faces in the room.

"Santino," Lysander said calmly. "Tell us again what it is Quentin is trying to accomplish with these abominations he's creating."

"Vampires are hard to control. I'm sure you all are aware of how strong the bloodlust is for a young one."

Lysander turned to me. "No, not really, I've never had a problem with that."

I smiled at his subtle compliment.

"What I am speaking of is the need to kill human beings for food," Santino said angrily. "Our organization cannot condone the death of a human to feed a monster such as ourselves."

"That's an interesting observation," Drew chimed in. A small smile pulled at the edge of his lips. "What exactly do *you* eat, Santino?"

Santino puffed out his chest and raised his head proudly. "I drink the blood of animals: cows, chickens, and pigs."

"You're forgetting to add vampires to that list," Nicholas added smugly.

Santino's chest deflated a little, but the haughty expression didn't leave his face. "Well, yes. That is part of my reward for destroying monsters. Animal blood alone cannot sustain me the way human blood would. It's a compensation that works to the organization's advantage."

"Have you no respect for what you are?" Nicholas snapped, baring his teeth in a predatory, threatening sneer.

Fallon edged sideways in her seat, leaning closer to Crystal, who sat on the couch next to her.

"I have the utmost respect for what I am able to accomplish with this … affliction. You forget that I was brought into this life for the sole purpose of ending yours. It's a fitting treat that I can savor the blood of my enemies while bringing justice to the world."

The next moment was a blur. The coffee table in the center of the sitting space flew toward the wall, the thick glass cracked as it landed. When I looked back, all four men in the house had shifted positions. Nicholas had lunged forward, his teeth bared and ready to strike. Lysander must have caught him before he could attack Santino. I didn't even have time to feel the breeze left in his wake.

"Nicholas. Patience. Now is not the time." Lysander had made himself a wedge, standing in front of Santino with his hand pressing against Nicholas' chest. Drew was standing just behind Nicholas with a hand clamped around his arm, pulling him backward.

"You heard him. He'd be perfectly happy feasting on our blood," Nicholas rasped.

Lysander snarled at them all. "We can argue later about who and what we eat. Let us discuss the matter at hand and leave our differences for after."

Murmurs of acceptance filled the room. The men all returned to their seats. Nicholas slumped backward into the couch. Rozaline reached out and grab her mate, pulling him close to comfort him.

Lysander again motioned to Santino. "Why is the threat so dangerous now? Why did you not take care of this when you were first made aware of the problem?"

"In truth"—Santino's shoulders slumped a little. He breathed out a sigh and looked down—"I was unaware until it was much too late. After I healed from our last little fight, Quentin sent me on various assignments. He kept me busy, eradicating a pack of werewolves in Colorado for a few months while he performed his initial experiments."

Crystal gasped. "No, not Gareth's pack!" Crimson tears glistened in her eyes. "They were a peaceful group. They hunted animals in the woods. Not people! How could you?" She raised her hand like a claw, baring her sharp nails, and lunged forward to swipe at Santino's face.

Drew grabbed her around the waist before she could make contact with him, and pulled her back to the seat. "Easy, love, you will have a chance to get him later."

Werewolves? Why hasn't Lysander told me about them before? I shot Lysander a puzzled look, but he wasn't paying attention to me.

Santino didn't move from his spot. Not when Crystal threatened him or when Drew made his comment. He sat quietly, waiting for the commotion to end before speaking again. "I had reports of murders in the area, so I did my duty."

"And you call us the monsters," Crystal yelled. "What proof did you have it was them?"

"I don't need proof. There were murders and a large pack of dangerous sub-human animals nearby. I cannot condone the slaughter of innocents. Those beasts needed to be put down." Santino turned away from Crystal, focusing on Lysander. "As I was saying, I was kept preoccupied with my missions. It was not until I had returned that I was made aware of Quentin's plans."

"Why didn't you stop him then?" I blurted out.

"I denied him my blood. What else could I have done?"

Rozaline huffed in disgust. "You could have destroyed him. He was effectively killing off your team with this ... mixture he gave them. Isn't that what you do? Destroy the monsters harming innocents?"

"I cannot harm a human. I'm honor-bound to protect them. I will have to answer to God for my crimes. I will not go to Him with blood on my hands."

"Even when this human is killing other humans?" Rozaline asked.

"You must really be buying whatever it is your organization is feeding you," I added.

"I swore an oath." Santino turned toward Fallon. "I'll not harm a human. If I break that oath with

Quentin, what is to stop me from breaking it when my thirst demands it?"

"So you call us in to kill him? I think your morals have been skewed," Drew said sarcastically.

Santino shot to his feet. The rest of the group twitched nervously as he moved. Various low growls and snarls emanated from the couch.

Santino folded his arms behind his back and paced along the wall of bookshelves. "I do not ask that you kill him. I wish to take him back to Rome and let his punishment be delivered by the leaders of my organization. What I'm asking is your help in ridding the world of these abominations he has created, and to help me take him into custody."

"Won't they just die out on their own?" I asked.

Santino stopped his pacing and shot me an angry glare. His upper lip quirked up, not quite a snarl, but almost so. "We don't know how long that will take. And with your fresh blood, he could keep them alive for quite a while. Think of the damage they could do if they got out into the city. Already some have escaped Quentin's watch. We need to act fast and destroy them all in one targeted assault. I will handle Quentin from there."

"Why us?" Nicholas asked. "Why not create a new group of vampires on your own to take on this supposed threat?"

"A group of newly turned vampires would just exacerbate the problem." Santino turned toward one of the bookshelves and fingered the spines of a few of Lysander's older-looking books. "You all are much more experienced, as well as being brave and capable fighters." He nodded to Lysander. "You did best me and my previous group of hunters during the attack of Kallisto's coven. I know you can handle this challenge."

"And what happens after? Won't you return to hunting us again?" Lysander asked.

"I will always hunt evil. But I see that there might be some good in the supernatural world too." Santino sighed. "I would give you my word to leave you and your... clan alone."

The room fell silent. Everyone seemed to be eyeing everyone else, waiting for someone to make the first move or respond.

"We will put it to a vote," Lysander said breaking the silence. "Will we help Santino?"

Crystal shot Santino a hateful stare. A trail of red tears stained her face. Drew still held her tightly about the waist. I doubted she was going to vote for anything to help Santino out.

Nicholas too glared coldly at Santino.

Santino crossed his arms in front of his chest. He closed his eyes and let out a long, slow breath. He actually appeared worried, as if waiting for the axe to drop, a look that didn't suit such a feared warrior. The lines and scars on his face seemed to deepen as his mouth pulled into a tight frown.

Tension ran thick in the air. Fallon adjusted, looking uncomfortable in her seat.

I tapped my foot a few times and bit my lip. Someone had to say something, but no one, it seemed, wanted to be the first to speak up; not that I really blamed them. He was, after all, our sworn enemy.

"I'll help fight," I said finally, breaking the silence.

Lysander stroked my knee with his hand. I turned to look at him and he smiled.

"I'll help Lysander, if he intends to go into battle," Drew said confidently with a nod at Lysander.

Rozaline chimed in too after a few more quiet moments. "I too will help Lysander," she said his name poignantly. "And back him up if he wishes us to fight."

Lysander looked at Nicholas. "Will you fight with me, old friend?"

"I'd rather not make a pact with the enemy, but if you go into battle, I will be at your side."

The only one left was Crystal. She looked like she would rather kill Santino than work with him. She sat there with gritted teeth, eyes shooting daggers at him.

"Crystal, we will not ask you to fight if you do not wish it," Lysander said calmly.

She turned to look at Lysander and took a deep breath. "I will assist you and the clan, but I will not associate with him."

"Understood." Lysander nodded.

"Well that settles it then. We fight," I said.

"You are forgetting your little friend here." Santino motioned to Fallon.

"What? She can't fight, she's out of this." *What's he playing at? She's mortal.*

"Yeah. I'm done with this supernatural bullshit. I'm cool with Alyssa being a vampire, and you all are really nice, but I don't want to get involved in this war or fight or whatever the hell you guys are doing. Leave me out of this."

"I will need her help to infiltrate Quentin's operation. I need a viable excuse for my absence," Santino said. "Tracking her down and returning her with valuable information will seem plausible."

"Wait, you're going back there without us?" I yelled. "With my friend? No way."

"Hell, no! I'm not doing this," Fallon yelled as she jumped to her feet.

Santino caught her by the wrist and she yelped. "Let go of me."

"If I go back with her and an excuse to explain my absence, I can make it easier for you to get in. Otherwise, Quentin will be expecting an attack. If things look too suspicious, he'll be on guard. I assure you your friend will remain safe. He will not harm her."

"If he's as psychic as you said he is, then he'll be able to read her thoughts and know what we intend to do," I added.

"He can only read her current thoughts. He cannot look into her memories. I need her help to make the plan work. Quentin will not trust me alone any longer. She needs to feed him bad information. Let him read incorrect thoughts. Make him think she wants to see you all destroyed."

"No," Fallon whimpered. "You can't ask this of me." She fought against his grasp, trying to uselessly to pull her arm out of his iron grip.

"It may be the only way for this plan to work." Lysander said. "Santino is right. If he can create a diversion, a false sense of hope for Quentin, then it will make our attack a surprise. We have a greater chance of success this way."

I saw the fear in Fallon's eyes. This was more than she had ever expected to deal with in her life. She knew, as I did, that doing this would put her life in danger.

"Take me back with her then too," I said.

"No!" The response came from everyone in the room.

"We cannot allow him to take any more of your blood. None of you can come with us. I must bring her back and set the plan in motion. I must make Quentin think I am still doing his work. He must think she is ready to divulge secrets about you, so he can mount an attack. Only if he is busy with preparations will he let his guard down. That will give you the access you need to infiltrate and destroy his operation."

I stood up, looking Santino dead in his eyes. "Look, Fallon doesn't want to go. If you won't let me go with her, then come up with another plan."

Lysander's hand grazed the side of my arm. I turned quickly to look at him. "I'm not letting my friend be put in any more danger."

"Alyssa, Fallon, please listen," Lysander said soothingly. "I know this will be a difficult task, but neither of you can turn away from it now. Alyssa, you must take responsibility for bringing Fallon here. You have shaped her fate by introducing her to our world. And Fallon, you must accept that with the knowledge you possess, you must take on certain responsibilities."

"I'm scared," Fallon said, her voice cracking as she spoke.

"It is perfectly normal to be scared," Lysander said. "The danger to you should be very small. Quentin wants us, not you. Just do as Santino says, and you should be kept far from the actual fighting."

Fallon stood silent. Tears glistened in her eyes. Her body trembled and I could feel the fear radiating off her in in strong pulses. Her heart thrummed wildly in her chest. She wanted no part of this.

I felt like a leaden weight sat in the pit of my stomach. Lysander was right. I had set her fate in motion by bringing her into this world of mine. I wished I could take it all back. I wished I had never set foot back into that café.

Fallon gulped back her fear. I saw momentary resolve in her eyes. She didn't speak; she only nodded and sat back down next to Santino.

"It's settled then. The girl comes with me," Santino said.

"We will attack tomorrow night," Lysander said. "Midnight,"

"Come on, Miss Fallon, I'll give you your orders on the drive back."

I hear a soft whimper from Fallon as Santino took her and walked her to the front door.

"Midnight, Lysander, and not a moment later. I'll have Quentin preoccupied. Alyssa knows the location."

16

I listened to the clan making their plans for attack, all the while seething with anger over the fact that my friend had been used as a pawn in their strategy. Nothing I could have said would have changed it though. Once the clan had made up their minds, no matter the danger to Fallon, she'd been sent off ... with Santino.

On the drive to the hotel—our supposedly safe resting place for the day—I barely said two words to anyone. At that point, I wasn't sure if I really wanted to fight with them; I just wanted to get my friend back. Fallon's safety was my primary concern.

Upon arriving at the hotel, Lysander suggested we all get some rest and sent us off to our rooms. For me, that meant sharing with Lysander, my supposed mate. I wasn't feeling very lovey-dovey about him, though, and gave him the cold shoulder as we prepared to sleep.

I feared for my friend. She was in the hands of one of the deadliest killers known to our kind. She was being led back into the wolf den ... and we let her go.

No, not 'we,' Lysander did.

He ordered her to go. I could hardly imagine what she must have been feeling.

What if it was all a trick? Can we really trust Santino? He is a cold-blooded killer, after all. For that matter, what about Quentin? There's no telling what he's capable of. What if she's been tortured or murdered?

There would be no end to my guilt and grief if our plan sent Fallon to her death. *I should have never gotten her involved in our world.*

Frantic thoughts buzzed around my mind, keeping me from the rest I so desperately needed. I had to stop them before they made me crazy—or crazier. My stomach churned with fear and guilt. I paced the room, watching the edges of the curtains, noticing the shafts of light creeping inside. The dawn had already risen. There was nothing I could do for Fallon. I hoped and prayed that she would remain safe through the day.

With nothing else to do, I collapsed onto the bed. I tried in vain to close my eyes and succumb to a much needed day of sleep. Without it, I wouldn't be much help to anyone; though I doubted, stressed as I was, that it would actually come.

It pissed me off to no end that Lysander slept peacefully in the bed next to me. Anticipation had my mind racing between Fallon and the upcoming battle. I tossed and turned, remembering the zombie-like creature. A shiver of fear ran down my spine. Red, bloodshot eyes bulged from the creature's sockets. Abnormally long canine teeth protruded from his mouth. His skin pulled tight against his bones, making him appear no more than an emaciated corpse. And that scream, that terrible blood-curdling scream—like a rabid banshee.

Memory flashed to the strange news report I'd watched on TV—the dismembered corpse left out in the open on the street. Eye witnesses had seen the thing in action. How could the Acta Sanctorum even think to use them? They were more inhuman and beastly than vampires ever could be. Frightening images swam through my head. I remembered how it fought mindlessly; its fists like boulders as they slammed into me. Another shuddered ran through me, knowing we were going to go up against more of them come evening.

Then a new and terrifying thought invaded my mind. *What if Quentin used my blood on Fallon?* A horrid image of bloodshot eyes and abnormally long fangs, belonging to my best friend, haunted my vision.

I shook my head, trying to dislodge the image and thoughts. I didn't want to consider that possibility. No. Fallon would be safe, as promised, and I would get her out of there.

Lysander stirred next to me. I wasn't sure at that moment how I felt about him. He'd been cold to Fallon. He gave no second thought to sending her to her death. *How am I supposed to love and be a mate to this man who cared so little for my friend?*

"I do care, sweetheart," Lysander said softly. His voice startled me, but he smoothed away the shock with a gentle hand rubbing my back. "My little love, it is because I care that I am so strict. I do not wish to see harm come to you or anyone you care about." He dipped his hands below my shirt and traced invisible symbols on my skin. His soft touches caused a small shiver to dance up my spine. "I feel your pain and know it is terrible."

I rolled over and looked at him. His words were what I needed to hear, but his past actions left me wary of his real intentions. Lysander's face was calm. I gazed deeply into his eyes, willing myself to reach through our bond and sense his true feelings.

"I'm sorry I've hurt you, Alyssa," he said sincerely. "Please know I only want to protect you ... and your friend."

"You can't always force everything to be your way." I chose my words carefully, not wanting to incite another argument, but still hoping to make him understand how worried I felt. "We could have come up with a plan that didn't involve sending my friend into ... an uncertain situation."

Lysander caressed my cheek. "Yes, there may have been other options. Just as you might have found another option, instead of going to the café in the first place."

I rolled away with a huff, heat spreading to my cheeks. He was never going to let that go. Would I to have to deal with this chastising for the rest of my immortal life?

"Please, sweetheart, love, don't take things so harshly." He reached out and pulled me toward him. "You know I speak the truth. There could have been many other options to choose, instead of involving the girl."

"Her name is Fallon."

His eyes narrowed as he looked down on me. "The point is, we must play the hand we have been dealt. We cannot take back our actions no matter how noble or foolish they might have been. Fallon can be of great value to us now, if she does what we've asked of her."

I didn't know what to think. I was angry. I was sad. I was guilty. I had so many mixed emotions swimming around inside of me.

Lysander wrapped his arm around my waist and pulled me closer into his body. "Please try to understand." He nuzzled into my neck. "Alyssa, give up this stubborn streak for just a little while and see that this might work. See that your friend, Fallon, a human, might actually help us vampires out. That would do well to aid your desire to have us all as friends."

I hate it when he's right. And why does he have to be so sweet about it?

"Fine," I groaned.

"I feel your pain too. You worry for her. Just as I worried for you when you disappeared."

His breath blew across my ear as he spoke. A small chill, a ripple of excitement, awakened my body. I tried to fight back the sudden urge to run my hands over his tone body, and pull him close. Lysander had been running so hot and cold lately it was making my head spin. But emotional issues aside—ones he would never admit to— he was one sexy guy. My guy. Lying next to me wearing nothing but a pair of boxer shorts. That made it hard to remember that I was mad at him.

I took a moment to center myself, before my train of thought completely derailed. "It would be nice if you could show a little more of that worry and affection when I'm right here. You don't always have to be the tough leader-guy."

"How about I show you some now?" he said in a deep, velvety voice. "Should I show you how much I desire you?" His hand gently trailed down my stomach, just brushing the apex of my thighs.

"Why do you always try to end every fight by having sex?" I tried to sound annoyed, but the words came out as more of a purr. Warmth spread between my legs as my worry and anger began to dissipate. No matter how angry or annoyed I might be, I had to admit I loved his soft caresses. My body melted under his capable hands.

He tickled my skin with feather-soft touches, circling around my spreading warmth. I adjusted, parting my legs to allow him access to my most sensitive areas.

"Oh, were we fighting? Well, then, I guess this would be make-up sex. Isn't that what couples are supposed to do?" He nuzzled into my neck and nibbled at my pulse. "You know, we don't have to fight," he whispered, taking a finger and tracing it around my soft patch of curly hair.

"You're right. We don't always have to fight." I grabbed his hand to stop his teasing caresses. I could hardly think straight while he tempted my body. "You could lighten up a little on the tough guy act and give me a little more leeway."

Lysander sighed. "Sweetheart, I do. I know you think me harsh at times and perhaps dismissive of your thoughts and opinions, but that isn't the case."

"Wasn't it you who dismissed my worry about Santino in the first place? For weeks I had nightmares, and when I finally told you I might have actually seen him, you acted as if nothing was wrong."

He rose up slightly to meet my eyes. "Yes, and for that I am deeply sorry. I should have listened to you. You were right, and I was too short-sighted to see it. Part of the blame in this situation lies squarely on my shoulders. Had I listened more closely, you would not have gone out alone and found a reason to see your friend."

I huffed in annoyance. "Sometimes you get caught up in your age and experience and forget that others might have some sense of their own."

"I accept the blame for my part and hope that you will forgive me." He stroked my face again with the tip of his finger, running it down my cheek. "But you must also learn to listen to the wisdom and reason of others. Remember, there are more people to consider than just you and me. The rest of the Peregrinus are affected by our situation too. While they live with us, we are all one clan, one family. The needs and safety of the group are what must be considered."

I sighed. I knew he was right about that. My actions had involved more than just myself and Fallon. The whole clan was a part of this. But, just as Lysander considered the Peregrinus to be family, I too considered my friend in that category. He needed to know I would do anything to make her safe again, even if that meant putting my life on the line. No matter what ties I had to the vampire world, I still owed a debt to Fallon for dragging her into this mess.

"I hear what you're saying. I can't apologize enough for involving everyone in this. But Fallon is as close to me as family, and I need to know that you will protect her too, as if she were one of our clan. We have to make sure she is safe."

"You are as stubborn as the day is long." He nodded, and a playful smile stretched across his face. "I cede to your strong will, my love. If she is your family, then I must try to consider her mine as well. I will do all I can to ensure her safety."

"Thank you."

Relief washed through me, knowing we were back on the same side, so to speak, and seeing eye-to-eye about this.

"Now that we are back on good terms, shall I continue with your second request?"

I smiled. "Oh, and what request was that?" My body tingled with anticipation of his answer.

"You wanted to feel my desire, did you not? Come closer and taste me."

I rolled in close to his body. The thickness of his erection pressed against my thigh, heightening my arousal. I wrapped my arms around his hard body and buried my face into his neck, breathing in his deep, heady scent.

Lysander bent his head back, arching in invitation. I smiled, feeling the faint pulse there, just under the skin. I couldn't resist. I needed a taste of his honeyed blood.

"Drink from me, love," he whispered as his hand ghosted up my back to my neck. Gently he pressed me closer.

I bit down, flooding my mouth with his sweet essence.

His hands again trailed along my skin, dipping below the waistband of my pajamas. The tingling head rush from his blood hit me just as his finger found my folds. He parted them, searching for the spot that would make me melt.

I gulped at the fountain of his neck as he expertly flicked and massaged my clit. Wave after wave of pleasure wracked my body. He rounded my opening with his finger, before slowly dipping inside. I felt every motion, every move as he curled his finger, tickling my most delicate places. His blood, his touch, his hard body pressed against my sensitive skin—it was s decadent blend of sensual stimulation.

I lapped at the tiny pinpricks from my fangs, closing the wound and released myself from his neck. I felt I would shatter into a million pieces from the sensory overload.

Euphoria paralyzed me as he commanded my body. My breath came in short bursts. One finger soon became two as Lysander worked my body into a fury of delight.

His lips returned to my neck for a brief moment before traveling down to my breast. My nipples, now hard little pebbles, were so sensitive that the smallest touch felt like an electric shock zipping straight down to my sex. He nipped at them playfully, smiling as I bucked and moaned beneath him.

I praised his name, shouting it to the heavens as he brought me to climax.

But he was not done yet.

Tearing the clothes from my body, he eyed me with a predatory gaze. He rose above me and kissed a trail from my navel up to my lips. His body pressed against mine. I felt his erection, hard and waiting for me. His tongue delved into my mouth, playfully licking at my teeth. His arms wrapped around my body. Not breaking from our kiss, we rolled over in bed together and he guided me on top of him. His swollen tip pressed against my wet, needy opening.

He slowly slid inside of me.

"Oh god," I moaned as the wave of pleasure surged through me.

My body stretched to accommodate his girth. I savored the feeling, the momentary pause. He felt good inside of me, filling me completely as if we were meant to fit together, and through our bond I knew he felt exactly the same.

He thrust his hips, urging me to move with him. Following his lead, I rocked my hips, pushing him deeper inside of me, melding our bodies together.

His hands clasped my butt, guiding me, kneading my ass as we moved together. The wave of pleasure crested.

I moaned loudly, throwing my head back as the climax hit me and sent shockwaves of pleasure through my core. Lysander held me tight, letting out a low primal growl as he too found release.

For a wonderful eternity we lay in bed motionless, feeling pleasantly spent, until sleep finally took us.

17

Night arrived like an unwelcome visitor, waking me from my peaceful dreams. As much as I wanted to fall back into the serene bliss of sleep, I couldn't. As soon as my eyes cracked open, reality hit me and I remembered the impending battle and how dangerous our situation was.

Midnight, though still hours away, was fast approaching, and we needed to be ready.

Lysander had risen before me and was already dressed. He wore black from head to toe: jeans, turtleneck, and steel-toe boots. He caught my eye from across the room, where he sat at a small corner table, and smiled. I stretched and yawned, trying to shrug off the last remnants of sleep.

"You'll need to hunt tonight," he said as dug through a duffle bag at his feet. "I need everyone at full strength, especially you. I don't want to see you get hurt."

I nodded and slid from the bed, grabbing my clothes off the floor. "I'll hurry." I walked to the table to give him a good-evening kiss.

He looked up, meeting my eyes, and I caught a feeling of dread vibrating off of him. "I mean it. I don't want you to get hurt," he said. "Hunt fast, but pick clean blood."

I was momentarily taken aback by his serious tone. Through our bond I sensed his worry. I guessed that if it weren't for my friend being a part of this, he wouldn't allow me to join them in this fight.

"Yes, sir," I said and mock saluted him. I meant it to be playful, to lighten his tense mood, but the effort was lost on him. His frown deepened. With that, the smile on my face faded too. "I'll be back shortly, okay?"

I walked toward the bathroom to splash some cool water on my face and toss on something to wear while I hunted.

Santino expected us around midnight. That didn't leave much time to be picky, but then again we were on the Strip, a place known for having a wealth of unsavory characters. With minimal effort, it should be easy to locate a quick meal. After dressing, I took the elevator to the hotel lobby.

I wanted someone strong, yet untainted by drugs or alcohol. Lysander was right, I didn't need any negative effects in my system when we went into battle. The occasional lingering high that comes with inebriated blood might be too much of a distraction.

The casino, as usual, was filled with hookers, pickpockets, and cheats; all slightly evil in their own right, but not enough for me to take as my victim. Vampire or not, I still had some humanity left and didn't want to kill petty thieves. I needed someone who had more dangerous intentions. A real criminal. Someone worthy of the death my bite would bring.

As I wandered between the gaming tables, blackjack, baccarat, and pai-gow poker, the flood of human smells permeating the air tempted me. Each fragrant note played at my senses, calling out the beast within. I found myself stopping at the various tables, watching the players instead of the cards, savoring their scents. Occasionally the dealer would shoot me a curious glance. I wondered if I appeared strange; perhaps he saw me for the creature I was, or maybe he was just waiting for me to buy in to a game. Deciding it would be better to go someplace less conspicuous, I ventured outside, hoping to find quick prey.

After the fiasco with being trapped and bled out by Quentin, I hadn't had a chance to hunt on my own. I'd sustained myself on the blood Lysander shared with me. As a very young vampire, I needed to hunt at least every other day. The elders could go weeks and sometimes even months without needing to feed if they wanted. I wasn't sure how they managed it, though. Just the thought of hunting had the monster in my head scream-ing for fresh blood. My mouth watered in instinctual anticipation.

Once outside the casino, I headed to the rear of the building. These large mega-hotels were easily accessible from the Strip, but behind them was a different story. A maze of quiet streets, meant only for employees, linked the various hotels. Mostly deserted and seldom traveled during the night, these roads usually attracted the types of criminals I was looking for.

Just as I rounded the corner, a loud yell caught my attention. It sounded like a frightened woman. I closed my eyes, reaching out with my senses, and listened closely. I could hear a distraught conversation, spoken in whispering growls, between a man and the panicking woman.

Perhaps my hunting will be quick tonight. I smiled widely, hearing a muffled whimper, and licked the tips of my fangs in anticipation.

I stalked toward them, keeping to the shadows. The sound of whimpering grew louder. I sniffed at the air—a thick, sweet scent wafted from a row of bushes. I inched closer and spotted two figures struggling on the ground.

The man looked strong. A thick, bulky head and neck sat atop a mountain of muscles. He bent over the helpless woman, who was no more than squirming skin and fabric beneath him.

With a silent snarl I pounced, driving my fist across the back of the man's head as I swept past. His body slumped and lay still, like the sack of shit that he was. I hoped I hadn't hit him too hard. I needed him knocked out, not dead.

Thankfully, the woman was too concerned with her sudden freedom to question what had just happened. As soon as she realized her attacker was unconscious, she squirmed to get up, heaving his limp body off her. She swiped the back of her hand across her face, wiping away the streaming tears, and scrambled to her feet. She spat on his limp form and delivered a swift kick to his stomach before tearing off toward the Strip—running as fast as her legs could carry her.

When the woman was out of sight, I walked over to my victim, who was now nothing more than a lump of flesh on the ground. I had hit him just a little too hard. He was still alive, though probably brain-damaged—not that it mattered anyway. He was unresponsive, unconscious, and drooling. Shaking my head at my own overzealousness, I grabbed his hair, yanked his head and thick neck sideways, and sank my teeth in deep.

Sweet, hot blood flooded my mouth. Like a thirsty person in the desert, I gulped it down. His heart beat strong, pumping the blood into my mouth as quickly as I could gulp it.

The unconscious man slipped further away from life. Weakness settled into his heart. It faltered. The tell-tale erratic thumping signaled the end. The human body can only withstand a certain amount of blood loss before the pressure bottoms out and the heart stops. I had drunk him well past that point, but I needed every drop.

I released him, bit my tongue, and then swirled my blood and saliva over the fang marks on his neck. That would remove any evidence of my attack.

Renewed by his blood, I left him to rest behind a heavy row of shrubs before returning to Lysander and the clan, ready to take on Quentin and the zombies.

18

When I arrived back at the hotel room, I found Lysander sitting on the bed, polishing a large dagger. I stopped for a moment, watching the motion of his hands as he stroked the blade with a soft cloth. The light reflected off of the highly polished metal, casting a glow all around it. The dagger was large, and seemed to be one solid piece of steel from tip to end. The handle was grooved and rounded, with the head of a dragon transitioning into the polished, slightly curved blade. Two tiny sapphire jewels were set as eyes in the dragon's head. The blade itself had the design of a flame carved in it, as if the dragon hilt was breathing fire.

Lysander turned and smiled up at me. "It is part of a set," he said as he ran the cloth across the blade one last time. "We will be fighting with old-fashioned weapons this evening. If these creations are as hardy as vampires, removing their heads will be the only way to ensure they are truly dead. "

"May I?" I reached out and gingerly picked up the dagger, expecting it to feel heavy in my hands. It certainly *looked* that way. Surprisingly, it felt light as air. No doubt my vampire strength had something to do with this; the thickness of the hilt alone should have felt like a barbell in my hands. Waving it around in front of my face, I enjoyed how fluidly it moved, slicing through the air like an extension of my hand.

"It's beautiful, Lysander."

"You may use that one. I shall use its match." He pulled out another dagger from the black duffle bag on the bed.

"Thank you," I said with a smile. I cut the air again with the blade, admiring the sapphire eyes sparkling as they reflected the light.

"Let us practice with it. You'll need to be accustomed to it for tonight. Be ready to remove the head of those beasts."

I shuddered, remembering the screaming beast that had attacked me before. It was strong and fast. Santino had been there and pulled the thing off of me. A small worry had me wondering if I would truly be able to handle one on my own.

Lysander stood in front of me. "Come, let me see you in action." He held his dagger poised and ready in his hand. "Take a swing at me."

"Really? Right here … in the room?" I suddenly felt awkward and clumsy. I brought the blade down to my side and tapped my knee with the point.

"Yes. Right here. Right now." His face became stern and all emotion disappeared from his eyes. "And don't play with it. That dagger is not a toy. Hold it like you plan to use it."

I gulped. Bringing the dagger to waist-level, I held it, point upwards, with the blade facing Lysander. "Is this right?"

He scoffed. "You look ridiculous. Don't grip it so hard. Keep your wrist loose. Put your weight on the balls of your feet. And bend your knees a little. Be ready to defend without warning." He took a swing at me, his arm moving in a fast, blurry downward motion.

Instincts kicked in and I brought the blade up just in time.

"Good. Again." He took another swing, this time, stepping in close to me.

Unprepared for the second attack, I wobbled where I stood, taking a step back to avoid falling over. I tried to block; our two blades *clanked*. Mine broke free, flying from my grasp to the floor with a dull *thud*.

"You are going to have to do better than that," Lysander cautioned. "If you keep up your current level of competence, you are as good as dead." He crouched low, at the ready. His blade held firmly in his right hand. With his left, he pointed to my fallen dagger.

I know I can do better than this.

Not breaking eye contact with Lysander, I bent down to retrieve my fallen blade. "Let's go again," I said, matching Lysander's serious face with my own resolve.

His eyes narrowed and his mouth formed a cruel slash across his face. "Okay, take a swing now. Attack me."

I brought the blade up with me as I stood. Holding it firmly in my hand, I swiped at Lysander's chest.

He blocked easily with a smooth, fluid motion, pushing my dagger and arm to the side as he rotated around me. I stumbled, then caught my balance.

Arching his arm as he spun Lysander brought his blade back down.

This time, though, I was not caught off guard. I watched the angle of the blade and was ready to defend. I twisted toward him and brought the dagger up, just in time. The *clang* of metal on metal echoed in the room as our daggers collided.

"Very good, Alyssa." Lysander bowed his head briefly in recognition of my achievement.

That little gesture sent a flutter through me and made me feel a bit better about taking on the zombies. If I could defend against Lysander, that had to count for something, right? Feeling a little cocky, I took advantage of his momentarily relaxed stance and swiped at him again.

He leaned back just out of my reach. "Good instinct. Never give up an opportunity to attack."

I blushed at his approval and turned away to hide my reddening cheeks and the smile stretching my lips.

I realized a fraction of a second too late that he was probably going easy on me. Without warning, his foot swept my legs, sending me crashing to the ground.

I groaned as I hit the floor, but didn't drop my weapon. Rolling over, I scrambled to my knees.

"That's another thing you should know. Never turn your back on an enemy," he said as his arm snaked around my middle and his blade pressed against my neck.

"Point taken." I gulped. The blade bit into my skin. My heart skipped a beat.

Lysander lifted me to standing and dropped his dagger on the bed. "Always be aware of where your enemy is. You must be alert. Never give an enemy a way to surprise you."

I turned around to face him, our eyes met, and I saw again a hint of the worry he'd been trying to hide all evening.

"I wish there was more time to practice."

"You could stay behind," he said softly.

"No," I said a little louder than I wanted to. I was worried too, but I couldn't walk away from this fight. "I've got to make sure Fallon is okay. I have to help you and the clan. I'm not staying behind. Just because I'm the youngest member of the clan doesn't mean I'm incapable of fighting."

"That's not what I was trying to say. I just want to ensure your protection. That's all I'm concerned with."

"This isn't my first fight, Lysander." I shot him an angry glare. "I was there at Kallisto's, if you remember."

"Yes, I do," he said with a sigh. "All the more reason for me to worry. I cannot have you charging in after Fallon, like you did for me."

"You're mad that I went back for you?"

"No. But you need to think before you act. It doesn't always end well when you do things on impulse."

I groaned and buried my head into his chest.

He stroked my back. "Just stay close to me, love." His voice was no more than a whisper. "I will do my best to protect you."

I looked up, meeting his gaze. He caressed my face with his hand.

I dropped my dagger on the bed, wrapped my arms around him, and leaned into his chest. "I'll try not to get into too much trouble tonight."

He laughed. The sound rumbled through his chest. "That's all I can hope for."

The door lock clicked, and I looked over, seeing the handle turn. A second later, Nicholas and Rozaline strolled in, dressed in black from head to toe.

"Perhaps you should change to be a little less conspicuous." Lysander said, pulling away from me and walking to the bed. Reaching into his bag again, he pulled out a folded pile of black clothes and handed them to me.

Yes, because black is the only thing fashion-conscious vampires wear to an ambush. "Thanks, Lysander." I smirked and walked toward the bathroom to don my new outfit.

Rozaline caught me by the shoulder as I reached the bathroom door. "Can I talk to you for a moment?"

My eyes narrowed as I caught her tight lipped-expression. I had a feeling that whatever she wanted to talk about couldn't be good. Nicholas stood behind her looking smug. That only added to my suspicion. When I turned a questioning eye on him, though, he walked away without a word.

"Sure, let's talk in a second." I motioned to the bathroom. "Lemme just get dressed."

"I'll help you."

I cocked my head sideways. "Must be an urgent discussion. Okay, c'mon."

Rozaline followed me into the small bathroom and shut the door behind her. "I know I cannot stop you from going with us. Nor would I want too. You are a member of this clan and deserve the right to fight. But ..." She took a deep breath. Her hand reached up to one of her crystal point necklaces. She held it and thumbed the length of the crystal, rubbing it as if it were a worry stone. "You are brash and rush in for action where a calm head is needed."

I remembered our previous fight with the Saints and the wounds I'd inflicted on Rozaline. No evidence was left on her immortal skin, but the look on her face told me she still remembered the pain.

"I need you to promise me something." She dropped the necklace, which fell back to her chest, clinking softly against her other crystal points as it settled into place.

"Listen and follow orders. No matter what happens. You have the heart of a warrior, but not the training. Listen to Lysander and Nicholas. They will lead us in this fight."

I nodded. She was right—I did have a tendency to rush into things. "I'll listen as well as I can." Suddenly, Fallon's frightened face flashed in front of my eyes. I had a feeling that Rozaline's little chat was not just to prevent me from rushing into things; it might also be a warning that Fallon might not be saved. "I know the clan is not too happy about Fallon. Promise or no, I'll make sure she gets out alive."

Rozaline sighed, her shoulders slumping slightly. "I know you think we're all against you. Trust me, this is not the case. In fights like these, though, survivors may be few, and I need you to be prepared for that. Any one of us could find death."

I gulped and turned away, pulling my shirt off over my head. "I can't let her die. It's my fault she's involved. I will get her out."

"Then be smart in your actions." The door opened and shut again behind me. By the time I had pulled on my black turtle-neck shirt, Rozaline was gone.

19

The time had come. As midnight drew close, we all packed into Lysander's Jeep, and I directed us to Quentin.

We circled the industrial building once, surveying the area. Just as it had been a few nights earlier, the place looked desolate and forgotten. Rodents scurried in and out of storm drains, and trash lined the streets.

Last-minute plans were discussed as we circled around the building a second time, and it was decided, for ease of escape, that we park a few streets away from Quentin's building. As we exited the car, an eerie calm surrounded us and a feeling of dread washed over me. Flashes of memory brought back the echo of pain from the gunshots I'd received the last time I was here.

"Be careful of traps," I found myself whispering.

Lysander grunted in acknowledgement but didn't speak. He carefully surveyed our surroundings.

The whole area reeked of piss and garbage. A hot breeze blew past me, carrying with it all manner of foul odors. It sent a small shiver of dread snaking down my spine. My heart sped and a lump formed in my throat. I sensed something wasn't right and wondered if we were being watched.

Lysander and Nicholas took the lead and guided us down an alleyway between two old warehouse buildings. We exited into a parking lot directly across the street from Quentin's compound.

I spotted the Jeep Liberty that Santino had been driving. It was parked just outside an entrance to the building.

A lone guard stood outside with a large rifle-like weapon.

From our distance I couldn't tell if he was human, vampire, or one of those creatures. Knowing the Acta Sanctorum used all of them to fight us, I stopped and closed my eyes, trying to sense what the creature might be. With the sour stench of death wafting in the air all around us, I couldn't tell by scent, and with all of the other vampires around me, I couldn't sense anything either.

Lysander and Drew seemed to be doing something similar, trying to sense our surroundings. When I looked to them they both had their eyes closed and noses pointed up in the air. I hoped their senses were more in tune.

Rozaline and Crystal kept watch at our backs. I turned to see them scanning the deserted alleyway we had just left.

Nicholas whispered something into Lysander's ear, too low for me to hear.

Lysander nodded, looked to Drew, and pointed to the right. As if following mental orders, Drew and Nicholas took off in a flash.

I wish I could read thoughts. It would make this so much easier.

"What are they doing?" I whispered.

"They are checking the perimeter," Lysander answered. "We need to know how many entrances there are, and who or what is guarding them."

After a few quiet moments, Nicholas and Drew reappeared.

"There are two other entrances; each one has a guard just like this one," Drew said to Lysander. "They don't appear to be tainted."

"Sounds like evil henchmen number twelve to me," I turned and whispered to Crystal. "You know, like in the movies. Poor bastard doesn't even get a name. He's just there to get slaughtered." I'd hoped to lighten the mood a bit. We hadn't even made it inside, and already the tension was starting to get the better of me. I felt nervous and shaky.

Crystal smiled and nodded, but didn't laugh at my joke.

Lysander shot me a disappointed look. "If they are human, we can incapacitate them. We're not here to murder everyone. We're here to remove the threat against us."

"Sorry," I mumbled feeling instantly ashamed for my off-handed comment.

He pointed to the door I had been staring at. "Since there is only one guard, we will take this entrance ahead of us and remove that guard."

Nicholas moved in a blurry flash. He struck the guard, sending him crashing to the ground with a dull thud. Nicholas bent down, checked the body, and then waved us over.

We followed as silently as we could, creeping down toward the door, using the shadows to remain hidden.

Nicholas dragged the body behind the Jeep and took the rifle as his own. He sniffed the air as he walked back around the vehicle. "Something's coming."

"Weapons," Lysander whispered.

I reached down toward my belt, unsheathing the dragon fire blade Lysander had given me.

"Where's Santino?" I asked.

Lysander growled. "Not sure, and that is very disturbing." He looked up, his eyes scanning the surroundings. I followed his line of vision to a blinking security camera.

"Oh crap." I barely got the word out before a loud screeching noise sounded above us. My head shot up just in time to see the large, hulking form of one of those creatures falling from the sky.

"They're coming from the roof," Nicholas yelled.

I took cover under the small metal awning above the door just as three more creatures descended on us, all landing hard on the ground. They rose up to full height and let out loud shrieks in unison, like wolves signaling the hunt. Their ear-piercing wails felt like spears being thrust into my ears.

One of the creatures locked its blood-shot gaze on me. It raked my face with a claw-like hand. I screeched as the claw tore into my skin, and pivoted out of the way before it could land another painful blow.

The creature moved as fast as I did. It backed me in to the wall before I had time to defend myself. A meaty fist landed a hard punch straight into my gut. I crumpled forward. Pain exploded through my shoulder. I felt its teeth tearing through my flesh.

I moaned and jerked, trying to struggle free. Suddenly, I remembered the dagger in my hand. I thrust it forward, putting all of my weight behind it, and buried it into the soft belly of the creature.

It stiffened, and then threw its head back, howling like a feral beast. Its bloodshot eyes darkened with rage.

My heart pounded, threatening to explode from my chest. Fear and survival guided my movements. In a fluid motion, I pulled back the knife slashed in a wide arc, slicing straight across the creature's throat.

I took a few calming breaths, watching as the creature staggered backward. Blood poured from its gaping wound; like a waterfall, flooding down its body. It reached out again as if to grab me. Before its fingers could reach me, I lifted my foot and with a hard thrust, kicked it dead center in the chest. It wobbled backward, arms windmilling as it attempted to keep upright. Once more I kicked, sending the beastly creature crashing to the ground. I leaped on top of it and plunged my blade deep into its chest.

After a few moments, its limbs stopped flailing and the creature went still.

Panting, I looked up to see how the others were fairing. Nicholas stared at me, his face contorted with an unusual smile.

"Now, cut off its head," he said.

I nodded, and grabbed the dagger still buried in the chest of the creature. I stepped on its chest and I yanked the blade free. The zombie creature didn't move or make a sound. It looked dead, but there was only one way to be sure. I clutched the hilt tight in one hand and with a swift slice, severed the creature's neck.

"You might make a worthwhile warrior yet," Nicholas said extending a hand to help me stand. "Good job."

That was the first time Nicholas had uttered a genuine compliment to me. I was stunned and momentarily dumbfounded. I accepted the offered hand, wincing as I stood, then wiped the dagger off on my pants and sheathed it.

Lysander studied me with concerned. "Are you okay?" He reached out and gingerly touched my shoulder.

It throbbed from where the soldier had bit me. I shrugged and moved my arm around, testing it. Movement hurt, but not too much. I knew the wound would heal quickly, though the pain might linger a little. "I should be fine."

The group standing around me looked battle-worn already. Drew panted, out of breath. His shirt was ripped across the stomach, revealing a wound already in the process of healing. His skin knitted itself back together before our eyes. Crystal stood next to him, pulling her blood-matted hair away from her face and into a ponytail.

"I guess you guys killed all of those other things?" I asked.

A collective nod came from the group. Rozaline gave me an approving smile.

"Something is not right," Lysander said. "Santino was supposed to meet us here. We do not know if this is treachery, or if Quentin is on to our plan." He pulled me in close.

"We need to split up." I suggested. "Lysander and I can go after Fallon. Nicholas can cover our back. Rozaline, Crystal, and Drew can look for Quentin and Santino."

"No," Nicholas grunted. "I'm guessing that where Fallon is, Quentin is. And wherever Quentin is, Santino won't be far. We need to kill the soldiers first. Remove the threat before we go after the ring leader."

"And what if Quentin hurts Fallon?" I whispered.

Lysander lowered his voice. "Nicholas is right. We must assume he won't. Removing the threat of his army is imperative. Quentin is human. He will be easier to kill alone. Knowing that, he will guard himself heavily against us."

I didn't like wasting time before finding Fallon and destroying Quentin, but it appeared there was no other choice.

Lysander squeezed my good shoulder. "Let's go."

Nicholas slowly opened the door. We all listened for any sound of danger. He led the way into the dimly-lit warehouse and down a long corridor with various adjoining hallways. My shoes squeaked against the polished concrete floor.

"Humans," Lysander whispered.

As he said the words, their scent hit me. It was strong; I could tell there was more than one nearby. The smell made my mouth water. I was thankful I'd fed before we left.

We approached the intersection of two hallways and found the source of the smell. Two young men, barely old enough to be drafted into an army, stood chatting against a wall. Wearing tacky pea-soup khaki pants and matching shirts, they looked less like soldiers and more like a crew of janitors. Only the rifles in their hands gave away their real purpose.

Nicholas' hand went up, signaling a halt. We stood just at the edge of the intersection as he walked around the corner.

I peeked around to see how Nicholas would handle this situation. Just as I had expected, he strode toward them without an ounce of fear.

"Where's Quentin?" Nicholas snarled at them. The sweet aroma of their fear instantly permeated the air.

The two men trembled as Nicholas bared his fangs and fixed them with a bone chilling stare.

"Upstairs lab," one of the men squeaked.

I had to stifle a laugh.

Nicholas smiled; his long fangs glistened under the flickering fluorescent light of the hallway. In a blurry rush, he sank his fangs deep into the neck of one of the guards while he smashed the other one's head into the wall.

I watched hungrily as Nicholas fed on the soldier, licking my lips.

Rozaline placed a hand on my wounded shoulder. Pain snapped me back to reality. I turned to her, and she shook her head. She didn't need to say anything. I knew exactly what her silent warning meant: 'I needed to keep my head straight.'

I turned back to Nicholas as he dropped the soldier to the floor. His eyes closed, and he tilted his head back. A look of deep satisfaction swept across his face as he licked the blood from his lips. "Thanks for your contribution to the cause," he sniggered, turning to walk back to our group.

Lysander growled as Nicholas rejoined the group. "That took too long."

I sensed the restlessness coming from the other members of our group. Crystal, Drew, and Rozaline all radiated nervous energy. It put me even further on edge.

Nicholas wiped away a drop of blood from his chin. "At least we got some information. Quentin is upstairs."

We left the two men in a heap on the ground as we continued on. Surprisingly, the hallways were empty. *Where are all the guards?* It seemed strange that the place was left so unguarded. *What if someone walked in? What if…*

"The guards are not for Quentin's possessions, they are there to protect him." Lysander said in a hushed voice. "They are here to stop the monsters from accidentally killing him. I am willing to bet the closer we get to Quentin, the more of these… things we will find."

We came to the end of the hallway. Nicholas again motioned for us to halt.

Zombies, lots of them. I could smell them reeking of death and hear them thrashing about behind a set of a large double doors. I pulled out my dagger, holding it at the ready. Their footsteps echoed as they paced back and forth. My hand tightened on the hilt of the knife.

"I'm guessing that behind that door is Quentin's army," Nicholas said with a deep sigh. "Mindless zombies fed off Alyssa's blood. He's created quite a gauntlet for us to get through. He'll no doubt be holed up somewhere on the other side of this mob."

Leaning my head around the corner, I saw the door chained and locked. No guards stood outside.

An eerie feeling crawled down my spine. It curled into my stomach and weakened my knees. I tried to gulp back my fear, further tightening my grip on the blade.

This seems too easy. Too simple. Something is wrong here.

Nicholas and Lysander whispered something to each other.

Lysander urged us forward. "Let's go."

Drew broke the chains with a quick jerk and forced the door open.

As the door swung wide, a flood of drooling, flailing men came rushing out. The shrieks were terrible. High pitched, ear shattering wails erupted from the zombie-like creatures. Their clawed hands raked at us, their intended victims.

Activity was a blur all around me. I backed toward the wall and raised my dagger, swiping it wildly around me to ward off any attacker. There were even more than I'd expected. Frantically looking around, I hoped to find some back-up as a large hulking creature bore down on me. I spotted Lysander nearby, but he was wrestling with two of the creatures. He had already removed the limb of one when another came crashing into him. They writhed and wrestled on the floor.

I swiped my blade again, catching the creature across the face as it lunged toward me. Pivoting out of the way as it crashed into the wall, I spotted Crystal. She couldn't help me either. She was busy fending off an attack from one. Drew was cornered with three.

I turned around, spotting Nicholas and Rozaline fighting back to back, moving in slow circles as they were surrounded by a few more.

"Alyssa, watch out!" I heard someone scream, but I couldn't tell who had said it. As I heard the words, something came crashing into me hard. Stars danced before my eyes. My world distorted. I fell, smashing into the concrete floor. A moment of blackness followed a throbbing pain in my head.

By the time my vision returned, I felt something tearing through my already wounded shoulder. I focused through the sting, seeing the head of one of the creatures latched on to me.

Like a rabid dog, the thing bit me over and over again, shredding my skin. Blood coated his face and clothes like war paint.

I struggled to roll and move; anything to gain leverage, to move this creature off of me.

Yelping, I rolled my hand free and was able to reach for my fallen dagger. I pulled it in one quick motion and stabbed and slashed blindly at my attacker.

It seemed unaffected by my attempts. Its blood splattered as the blade made contact with its skin, yet it didn't wail or move away from the damage I was inflicting on it.

I continued to hack and slash as I writhed underneath the zombie thing. All of my companions were busy with their own beasts to slay and couldn't help.

It tore into my neck, its teeth like razors, fraying my skin. Blood oozed from my wounds. My head became a heavy weight as weakness threatened to sink in. Only the worry of Fallon kept me going. I needed to find her. I needed to get to my friend and make sure she was okay. That thought alone gave me strength. With a surprising new vigor, I broke free from the zombie's grasp. I used every ounce of rage inside of me to fuel my motions. As I rolled away, I brought the blade down hard and cut into the beast's neck.

Finally the creature reacted, crying out as if it knew its final death was here. Its red bloody eyes darkened moments before its body slumped to the floor.

I caught my breath to calm my pounding heart and assessed my surroundings. Lysander still fought against one zombie. Another lay dead at his side. Nicholas and Rozaline were both attacking the last of their creatures, and Drew and Crystal still each had one left to battle with.

My arm felt sticky and wet. I turned my head, looking at my shoulder. My stomach lurched at the gruesome sight. It reminded me of ground beef, bloody and unrecognizable as its original form.

I shouldn't have looked. Blood dripped everywhere. It was always worse when you knew exactly how bad the wounds were. *Mind over matter!* Suddenly very dizzy, I swayed where I stood, feeling the effects of my weakened body. I knew I couldn't stand much more blood loss. I would fall into paralysis soon if I didn't stop it.

Using the only thing I could think of, I tore my shirt and wrapped my arm as well as I could in the fabric.

A loud female scream echoed through the hallway. It wasn't Rozaline or Crystal. I turned sharply to face the sound.

Fallon.

Dizziness dissipated as quickly as if someone had flicked a switch. Fear fueled me with adrenaline. I knew I had to go after her. Quentin could be torturing her or killing her at that very moment. I couldn't wait. Every moment, I felt, was precious. The clan had things well enough in hand. With only a few more to fight, they should easily be able to catch up and help take down Quentin.

"I'm going after her," I yelled back to the clan and took off, without a look back, down the hallway in search of Fallon.

20

Dizzy with blood loss, my brain worked in slow motion; it was fear alone that fueled me, driving me toward my purpose. Fear for Fallon. I ran blindly through the halls, not really knowing which direction to go.

A pleading wail echoed in behind me—Lysander begging for my return. I couldn't stop. Every moment could be Fallon's last. I knew the clan could handle the few beasts that were left. If I could handle one, young as I was, they could do it with their ancient blood.

I stopped at the intersection of two halls and sniffed the air, hoping to catch a trace of something: Fallon, Quentin, anything that might help me figure out which path to take.

My nose picked up the sweet smell of a human. From the strength of the thick aroma, I judged that the person was somewhere close by. If Nicholas was right, the human guards would be closer to Quentin, protecting him in case the zombies turned on their master. I took off in a flash, rounded the corner, and plowed into a waiting soldier. He was alone.

Like the other human soldiers we'd met earlier, this one was young—too young to be fighting someone else's battles. He still had acne spotting his tanned, youthful face. I felt sorry for him; he'd probably been brainwashed by the Acta Sanctorum and told we were nothing but monsters. But sympathy aside, he was still a danger to me.

He wore the same pea soup-green outfit as the ones we'd met before, with the addition of a loose-fitting canvas jacket to match. This soldier, however, didn't carry a rifle. He raised his weapon, a small handgun, and pointed the muzzle at my stomach. "A close range shot might not kill you, but it will put you on your ass long enough for me to take your head." He sneered at me as he talked, but the slight tremble of his hands gave away his nervousness.

He was right though. A close-range shot would put an end to my rescue attempt. I needed to play along, to give him a sense of hope, make him think he had the upper hand, and distract him long enough to get his gun. I lifted my hands up in surrender, and tried to look as innocent as possible. Biting my lip, I softened my expression and let my eyes appear wide, as if I were fearful of him.

My arms trembled and I allowed my voice to crack as I spoke. "Please, don't hurt me."

His face softened a little, yet he still firmly held the gun at my stomach. Slowly I focused my gaze, locking on to his eyes.

I was surprised that he didn't try to look away. *Not very well trained.* He stared intently at me, as if having a contest for dominance—a terrible mistake.

I didn't have to be a mind reader to know that he was unsure of what to do next. His face told me that much. A slight quiver of his lips gave away his anxiety. His stony expression was nothing more than a paper mask. I reached out with my senses, delving through the windows of his eyes into his mind. I felt his fear, his anticipation. I doubt he had really expected to come face to face with an unfriendly vampire.

I let my mind go blank, releasing a wave of calm, and let that feeling flow to the soldier, enveloping him like a warm blanket.

"Please," I said in a whisper. "Put the gun down."

I called up all of my remaining energy and spoke the words in his mind. *Drop the gun, I won't hurt you. Everything is okay.*

It took too much of my energy, maintaining the mental connection between us. My head felt heavy from the loss of blood. I swayed where I stood, fighting to keep upright while still holding my control over the soldier.

Give me the gun.

His shoulders sagged and the gun lowered in his grasp, yet I still felt some resistance. This shouldn't have been so tough. He was barely a man. At that moment, I knew even if I did make it to Quentin, I wasn't going to be able to fight. I definitely needed blood.

Focusing all of my remaining energy, I intensified my controlling stare. His face finally blanked of all emotions, his eyes drooped, and his mouth softened. I'd gained the control I needed. "Give me your gun."

He released the gun from his grip, and it fell into my awaiting hand. His sweet scent flooded the air around me, overpowering my senses. His blood called to me.

The beast inside of me cried out with need. *Just a sip.* I gave in.

I bent my head, sinking my teeth deep into his shoulder. Even though I didn't sever a major vein with my bite, the wound gushed liquid rejuvenation. His heart beat frantically, pumping his blood into my awaiting mouth like a hot, bubbling geyser. I heard a faint whispering cry in my mind. He feared for his life.

My mind must be getting stronger. I not only felt his terror, but could swear I heard his internal screams.

His blood was like a soothing syrup that instantly subdued the aches and pains of my wounds. It warmed me as I drank, revitalizing me. The monster inside of me urged me to drink all that I could. I was certainly tempted; I needed every drop to regain my strength, but the weakened thump of the soldier's heart told me he would die if I did, and I had no intention of killing this misguided kid. He wasn't a real soldier or a hardened criminal, just an unfortunate boy who had gotten mixed up with a fanatical organization.

I bit my tongue and spread my blood and saliva across the wound to close it. Then, with all the willpower I could muster, I tore myself away from his neck, even though the monster inside of me screamed for more. I'd drunk enough to clear the dizziness in my head and calm the sting of my wounds; that was sufficient for now. I needed to move on.

The soldier appeared dizzy; his head lolled to the side as his eyes glazed over and started rolling backward into his head. Limp in my arms, his body threatened to collapse. I supported his weight, allowing him to slide down the wall gently.

He made a few incoherent noises before finding his voice. "You . . . didn't . . . kill me," he rasped.

Now that I'd regained more of my strength, I let him feel the full intensity of my mental influence. Locking on to his squinting eyes, I delved deeply into his mind to make sure my message stuck with him. "No. But if you try to hunt me, or any other vampire again, I will."

His eyes closed and he slumped over. I listened to make sure his heart still beat. It was faint, but I could still hear the whispering thump. He'd live, and hopefully, if he was smart enough, he'd heed my message and leave the Acta Sanctorum.

I winced, testing my injured shoulder. The fabric of my shredded shirt stuck to the inside of the wound as it tried to close on itself. If I left it, it would fester until the fabric worked its way out. Not something I wanted to suffer through.

I ripped away the fabric, cringing as it briefly reopened the wound. I panted, biting back a cry as the sting ran through my body like a lightning strike. I took the unconscious soldier's jacket to cover me and hoped the wound would be healed by the time I made it to Quentin. Even if it weren't, the jacket would conceal the injury. I needed to at least appear healthy.

Sliding the gun into the waistband of my pants, I took off again, trying to find the right path to Quentin.

I ran through the corridors, smelling, listening, looking, hoping for any sign to tell me where to go. Fallon's scent was everywhere. He must have taken her all over these halls.

A set of double doors with glass windows caught my attention. Behind them appeared to be a stair case.

Ripping open the doors, I caught Quentin's scent, then Fallon's, and Santino's. Fear raced through me, sending terrible images of what could be happening flashing through my mind. *Oh, God! I hope Fallon is all right.*

I launched myself up the stairs two at a time, practically flying up to the next floor.

The double doors at the top of the steps had windows, allowing me to see the large room on the other side. I peered through the corner of the glass windows, hoping not to be spotted. Fallon was tethered to the wall, her neck collared with a large steel ring, her arms bound in chains hanging from the ceiling.

She was not the only one chained in this fashion; there were others. A pair of human soldiers were secured against the back wall, and Santino too hung from a set of shackles, next to Fallon. His head tilted upwards as if he were acknowledging my presence, but he did not meet my gaze.

My heart sped as realization struck me. Our plan had failed before it had even begun. Quentin must have known Santino was a traitor and had used him as the bait to bring in my entire clan.

Before I could think of what to do, Quentin's face appeared in the window. He laughed, a cold sound that sent a shiver of fear down to the churning pit of my stomach. "You can come in. I've been expecting you." He jerked open the door, grabbed my shirt, and yanked me inside.

Caught off guard, I stumbled under his grip and crashed hard on my hands and knees. My weakened arm buckled underneath me and tumbled further to the ground.

"Pathetic," Quentin scoffed.

I groaned as I pushed myself back up, using my better arm to support most of my weight. "You're too cocky, Quentin." I remembered something Lysander had told me: *Beware hubris, for Nemesis is always close behind.* He'd always used it to reprimand me for getting too cocky. I hoped his words were true. Quentin deserved retribution.

"I have every right to be," he teased. "I'm about to finally rid this city of its monsters and bring about the newest warrior of our organization."

I wobbled as I got to my feet. "You will fail."

"And who will stop me? You?" Laughter bubbled up from his chest. "Santino, perhaps?" He bent down and picked up my fallen gun and emptied the clip into Santino's chest. "I doubt it."

I gasped, eyes wide in shock.

Santino groaned; his body shook with each bullet's impact. Blood poured from his chest, and he sank down to his knees. He hung limply from the chains, the only thing preventing him from resting completely on the floor.

"Not a very fearsome warrior now, is he?" Quentin scoffed. He walked over and kicked Santino in the ribs. "I'm sick of you always lying down on the job. Your usefulness has come to an end." He let out a maniacal laugh that grated on my nerves.

Fallon whimpered, but a gag filled her mouth preventing her from speaking. Beads of sweat dripped down her face. Her heart raced so loudly I could hear it thundering like a drum roll.

I tried to make a move toward Fallon, but Quentin inserted himself between us. He reached for another gun holstered against his chest. "I don't think so," he said, pulling it and aiming at Fallon. "I'm not stupid. I know this gun won't kill you or that lump right here." He kicked Santino's motionless body again. "But it will kill your precious human. Let's have a chat, you and I." He motioned with the gun, pointing to a medical table in the center of the room. "I'm going to need some more of your blood."

I gulped back a knot forming in my throat. "Why me? You have plenty right there." I glanced back at Santino's limp figure, desperately hoping he would get up. My heart pounded against my chest.

"Not all vampire blood is good for my experimentation, but yours has been especially helpful. You're weaker than the others... and so easy to manipulate." He chuckled. "Your young blood doesn't react as quickly on my soldiers, allowing me to stay in control of them longer. I'm going to use you and farm every last drop of your weak blood."

Anger ripped through me, temporarily replacing fear. "I'm not so weak."

"Oh, but you are; weak and easy to manipulate." He patted the gun in his hand. "Twice now I've gotten you to walk willingly into my lair. Your stupid affection for this human girl has been quite helpful to me. Not only have you provided me with blood, but you have brought me an entire nest of vampires to dispose of. I should thank you."

My thoughts turned to Lysander and the rest of the clan. Surely they would have finished with the mob downstairs. I hoped they would find us soon. I just needed to hold Quentin off for a little longer.

Fallon moaned and struggled against her chains. I noticed the other two men chained to the wall were fighting against their chains too. Gags in their mouths prevented me from understanding their moans and wails. It wouldn't take a genius to know they realized what Quentin planned to do with them. No way were they willing participants.

"You won't be getting any more of my blood, Quentin."

Quentin lifted the gun again, pointed it at Fallon. "Won't I?" He shot her once in the arm.

A loud muffled scream came from her. Blood oozed from the wound, staining her shirt as it ran down her arm.

A low rumbling, feral sound tore from my throat. Anger ripped through me. I lifted my hand to strike at him just as he turned. He looked me straight in the eyes, and I froze. He still had the gun pointed at Fallon, and his finger was ready to squeeze the trigger. I worried I wouldn't be quick enough, and he might get off another shot and hit her in the chest.

"Do we have an understanding?" he asked.

I filled my mind with anger, hatred, and pictures of the various ways I could kill and dismember Quentin. I sent those feelings and images to him, willing him to feel fear.

No echo of these feelings showed in his cold eyes. He remained calm and unaffected by my efforts.

Fear me, human.

His mind responded back as Lysander had done on so many occasions. I heard his voice as a whisper in my head. He simply said, *No.*

I knew now what Santino meant by Quentin being special. He was as unaffected by my mental control as he had been by Santino's, a man of much stronger power.

"Glad you understand me." That haughty smile crossed his face again. I longed to remove it and extinguish the light from his eyes, but didn't know how to do it without sacrificing Fallon in the process.

The smell of her blood wafted to my nose. I looked to her pale face. Fear was etched across her features.

What would Lysander do? What would the Peregrinus do? They would certainly sacrifice Fallon for the good of all others. I knew I should attack him. He was human after all. One well-placed bite, and he would bleed to death. I could end his reign of terror and maybe even send a crushing blow to the Acta Sanctorum with one strike.

For all the reasons I should have lunged at him, I couldn't force my muscles to move. I couldn't kill my friend. Maybe he was right—I was weak and easily manipulated.

"I think we might come to an agreement," Quentin said, no doubt reading my mind. "I'll let your little friend go"—his eyes narrowed as he focused on me—"after you give me your blood and the locations of all the vampire safe homes in this city."

"You know I won't do that," I snapped at him.

Without a word, he pointed the gun and shot Fallon a second time. "I don't really think you have an option."

The sound of Fallon's muted cries wrenched my heart. Tears poured from the corners of her eyes. She strained against her chains again. A second stream of blood ran down her body, soaking her shirt.

I wished I hadn't left the others downstairs. Something was wrong. They should have been able to finish off the remaining zombie creatures by now. Each of them was stronger than I was, and they'd only had one to deal with each by the time I'd left.

Why aren't they here to help me?

Quentin laughed—a loud, insane, maniacal laugh. "Your friends are no doubt dead. You think I would be so foolish as to send my best fighters in first? Once the new recruits softened them, I sent in my finest soldiers.

Your blood went pretty far. I was able to convert fifty men from that one pint."

My heart ached, ripping itself to pieces as I stood there. My lungs refused to take in air. *Lysander! No!*

I'd unwisely assumed that Quentin's mob would be easily defeated. I thought the others would be able to take care of them while I went after my friend.

I shouldn't have left them like that.

An image of Lysander filled my head; bloody and beaten, muscles and flesh shredded on the floor, he lay as if dead.

"Your friends downstairs cannot help you. But you can help this one last friend of yours. She will need medical attention soon or she will die. She is losing quite a bit of blood. Can you smell it?"

Yes, I could smell it. I had to breathe through my mouth to avoid temptation. Friend or not, I still needed blood in my weakened state, but I wasn't about to let that cloud my judgment.

Lowering my head, I stared at the floor. My heart thumped painfully hard in my chest. Crimson tears welled into my eyes, blurring my vision and casting an ominous red filter to the room.

Emptying my thoughts, I tried to reach out with my mind. I tried to sense the presence of anyone or anything nearby. They had to be alive. There was no way they were dead.

Between the tempting smells of blood and my anxiety, I couldn't clear my mind enough to sense anything other than the beating hearts of the humans all around me.

A small twitch caught my attention. Santino. His arm struggled against the shackles, yet the rest of his body lay motionless. I knew he had lost quite a lot of blood, and I was surprised he still fought the paralysis.

With age comes great strength. I remembered the words I had heard Rozaline speak a long time ago. I always knew ancients held a lot of strength, but to see Santino, bled out and shackled like this, and still fighting, said a lot to me about the limitlessness of that strength.

"Get up, Santino. You can do it," I cheered, filling my mind with an image of Santino rising to his feet. I sent the image to Quentin, knowing he would already be eavesdropping on my mind. I imagined Santino towering over him, straining the shackles at his wrists to the breaking point, his teeth bared and ready for the kill as his eyes zeroed in on Quentin's neck. "Kill him, Santino," I shouted.

Quentin's face contorted with confusion.

Santino moved his arm again, more of a flopping motion than an actual movement, but it was enough to make noise. The links of his chains clanged together as they collided, adding to the believability of my ruse.

Again, I sent the mental image of Santino, blood-thirsty and filled with rage, rising up to his full height behind Quentin.

The distraction was enough. *Curiosity killed the cat.* It's an old saying and such a true one.

Quentin eyed me curiously, as if wondering what to do. He'd have to turn away from me to confirm the images I'd projected in my mind. I focused hard, trying to send a clear picture of Santino, ready to strike. After a moment of debate, he looked over, and I sprang forward. Without hesitation, I did what instinct had been screaming at me to do.

My body collided with his, and my teeth found his flesh. I clamped down on his neck. Quentin yelped in pain. The sound vibrated into my mouth with his hot blood and a rush of pure energy.

Time seemed to slow as we fell. The sound of a shot firing rang in my ears.

Warmth trickled down my spine as we both hit the concrete. My teeth, still firmly entrenched in his neck, ripped away his flesh as I was flung to the hard ground with the jerk of impact. Blood shot out in a spray, coating my face. I looked over to Quentin and saw his eyes roll back into his head. His body twitched, arms and legs flailing. His face paled as it became freckled by the spray of his own blood.

A sticky, wet, warmth pooled under me. A cold prickling sensation began spreading throughout my body. I looked down and spotted the fountain that was my chest, pouring blood out onto the ground. The gun shot must have blown a hole straight through me.

Dizziness set in again. I couldn't fight it this time. The heaviness of my eyelids was too great.

At least Quentin should be no danger to anyone now.

My eyes rolled back, and I let darkness take me.

21

I toed the line between peaceful, numb unconsciousness and painful reality. As if floating, I felt
weightless and detached, unencumbered by the
problems and pain of the world. Was I finally dead? Was
this death, real death? Would I be carried to the infa-
mous light that people claim is supposed to greet you as
you cross over into the afterlife? Was that just a myth?
There was no light to be seen in this peaceful abyss. The
world was dark and fuzzy, as if I'd been cocooned in a
warm fleece blanket.

I was not alone, though. I sensed the presence of
others around me. Distorted voices called out to me, as
if shouting from a great distance, begging me to return
to reality. I struggled fight the tempting pull of the
peaceful welcoming abyss. I tried to open my eyes, but
my body wouldn't respond.

Unseen hands grasped at my limbs. Large fingers
parted my dry, parched lips. My teeth found flesh and
pierced it.

Cool, thick liquid drizzled into my mouth, pooling at
the back of my throat. I struggled as instinct told me to
swallow but my body refused to cooperate. A soft

tingling sensation accompanied the cool, refreshing liquid. I felt it run down into my stomach, like ice water. It diffused through my body, sending chills to my limbs, reawakening them. My wounds too found fresh new life, revitalized by the liquid pumping through my veins. Weak numbness quickly became a searing pain that radiated out from my chest as if I was being dealt fresh new wounds to replace the ones that had sent me to my death.

But I wasn't dead. Was I? Dead people don't feel pain. I didn't want to feel pain anymore. Stabbing, burning, stinging; all the hurts I didn't want to feel anymore came back. My chest ached with a thumping pulse like the slow beat of a heart. Each beat sent a shock through my body as if the very blood in my veins was injured. It was a torment I didn't want to take. I wanted my peaceful, warm, and fuzzy numbness back. I had nothing left to hold me to this world. Lysander and the clan had met their deaths, and Fallon too was probably waiting for me the other side. She'd lost so much blood.

The distorted voices surrounding me became louder. I heard my name being repeated over and over again as if someone was calling out to me, but I couldn't tell who it was. The voice was muffled and indistinguishable as either male or female. I gurgled the liquid in my throat as I attempted to respond. I wanted to answer back, to scream out in agony, but I had no voice.

Unconsciousness, unrelenting in its siren song, continued to call me back into the abyss. I willingly followed, hoping to end the pain.

***

"Alyssa, come back. Please come back to me," a soft sobbing voice called out. It pierced the black emptiness in my mind, rousing me.

Gentle warmth enveloped me. I recognized the sensation. The same one that Lysander and I had shared through our bond.

Lysander?

His voice invaded my mind. *I'm here, love.*

I felt his presence and knew, without having to open my eyes, that he was with me.

It can't be. He's dead.

A strong, rough hand stroked my cheek. A man's hand. Large fingers parted my lips and a heavy weight pressed down on them. Again I felt the cool trickling of liquid down my throat.

Sudden realization that Lysander was with me, in the flesh, and he hadn't been killed by Quentin's creatures filled me with a new desire to awaken from the peaceful numbness.

I had to see him with my own eyes. But my eyelids, still too heavy, wouldn't open yet. It took all my strength to swallow, but I did, knowing it would help rouse my body. After one choking gulp, the tingling began again. It gradually diffused through my body, traveling to the ends of my limbs. I stiffened, waiting for the pain to follow the reawakening of my wounds. The dull ache started in my chest, but thankfully didn't intensify. It throbbed with the deathly slow beat of my heart. Each thump ached with the soreness of overworked muscles. A small measure of strength returned to me, enough to make the act of swallowing easier. I gulped down another mouthful of the revitalizing elixir, Lysander's blood.

"Yes, drink," he said softly. "Good. Take all you need from me, love."

His voice was music to my ears. His hand stroked my cheek again. The soothing cool touch helped to ease the pain.

I let his life-giving blood fill my mouth before gulping it down. Each swallow slowly brought me back to reality.

I became aware of the soft pillows at my head and the warmth of the plush blanket covering me.

Home?

"Yes, my love, you are home." His voice cracked as he answered my unspoken question. He sounded as if he had been crying.

The weight lifted from my eyes, and I cracked them open. Faint, blurry light seeped in, and Lysander came into view. His messy waves of coffee-colored hair fell around his face like a hood as he looked down at me. Crimson tears had left their mark his cheeks, drawing a roadmap of his sadness in dried blood on his pale face.

He gave me a warm loving smile, the corner of his mouth quirked up just enough that I could see his fangs. I gazed into the beautiful pools of his twilight eyes, studying him, making sure he was really there and not some figment of my imagination.

What happened? How long have I been out?

He lifted his wrist from my mouth and bent down, weaving his arms underneath me, and pulled me tight against his chest. I was like a rag doll in his arms, weak and pliant. Even if I hadn't just come back from the dead, I would still be putty in his hands. He could hold me like that forever. I felt overjoyed that he had survived. If I had any strength of my own, I would be clutching him just as tightly.

"Oh, thank the gods," he said in an exhaling breath.

I cleared my throat, testing my ability to speak. "You're alive!" I rasped, finding it hard to speak. "I thought you were dead. Quentin said—"

He buried his head in my neck, kissing at the slow pulse there. "Shhh. It's all over. I'm here."

I melted into his body, allowing him to support me, unsure if I had the strength to sit up on my own. I nuzzled into his bare chest, savoring his masculine scent, enjoying the small hairs tickling my nose.

Lysander rocked with me in his arms as if I were a child. "Please don't ever scare me like that again," he whispered into my ear.

Tears formed at the corners of my eyes as the weight of a multitude of emotions rushed through me. Like the breaking of a dam, I felt relief, happiness, sorrow, and then fear. I should have never left the group. I should have listened to Rozaline's warning. I came so close to losing everything I had left in this world because of my reckless haste.

"I'm so sorry," I sobbed.

"I know." He smoothed a hand down my back. "We will discuss all that later. For now, I just want to hold you."

That was a conversation I didn't look forward to, but I accepted his desire to hold me, as it matched my own to be held. Still I wanted to be sure everything and everyone was okay.

"What about Fallon?" I asked. "Is she alive?"

He pulled me closer, crushing me to his hard body. "She's fine. But you were not." His chest vibrated my ear as he spoke. "You had us all worried. I thought you might never wake again."

"How long was I out for?"

"We brought you home yesterday, just before dawn." He spoke softly. I felt the brush of his lips against my forehead. "The bullet nearly destroyed your heart, and by the time we found you, the blood loss was…" He took a breath. "None of us … we didn't know if there was enough of your heart left to regenerate the organ."

I could only imagine what that bloody scene would have looked like.

"I thought we could heal. You said—"

"Our wounds heal. The skin can seal itself back up. We cannot regenerate missing organs or limbs."

Lysander had once told me that a stake through the heart would do nothing more than irritate a vampire. I never thought to question it further, feeling fairly secure in my immortality.

"So if my heart had been completely destroyed …" The weight of the words sank in as I said them. "I'd be dead?" I really wasn't as indestructible as I had thought. The pain I felt was clue enough to the extent of my wounds and explained why each beat of my heart still ached.

It shocked me to know how fragile I could still be. It made sense, though. Old myths usually included cutting out the heart of a suspected vampire. There was always some truth hidden in old stories handed down through the generations.

Lysander nodded against my forehead. His hand ghosted up and down my arm.

I looked up, meeting his eyes, and whispered, "Thank you."

Confusion clouded his watery eyes. I saw the tracks of a fresh tear that had run down his cheek. "For what?"

"For being alive. For coming to my rescue again. For … just you."

"No, thank *you* for being strong enough to survive. I may not show it well, but I love you. You are my world. I don't know what I would do if I lost you."

"I know you love me, and I love you too. I was ready to cross over when I thought you would be there, waiting for me on the other side."

"Let us hope it never comes to that." He kissed my forehead again. "But know if it does, I will be there patiently waiting for you."

As morbid as that thought was, the sentiment did make me feel a little *warm and fuzzy*. I hoped, though, to not have to test his promise anytime soon. I'd come close to death enough times recently to not want to deal with the prospect of it for a very long time.

"Speaking of death… what about Santino? What of the rest of the clan? Are they okay too?"

"Relax now, Alyssa. Everything is fine, but you need your rest." There was an air formality to his voice that made me worry. I wondered if he was hiding something. Maybe he just wanted to have me to himself for a while. Either way, I didn't have the strength or the desire to press the matter further.

I allowed him to hold and rock me as I pondered his words. I'd ask again after a little nap.

22

A knock at the door pulled me out of deep sleep. I blinked my dry eyes and glanced around the dark room. I wondered how long I had been asleep. Surely it was night time now. No light seeped in from the corners of the curtains. Lysander's arm tightened and pulled me closer. Instantly, I was comforted by his strong embrace and for a moment pondered returning to sleep and investigating the noise later.

Just as I was resting my head back into the pillow, the door creaked open. A faint ribbon of light danced across the bed.

"Lysander, Alyssa, I'm taking off now," Fallon said in barely a whisper.

Excitement and a wave of relief swept over me upon hearing her voice. If she was up and talking, then she was more than just 'fine,' as Lysander had suggested.

I shot up from the bed against the protest of my aching muscles and scrambled to find some clothes. "Wait, Fallon! Don't leave yet." I yanked open the dresser and grabbed a shirt, tossing it on as I fumbled my way to the door, tripping over my feet in clumsy haste to see her.

I threw my arms around Fallon's neck and squealed, "Oh thank god you're alive."

She whimpered under my tight grip. Realizing my strength had returned, I let her go, hoping I hadn't crushed her. Her face contorted in pain and then relaxed.

I was so relieved to see that she was alive. She looked a little paler than normal, and her arm was cradled in a sling.

"You were shot, twice. Are you sure you're okay?"

Her face flushed red for a moment. "Yeah. You didn't tell me vampires could heal wounds."

I shot her a quizzical look before realization hit me. Our saliva has some healing properties.

"Nicholas took care of my arm." She bit her lip. "He … well … sort of … licked my wounds clean." A slight shudder rocked her body.

I could just imagine what that must have been like for her. A vampire licking her wounds clean. I'd probably shudder too. I hoped Nicholas hadn't been too much of a jerk about it. I could easily see him making a big show of it to freak her out, relishing the sight as she cringed and tried to pull away from him. He did like to rub people the wrong way, just to see their reactions.

Fallon lifted her bandaged arm. "This one still hurts. They had to extract the bullet." She gritted her teeth as if remembering the pain. "Still a little tender, but the skin has healed."

"Well I'm glad you're okay. I thought everyone had died."

"It wasn't any fun, but I'm good now. In all honesty, I was more worried about you. You looked truly dead by the time the clan found you. They all tried to give you blood, but you didn't respond. It was really scary. Lysander lost it." She shuddered again. "That man is pretty scary when he is mad. You don't want to know what he did to Quentin's body. Took both Nicholas and Drew to hold him down until he was calm enough to move you."

I blushed. Not because Lysander had gone into a murderous rage, but because everyone, it seemed, had been so worried about me and did all they could to bring me back from the edge of death. "Seems I owe everyone a great big thank you."

"Not me. I owe you all the thanks. You really came through for me." She beamed with pride.

"And with all this appreciation, you were just going to leave without saying goodbye?" I cocked my head and arched an eyebrow at Fallon.

"Yeah, I was going to pack up my stuff at home." A mischievous smile pulled at the corners of her lips. "Didn't Lysander tell you?"

I jerked my head around, looking back toward the bed. Lysander was sitting up, stretching his arms wide with a yawn.

I narrowed my eyes at him. "Tell me what, honey?"

His face was a mask of innocence. "Fallon has agreed to take care of our home during the daylight hours."

"You're moving in?" I squealed, turning back toward Fallon.

"Yeah. But don't get any ideas. I'm not trying to become one of you guys. I just want to be able to be close to my friend. And well, this place totally puts my rat-hole apartment to shame." She finished with a snort.

I was beyond words. I had to pinch myself to be sure I wasn't still dreaming. Things were better than I had hoped. I got to keep my friend and my clan together.

"So, okay, I have to go pack." Fallon turned on her heel and walked down the hallway and out to the living room.

I hastily found a pair of jeans and turned back to Lysander. "So you've finally accepted her?"

"Yes, and you were right, I should have done so earlier. In some instances, vampires and human can be good friends and allies. Besides, I know now that I cannot keep you from her. Your friendship is too strong a bond. And I am certainly not willing to risk your life again to test it." He stood up from the bed and wrapped his arms around me. "Fallon is a good person and one tough woman. She has more than proved her mettle with me. I know we can trust her."

"Thank you."

"Go out there," He whispered in my ear. "I'm sure the rest of the clan is anxiously awaiting news of your good health. I'll be out in a minute."

I nodded and walked out to the living room.

Surprise stole the breath from my lungs as I spotted Santino, alive and well, perched on the edge of the couch. Even more shocking was the fact that he was writing in one of Lysander's large books. I'd never seen anyone but Lysander scribbling in those pages. They were his history, his memoirs, the place he chronicled events he witnessed to keep track of the future.

"What are you doing?" The words left me before I could filter out the rude accusatory tone.

"Filling in the gaps in Lysander's information about me and the Acta Sanctorum." He grunted.

Well, that was nice of him.

"Thanks, I guess." Information was always handy to have. And I'd noticed the limited amount of information Lysander had accumulated when I myself had searched through the books. It still felt odd, even though we had worked together for a common purpose, seeing Santino acting as an ally.

He finished a note and set down his pen. "Lysander asked me to do it." He looked up, stone faced at me. I couldn't gauge if he was pleased or not to see me. I was certain my own facial expression gave him the same impression.

"Don't worry. I'll be gone soon," he said curtly, then lowered his head back down and started flipping through pages.

"For what it's worth, thanks for your help back there."

"I didn't do it to help you kill him. I wanted to take him into custody, back to Rome." Santino set the book down on the table and shot me an angry glare.

"I don't remember killing him, just knocking him out."

He snorted and leaned back into the couch. "You tore out his throat when you collapsed together on the ground. He bled to death before anyone else showed up."

"And what of the rest of his creations?"

"Lysander and the others took care of them."

"And your Acta Sanctorum?"

Santino grunted, and his eyes shot to the ceiling. "Won't be going back there now. They'd never take me back for killing Quentin. I set his lab on fire. Vampires will be blamed, of course." He waved a hand dismissively. "It will be assumed by the Order that I am dead, and I don't plan on changing that opinion."

"What are you going to do, then?" I certainly didn't see him gaining a place with us in the Peregrinus clan. He may have worked with us this time, but I doubted that would be enough to erase the prejudice created by his reputation.

"I'll rest a bit longer." He stretched out long ways on the couch. "Then take off on my own. Maybe go into business for myself. I'll keep my word though. Your clan is safe. I know you are not the monsters I was trained to believe you are. But there *are* monsters out there."

I crossed my arms and nodded. "Fair enough. Good luck. Don't take this the wrong way, but I hope we never have to see each other again."

Santino let out a deep belly laugh. "None taken. The feeling is more than mutual."

A rough hand clasped my shoulder. I jumped in surprise.

"Well, look who's come back from the dead," Nicholas said.

I turned to find a smile painted across his face. "Thanks."

He let out a laugh. "Don't thank me yet. It seems you have a mind to be a lone warrior. Has Lysander told you of your punishment yet?"

Blood drained from my face at the mention of punishment. Lysander had mentioned wanting to discuss something with me. He wasn't happy I had run off. I hoped for just a smack on the hand, but doubted I would get off that easily—not after seeing how happy Nicholas was about it.

"A month in the stocks," I said with a nervous chuckle.

"Oh, we've got something better in store for you," Lysander said as he joined us in the living room.

Nicholas leaned into my ear. "Since you seem to think you can take on the world, little warrior, it's now my job to train you."

"Nicholas will be teaching you the finer points of hand-to-hand combat." Lysander said. "So the next time you decide to run off by yourself, we won't find you in a pool of your own blood."

I gulped.

Nicholas' eyes lit up as he smiled at me. "And I won't go easy on you."

I could only imagine how much fun he was going to have putting me on my ass. I deserved it though. I'd done a lot to cause trouble in the clan. I feigned a smile of my own and clasped my hands behind my back, twisting my fingers together. "Great. Looking forward to it."

"We'll start tomorrow night. You get one more night to heal up, little warrior, before I break you again." Nicholas patted me on the head as if I were a child.

I cringed. This was going to hurt.

"Alyssa, can you come here for a moment?" I heard Rozaline call out from the back bedroom. I cringed, wondering if she too would participate in my punishment. She had warned me not to go off on my own. I prepared for another well-deserved earful as I walked back toward her bedroom door. Rozaline, Crystal, and Drew were all casually lounging on the bed as I entered.

"I'm sorry, Roz," the words sprung from my lips the moment I locked eyes on her.

She stood and closed the distance between us, assessing me with neither anger or relief showing on her face. After a moment of awkward silence, she sighed quietly. Reaching around behind her neck, she unclasped one of her necklaces. Light twinkled off a yellow crystal point pendant as she lifted it from her chest and handed it to me.

"I knew you wouldn't listen. I feared it would lead to your death." She wrapped the silver chain around my neck and clasped it. "This is for you. Citrine is not only for luck, but for clarity of mind. You must learn to think things through. You are too brash, and one day things might not work in your favor. When that day comes, hopefully this will give you a little more luck." She hugged me close.

I had no words to say. "Thank you" didn't quite cover it. "Sorry" was an understatement, and at this point it would do no good to erase the damage done. I couldn't assure her I would never find my way into trouble again either. As Lysander liked to say, I was a magnet for trouble. I settled for silent nodding as my response and wrapped my arms around her to return the hug.

Crystal and Drew both smiled from the bed. They looked relaxed and comfortable, lying together reading a magazine about traveling. Thankfully, they didn't show the slightest hint of wanting a turn to chastise me. Knowing them both, they probably felt I'd heard and been through enough.

"Why are you all in here?" I asked. Normally the living room was the place everyone congregated—with Nicholas hogging the television.

The smile melted from Crystal's face. "I won't leave until he does." Hatred poisoned the normally carefree tone in her voice.

"Santino," Drew added as if I couldn't guess who she was talking about. "He may have helped us, but she will not acknowledge him because of what he claims he did to the wolves in Colorado."

"Understandable," I said with a nod. "He said he was leaving soon."

"He's already overstayed his welcome," Crystal spat the words.

Drew shrugged, giving me one of those what-are-you-going-to-do looks. It shocked me to see Crystal holding such a grudge—valid though it was—but I guess Drew knew better how to deal with his mate. And I had to admit, too, it was nice to have a peaceful house right now, even if it was a strained peace with Santino here.

Crystal and Drew returned to reading their magazine.

Rozaline joined them again sitting on the end of the bed. "Want to join us?" she asked.

Before I could answer, I felt a cool touch on my shoulder. I turned to see Lysander's smiling face.

"Come back to bed. You could still use a bit of rest." He pulled me into his arms and whispered in my ear. "And I want a little private time with my mate, now that she's on the mend."

I let out a serene sigh and leaned into Lysander's body, allowing him to guide me back to the bedroom.

The pain still lingered in my chest, but it was more than bearable now. Things were definitely looking up. Quentin was gone, we'd survived yet another encounter with the Acta Sanctorum, and I had managed to keep my best friend alive. Of course, I'd almost died to accomplish all of this. It wasn't a perfect end, but I wasn't complaining.

Pandora's Box

Immortalis Book 3
SAMPLE CHAPTER 1

"You make living with vampires look easy." I chuckled, watching Fallon—my very *human* best friend—stake her claim in the den.

Since moving in, Fallon had taken over the empty room in our house, turning it into her own ultra-modern studio apartment: half bedroom, half office space. She'd even begun hanging pictures—something Lysander, had never done the entire time he'd lived here. On one wall she'd hung a large abstract painting in muted tones of blue and green. She was well on her way to making the room feel homey and completely separate from the rest of the house.

"I've had some pretty scary roommates in the past. You guys are nothing!" She waved a flippant hand in the air, downplaying the strangeness of our situation.

Fallon was a rarity, a human possessing knowledge of our kind, who hadn't been turned or killed. She was never supposed to know I was a vampire, but after a hasty retreat I'd made while dodging a hunter from the Acta Sanctorum, I accidentally let the cat out of the bag. My clan, the Peregrinus, weren't too keen on the idea at first, but after Fallon had showed them she was capable of keeping our secret as well as being helpful, they gave in and allowed her to stay.

"Oh, hey, has Lysander called the cable company yet?" Fallon asked as she shoved her head below a small glass-topped computer desk and began fumbling with wires.

For the last few weeks, Fallon had taken it upon herself to bring my two-thousand year old boyfriend into the modern era.

And he wasn't too happy about it.

You just can't teach an old vampire new tricks. I stood against the wall, remembering Lysander's first lesson with the computer. It had been hilarious. Not realizing his strength, he crushed the first mouse with a forceful click. The keyboard barely stood a chance.

Fallon had spent many days rebuilding her desktop computer after their last lesson. Still, she hadn't given up on him. You had to admire her persistence.

Cables snaked across the top of the desk while Fallon bumped and grumbled underneath. "Everything is plugged in. I don't know why it isn't working. Ah ha!"

I heard a loud *thump.* The whole desk shifted, and Fallon shouted, "Sonofabitch!"

"You okay over there?" I asked, trying to stifle my laughter and sound concerned.

"You know, Lysander may be old and wise and all that, but the man's an idiot when it comes to modern technology."

"No one's disputing that point. What did he do this time?"

Fallon pulled herself out from under the desk and scowled at me. She rubbed a spot on the top of her head, messing up her already wild, blond, pixie haircut. "Damn cable was plugged into the wrong hole. I don't even want to know how he managed to make it fit."

I shrugged. "Well, what do you expect, the guy's ancient."

Her deep-brown eyes narrowed as she shot me one of those *I-don't-think-so* looks. "That's no excuse

Alyssa. Living for two thousand years gives you plenty of time to learn things. You know, adapt with the times and all that jazz."

I nodded. She was right. But it did make me wonder, if I managed to live that long, would I be so out of touch? I hoped not.

Fallon stopped rubbing the sore spot on her head and pressed the power button on the sleek new, flat panel monitor sitting on the desk. Sighing with contentment as the screen came to life, she flopped down onto the office chair. "Time to start creating user accounts." She rested her hands on the desk and absently tapped a finger on the edge of the keyboard as if contemplating what to do next. "You know, it would be better if Lysander were here. I don't want to set up his account yet. He needs to learn how to use this computer."

"You're gonna have to wait then. He's off hunting."

The sweet smell of fear suddenly permeated the air. Human noses can't detect the subtle scent, but I wasn't human and the sugary fragrance teased my senses. Friend or not, I'm still a vampire, and instincts are hard to ignore. Hunting means blood. Fresh, human blood. Fallon knew this, but she had no reason to fear. As far as the Peregrinus were concerned, criminals were the prey—those deserving of our deadly kisses. No vampire in this house would ever harm her, especially since she'd been made an unofficial member (being human and all) after helping us with the Acta Sanctorum's last attempt to destroy us.

"At least he'll be in a good mood when he gets back," she said, trying to sound as if it didn't bother her. I could tell she was lying—beyond the smell of fear, I sensed her worry—but nodded as if I accepted her words at face value. It was understandable and expected of her to be squeamish on the whole blood thing. You can't truly appreciate the need for blood unless that's the only thing you can consume. For what it was worth though, she was handling it well.

"Guess I'll just check my email while we wait." She immediately began tapping away at the keys.

I shrugged and turned toward the futon, in the center of the room, spotting a cardboard box sitting on it. "Hey, what's this? More computer stuff?"

Fallon still tapped away at the keys. "Dunno. It was on the doorstep when I got home."

I walked over for a closer look. Oddly, there was no address or any kind of shipping information on the box. I picked it up and looked at the bottom, hoping to find a label there. What I found instead, was weird symbol: a large circle with what looked like a horizontal capital "I" dividing it, drawn in something maroon-colored. I hoped that was just a new Sharpie color, but after a quick whiff my nose said otherwise. Blood. Old blood.

"You didn't think it was strange?" I asked, a little annoyed that she hadn't mentioned this sooner. No tags meant that this hadn't been dropped off by the postal service.

We lived in the middle of a quiet suburban neighborhood, hiding in plain sight from the humans surrounding us. Thankfully, in a city like Las Vegas with a thriving nightlife, no one ever questioned our nocturnal habits. Maintaining secrecy was rule number one in our clan, and we did our best to remain inconspicuous. That meant whoever stopped by to drop this off must have known who and potentially what we were.

"Sorry, Lyssa, I had my hands full with the new monitor when I came in. Honestly, I had forgotten it was here until you mentioned it."

I hadn't been a vampire long enough to know all the ins and outs of our culture. Maybe this was a way new vampires announced their presence in our territory. Maybe our recent defeat of Quentin and the local branch of the Acta Sanctorum operation had earned us some respect. Maybe it was a parting gift from Santino, our old nemesis turned ally.

What's the old saying, 'curiosity killed the cat'? *But, does it kill the vampire*, I wondered.

Absently tapping my fingers on the box top, I debated how bad it might be just to take a peek. No strange odors emanated from the box. No ticking to indicate a bomb—not that I thought bombs ticked anymore, but I felt safer that there was no sound coming from the box. I picked it up and shook it. It felt light as air, and the contents didn't shuffle around much. Only a muffled thump indicated anything solid was inside, and whatever it was, it was packed to not break.

Curiosity got the best of me, I had to see what it was. I used my fingernail to open the tape across the top. A puff of dry air greeted me as I pulled back the flaps. Instead of packing peanuts, the box had been filled with some straw-like material, like the grass in children's Easter baskets. "Come check this out," I called out to Fallon while pushing aside the packing material.

She tore herself away from the computer and joined me, but the moment was anticlimactic. For all the mystery and ominous symbol on the outside, the contents were a bit boring. An ornately carved wooden box sat in the middle of the packing material; tied tight with a red silk ribbon. It was pretty, but not all that exciting.

I reached in, took hold of the box with one hand, and lifted it out. It felt strangely weightless to hold, as if the wood were hollow or perhaps not wood at all, but some kind of Styrofoam. I gave it a squeeze, gently though; I didn't want to accidentally crush it with my superhuman strength. It had no give. It was solid as a rock. I squeezed it a bit harder, expecting the wood to crack or groan under the pressure, but it too had no effect.

Maybe it's not so plain after all.

I shook it and held it to my ear to hear if there might be anything inside. Nothing.

"Let me see," Fallon said taking it from me. She traced the patterns that looked like ancient writing covering the small box. "It's really pretty. Should we unwrap it and see what's inside?"

"I'm not sure we should do that," I said, though I was hoping to learn the mystery surrounding its contents.

"It wasn't addressed to anyone specifically," Fallon said, eyeing the box as if entranced by it." So it was probably meant for all of us, right?"

"All of us" meant the other vampires that lived in the house, the Peregrinus clan: Rozaline, Nicholas, Crystal, Drew, and Lysander.

"Hmm, good point." I reached for the box but she pulled it just out of my reach. Her sudden movement shocked me.

"I mean, it's not like we're opening up someone's birthday present, right?" She continued to eye the box, her curious gaze becoming almost hungry as she inspected it.

"I don't think vampires celebrate birthdays."

"Maybe they celebrate deathdays," she quipped.

"We're not dead." I shook my head at her. "Beating hearts… remember?"

"I know, Lyssa. I'm just joking." She playfully tapped me on the shoulder. "Okay, let's take a quick peek."

"Maybe we should wait for the others to get here to open it? This was probably for Lysander," I said. "An antique for display or something. I doubt he'd appreciate us opening it." I could imagine it looking nice on his bookshelves. He was, after all, a historian and collected lots of old things.

Fallon started to untie the silk wrapper as if she hadn't heard me. As I thought, the carved words (at least, I thought they were words) were haphazardly etched into the wood all over the box. There appeared no rhyme or reason to their patterns. I had a feeling if I could read the writing, it would all make sense, but even not knowing exactly what it said, I could still appreciate the intricacy.

"Hey, are you listening to me? Fallon?" I snapped my fingers in front of her face to get her attention but she was so focused on the box, she wouldn't look up.

"Weird. It doesn't appear to have an opening. Looks like a solid piece of wood. There's no visible clasp or hinges either."

"Maybe it's not meant to be opened." That gave me a small measure of comfort.

Fallon still didn't seem to hear me though. She ran her fingers all over the patterns as if hunting for some hidden button or lock. After staring at it for a few seconds, she found what she as looking for, a hairline seam. It was barely visible within the patterns. "Must be like an ancient shoe box." Fallon chuckled. "Look. The top just fits over the bottom. Well, let's see what treasures are inside."

"Fallon, I've got a bad feeling about this. Let's not-"

Before I could get out another word, Fallon pulled the top off.

A cloud of dust *poofed* out, spewing dry chalky ash into my face.

I coughed as it choked out the air around me. My eyes began to water and a tear spilled over my cheek.

Fallon let out a violent sneeze that knocked her backwards into the wall. Her newly-hung painting fell with a crash. She dropped the box, spilling its contents, a gray pile of ash, all over the splintered canvas.

"Shit, I'm sorry," she said, shaking herself as if coming out of a daze. She bent down to clean up the mess. "I don't know what came over me. It was like the box was calling me, telling me to open it."

I felt a strange prickling sensation across my skin. The hairs on my neck stood on end as if electrically charged. The air around me felt as if it were growing colder, like someone had set the thermostat to zero. A shiver danced its way up my spine causing gooseflesh to erupt and spread down my arm.

My kind can always feel another vampire's presence. This eerily cold hair-raising sensation felt very similar, yet somehow amplified.

I turned to find Nicholas looking over my shoulder. It was if he had appeared out of nowhere. I jumped in place, startled by his sudden appearance, and bit back a curse. His scruffy face was mere inches from my neck, though his blue-gray eyes, a trademark of the vampire race, were locked on the box in Fallon's hand.

"What have we here?" he asked. "Been ordering junk from those websites again, little human?" He folded his arms in front of his chest. Nicholas wasn't a tall man, but he was muscular and looked very formidable and menacing when he wanted to.

Fallon finished sweeping the ash back into the box and replaced the lid. "No, the human has not been ordering junk." She shot him a taunting glare.

Human or not, Fallon didn't take Nicholas' crap. Once she learned he wasn't going to kill her, it became almost a game between those two: an ongoing battle to see who could annoy whom the most. It was fun to watch the two of them go at it, though somewhere in the back of my mind, I wondered if it might one day go too far.

"Someone dropped this on our doorstep." Fallon set the wooden box on the futon and picked up the corner of the cardboard box it came in, showing Nicholas the big red symbol on the bottom. "You're older than dirt, right? Maybe you can read this."

He opened his mouth as if to make another snarky comment and then closed it immediately. His eyes narrowed and his brows pulled together in deep concentration.

That startled me more than the odd chill in the air. Nicholas was always quick with an answer or some kind of quip. For him to be silent meant that this, whatever it was, was not the innocuous present I had hoped it would be and further confirmed my feelings of unease.

"Thanatos?" Nicholas whispered under his breath, as if asking a question rather than making a statement.

Fallon and I exchanged confused looks. I shrugged at her and after a moment of awkward silence, decided to ask the obvious question. "Who is Thanatos?"

"When did you receive this?" he asked curtly.

"It was on the doorstep when I got home from the store," Fallon replied. "I dunno, probably about seven o'clock or so."

"What were the contents of the package?"

"Just this box." Fallon dropped the cardboard box and handed the wooden box to Nicholas.

He took it gingerly, as if he feared to touch the ancient-looking thing.

"Who is Thanatos?" I asked a bit louder this time.

"Death personified." Nicholas's voice warbled, hinting his own worry.

A cold breeze blew through the den making the curtains covering the large, arched window dance. I looked up to see if the fan had been turned on, but it remained still.

"You mean Death, like the Grim Reaper?" I asked, my voice cracking as the eerie feeling of dread intensified to an overwhelming sensation.

"Exactly," Nicholas said. He too watched the curtains dancing at the window. "Though I doubt the person who sent this is the actual Thanatos of legend. But perhaps he is closer to the literal truth; something like we are, a vampire, a bringer of death."

I screwed up my face, confused as always by Nicholas's cryptic ways of explaining things. Did that mean he thought a vampire dropped it off, or that this box had something to do with vampires in general? "So did this belong to Thanatos?"

Nicholas suddenly looked more annoyed than worried. "Thanatos is the Greek god of death, Alyssa. That symbol is like a calling card."

"Wait a second," Fallon interrupted. "Hades is the god of the underworld."

Nicholas smiled revealing his fangs. "Correct. Two points to the little human. Perhaps you could teach your friend here a thing or two." He gave me a short sneer. "Hades is the ruler of the underworld, but Thanatos is the bringer of death. He is the one who sends the spirits to Hades."

"So are you trying to tell me the gods are real? And sending us warnings?" I asked.

"In my day, we believed the gods were as real as your next door neighbor. I, of course have never met one, but that does not negate the possibility that they might have some physical form. Remember, we were supposedly born of the Keres, grandchildren of the goddess Nyx."

I nodded, remembering Lysander's telling of our legend. Vampires were the offspring of the Keres, who were daughters of Nyx, Goddess of the night. The Keres were extremely bloodthirsty creatures who swarmed battle fields to drink the blood of fallen soldiers. They finished off the dying so their souls could pass on to the underworld. According to Lysander's story, one of the Keres had mated with a dying man and the first vampire had been born of that union. Immortal, like its mother, the new creation carried an insatiable bloodlust but took on the form and build of its human father. Nyx didn't wish the new creation destroyed and tried to hide it from the world. She cursed it to only be able to roam the night, where she could watch over it.

The lights in the room flickered for a moment. Again, Fallon and I exchanged worried looks. Nicholas' eyes narrowed. He glanced from me, to Fallon, then to the box in his hands.

"Whatever this thing represents—" Nicholas held up the box, "—it's very old. We will need to bring this to Lysander's attention as soon as he returns."

"We probably should have done that before we opened it." I turned to Fallon.

"I'm sorry. I couldn't help it. I didn't mean to open it. I don't know what came over me."

"There's nothing we can do about that now." A shiver ran down my spine as the words left my lips. Dread curdled in the pit of my stomach.

Fallon's computer beeped. The twangy, mechanical sound startled me from my thoughts. When I looked over, it was in the process of rebooting. The operating system splash screen flashed on the monitor.

Fallon scooted into the desk chair. "Why the heck did it do that?" She typed in the password as soon as the dialogue box came up on screen. "Something strange is going on here."

The Entire Immortalis Series can be purchased in individual books or on one complete boxed set.

Other Titles By Katie Salidas
Chronicles of The Uprising Trilogy 1

This trilogy can be purchased in individual books or on one complete boxed set.

Dissension - The great cataclysm wiped almost all life from the face of planet Earth, but tiny pockets of survivors crawled from the ashes, with only one thought: survival, at any cost.

But not all survivors were human.

In the dark, militant society that has risen in the aftermath, vampires, once thought to be mythical, have been assimilated and enslaved. Used for blood sport their lives are allowed to continue only for the entertainment of the masses. Reviled as savages, they are destined to serve out their immortal lives in the arena, as gladiators.

And there is no greater gladiator than Mira: undefeated, uncompromising...and seemingly unbreakable. When an escape attempt leads Mira into the path of Lucian Stavros, the city's Regent, her destiny is changed forever.

Lucian, raised in a culture which both reviles and celebrates the savagery and inhumanity of vampires, finds Mira as intriguing as she is brash. An impulsive decision - to become Mira's patron – changes more than just Lucian's perception about vampire kind. The course of his life is altered in ways he could never have predicted – a life that is suddenly as expendable as hers.

Can Mira prove to Lucian that all is not as it seems? Can Lucian escape centuries of lies, bloodshed, and propaganda to see the truth? Or will the supreme power of the human overlords destroy them both?

Complication - Narrowly escaping death at the hands of the Magistrate, Mira travels west, toward the coast. With three weakened human fugitives accompanying her, she searches for the mythical land of Sanctuary.

After encountering a pack of wolf shifters, headed by the charismatic—and brazen—Stryker, Mira learns that Sanctuary is real after all. Caldera Grove: home of the Otherkin. Hidden in the mouth of a dormant volcano, it has protected its residents from humans since the early days following the great cataclysm. For Mira— a vampire— Caldera Grove is a land of peace; an escape from the relentless persecution of the humans who once enslaved her, and an end to the daily struggle and bloodshed of being a gladiator.

For the humans accompanying her, Caldera Grove means death. Humans, greedy and untrustworthy creatures, are destroyed before they can penetrate its borders.

To plead her case for entry into Caldera, Mira must abandon her companions, albeit temporarily, and follow Stryker into the heart of the city. What she finds within Caldera Grove presents her with an unenviable decision between her own desires for freedom and peace, or honor and the human companions who risked it all for her.

Revolution - Peace is an illusion. Blood, violence, and death follow Mira like shadows.

Battle lines have been drawn between human and Otherkin, and a bloody war is on the horizon: one that will end in either a shift in the world's balance of power...or ultimate destruction.

In spite of their strength, powers, and a rage known only by the oppressed, the Otherkin are evenly matched by the superior numbers of the human army. To tip the balance in their favor, the Otherkin need more soldiers – and their only options are the Gladiators of New Haven city.

Mira is sent across enemy lines to recruit any able-bodied vampires to her cause. But what she discovers along the way will blur the lines between friends and enemies. Seeds of doubt weaken Mira's allegiance, and she finds herself torn between the old masters who used her as entertainment and the new ones who consider her as nothing more than a weapon.

As the war draws near, Mira will have to decide what she is truly fighting for.

About the Author

Las Vegas native, Katie Salidas is a Jill of all trades. Mother to three, Wife to one, and slave to the craft of writing, she tries to do it all, often causing sleep deprivation and many nights passed out at the computer. Author of the Immortalis series, Chronicles of the Uprising, and various other paranormal works; writing is her passion, and she hopes that her passion will bring you hours of entertainment.

Find Katie Salidas online at:
KatieSalidas@gmail.com

http://www.katiesalidas.com/

Facebook
http://www.facebook.com/pages/Katie-Salidas-Author/214780936916

LinkedIn
http://www.linkedin.com/profile?viewProfile=&key=58814031&trk=tab_pro

Twitter
http://twitter.com/QuixoticKatie